THE NOT SO SECRET EMAILS OF COCO PINCHARD

ROBERT BRYNDZA

RAVEN
STREET

Raven Street Publishing
www.ravenstreetpublishing.com
© Raven Street Limited 2021

Print ISBN: 978-1-8384878-0-5
eBook ISBN: 978-1-914547-00-3
ALSO AVAILABLE AS AN AUDIOBOOK

For Ján, whose help, encouragement,
and sheer brilliance made this book possible.

Thursday 25th December 20.01
TO: chris@christophercheshire.com

Dear Chris,

Merry Christmas? Mine isn't. The in-laws arrived last night. Meryl and Tony cycled down to London from Milton Keynes on their new tandem. They had to sit in the airing cupboard with the heating up for a good hour, thawing out. Rather cancels out their boast that they are carbon neutral! Rosencrantz picked up his nan, Ethel, from her nursing home, and she began with the usual, 'This might be my last Christmas,' before inviting herself for Christmas next year, and Easter, and Mother's Day...

Daniel was working late (the curtain didn't come down on his pantomime till eleven), so to inject a little Christmas cheer into the house, Rosencrantz, Ethel, Meryl and myself decorated the tree in the living room. Tony spent an age piling logs and newspaper in the fireplace, which at the touch of a match sprung into a roaring, crackling fire.

He excused himself when the decorating became competitive. We were divided into two camps style-wise. Ethel and Meryl favoured an all-silver display of baubles, whereas I wanted my usual array of multi-coloured baubles, tinsel, and the cross-eyed cotton-wool-bearded Father Christmas Rosencrantz made from bog rolls as a child. It was an exhausting series of compromises with no one wanting to spark a row so early. They are here for a week. I wish I had the guts to say, 'Back off, bitches!' However, I didn't, so we decorated one side of the tree silver and the other multi-coloured, with an agreement it would be rotated daily.

Rosencrantz sensibly joined Tony outside in the garden and helped him oil the tandem.

Christmas Day seemed to begin with promise. I had been worried about having to cook lunch, but I had a surprising saviour in the shape of our new Sky+ box and HD television. If it were not for them, I would have had much more criticism over my choice to serve individual Bird's Eye turkey dinners.

Thankfully, the hubbub surrounding the sixty-two-inch flat screen, and its surround sound speakers, drowned out the ping of the microwave.

Ethel was further diverted when Rosencrantz told her we had bought the box and TV using the advance for my novel, *Chasing Diana Spencer*. She couldn't believe I had been paid for 'that rubbish'. Still, it all covered up, quite nicely, the fact that I can't cook.

My presents were as follows:

1. Marlboro Lights. I don't know which is sadder – the fact that my son bought me four hundred fags for Christmas, or the fact I asked for them.

2. A pair of SPANX, which are giant stomach-flattening, arse-reducing, thigh-squashing mega knickers. I got quite excited. I've heard great things about them from Mr Gok Wan. Then Ethel explained where she'd acquired my

present – from a friend at her nursing home whose overweight daughter had just died in a car crash. 'She don't need 'em now,' she'd said.

3. Three pairs of thick black tights and a can of wasp killer, taped together as a set. 'They're for your varicose veins,' explained Meryl in a stage whisper over the airborne wrapping paper. I presume she meant the tights.

4. An iPhone. I will come back to this in a minute.

5. Your gift. *The Complete Sopranos Box Set* was wonderful, thank you. I told Rosencrantz I would now be able to join in with all the people raving on about how gritty and dark it is.

'Mother, we've like moved on,' he said, rolling his eyes. 'The Sopranos is so like 2007...'

6. Chanel No. 5 from Marika. I still can't reach Marika to wish her a Merry Christmas. Can you? Phone lines must be down. Slovakia is in the grip of a massive blizzard.

Meryl and Tony gave Rosencrantz *The Dangerous Book for Boys*. Which is lazy gift-giving, if you ask me. It's point-of-sale in almost every supermarket thus required no effort on their part. Ethel took one look at it and said, ''E's nineteen years old! It's not trees 'e's gonna be going up,' before handing over her gift, a Durex Vibrations Fun Pack. Meryl looked horrified. 'Well, 'e's a good-looking gay lad!' said Ethel. 'My present will keep 'im safer than your present!'

She had a point. Tony blushed violently and said he'd fetch more Buck's Fizz.

I gave everyone signed copies of *Chasing Diana Spencer*, since they've been too tight to actually buy it. M + T put on a good show of over-excitement. Ethel just dropped hers in her handbag without a glance at what I'd written inside. She was more interested in the book M + T had bought her, the number-one bestseller *Window Box Winemaking*.

'Did you know, 'er and Coco 'ave the same lit-ral agent?' said Ethel, pointing to the overly grand cover picture of its author, Regina Battenberg.

'Ooh, we love Regina Battenberg,' said Meryl.

'She was a scream on *Jonathan Ross* last week,' said Tony. 'Really gave him a run for his money.'

'Have you met her, Coco?' asked Meryl, in an awed tone.

I said we had been in the same branch of Waterstones for our book signings.

''Er queue must have been out the door, compared to yours,' said Ethel, with a glint in her eye.

Rosencrantz, seeing the first festive row brewing, suggested we wake up his dad.

It amazes me that all Daniel needs to do is lumber downstairs mid-afternoon in his dressing gown and he is greeted with such excitement.

'Mum, Sis, Tone,' he said, handing them little presents from his dressing gown pockets. Meryl and Ethel were squealing as if they were at the stage door after a David Essex concert. Daniel hadn't even brushed his teeth.

He gave me a kiss and pulled a little box wrapped in white ribbon out of his pocket. It was that certain shade of green which made me think Tiffany! We've met in Regent Street twice to look at the Christmas lights, and each time he has guided us towards Bond Street, and let me linger outside Tiffany, raving about a necklace. I whipped open the ribbon. The box fell apart, and nestling inside was... an iPhone.

'A phone?' I said, with forced gaiety.

'This isn't any phone,' said Daniel. 'You can use it to email and listen to music, can't you son?' He grinned, pulling an identical box out of his other dressing gown pocket.

'No way!' shouted Rosencrantz. 'NO FUCKING WAY!'

'We don't like toilet language,' said Tony, shielding Meryl as Rosencrantz jigged across the living room, narrowly avoiding the Christmas tree — which had been turned to its silver side for Christmas Day.

'You'll both need your phones to keep in contact with me!' Daniel exclaimed, grinning.

'Why do we need to keep in contact with you?' I asked.

'Well,' he said, 'I've just signed a contract, making me the new musical director of the *Whistle up the Wind* North American Tour 2009!'

Rosencrantz stopped jigging. They all looked at my frozen smile.

'What?' I said.

'*Whistle Up the Wind*,' said Daniel. 'It's a new musical.'

'Don't you mean *Whistle DOWN the Wind*?' said Rosencrantz.

'No,' said Daniel. '*Whistle Up the Wind*. It's sort of an unofficial sequel. Nothing to do with Lloyd-Webber,' he added. 'I start rehearsals in a couple of weeks...'

They all looked between his joy and my disbelief.

'This is my dream job!' he said impatiently. 'Launching a new musical... An American tour too. It's eighty grand!'

At the mention of money, everyone became animated.

Ethel tottered forward and clasped his face saying, 'Oh my clever boy. If yer dad weren't dead, 'e'd be so proud.' Grabbing her Bucks Fizz, she made a toast to 'Absent friends... and lots of dosh.' They all clinked glasses and I left the room. Daniel followed me into the kitchen.

'Do you like your iPhone?' he asked.

'Why didn't you tell me?'

'Come on Cokes, don't start,' he said. 'It's Christmas Day.'

'You choose to tell me, out of the blue, in front of everyone?'

'It was an exciting announcement!' he gestured with his arm. His dressing gown flopped open. He had nothing on underneath.

'What timing Little Danny has!' he grinned, raising his eyebrows and looking proudly at his tackle.

'Oh, put it away!' I said getting even madder. 'You were too scared to tell me, weren't you? Until you had the protection afforded by having your mother and Meryl here.'

'I need to be successful too,' he hissed, doing up his dressing gown. 'You spent all this year writing your book.'

'Why did I have to find out like this?' I said.

'You'd have tried to persuade me against it!' He was surging into a full-on rage now. 'You think I want to conduct the music for pantomimes every Christmas for the next twenty years?'

'It's great money, Daniel, and you're good at it.'

He kicked the pantry door and stalked around the kitchen with a red face.

'Ok,' I said. 'Tell me about it. Do you think it's a good script?'

He hesitated.

'You haven't even read it, have you?'

'It's eighty grand! I don't need to read it,' he said. 'Decision made.'

'Really? Wasn't *Metal Mickey: The Musical* meant to be fifty grand?'

'Here we go,' he said.

'*Rentaghost: The Musical* also went bust, owing you thousands,' I said, becoming shrill. 'And when *The Lady Boys of Bognor Regis* went into administration, I had to get another job to pay off the band's parking fines!'

'It was you who offered to lend them the Volvo, Coco!' he shouted. 'Their instruments wouldn't fit on the bus!'

'Daniel,' I said. 'I would love you to work on a successful musical, but sadly, you sign awful contracts and make awful decisions, usually ones which exclude me!'

At that point, Meryl came into the kitchen.

'Sorry to interrupt,' she said, 'but Mum has just sat on the remote control and now everything is in Spanish.'

Daniel glared at me and followed her out. I was expecting him to come back in and resume our discussion, but after ten minutes I found him sat on the sofa with Ethel.

''Ere Coco,' she said. 'Warm up some dinner for my clever boy, it's nearly time for the Queen's speech.'

Daniel refused to make eye contact.

'I need to talk to Daniel,' I said pointedly.

'Danny is watching the Queen,' said Ethel.

I stalked over to the Christmas tree and turned it round to the coloured side.

'You know where the microwave is,' I said.

I grabbed my Christmas fags, went out into the garden, and smoked on the steps by the shed. They should warn you, I thought as I looked out over the London skyline, that if you marry young there is a high chance your loved one might turn into a complete and utter prat.

When it got dark and I'd developed a rattling in my chest, I came back in. The Christmas film had just finished and Meryl pretended everything was fine by insisting we all play a game she'd brought called Rapidough. It's like charades, but your team has to guess what you are making out of modelling clay.

Meryl divided us into two teams. It was me, Tony and Rosencrantz versus her, Ethel and Daniel.

After several glasses of Drambuie, it was neck and neck...

I just needed to get my team to correctly guess what I was about to make and we would secure victory.

Meryl (the score mistress) offered me the cards and I picked one with the phrase 'cock and bull story'. Ethel took one look at my face and I saw her murmur to Daniel, 'She's gonna lose.'

I gave her a defiant smile.

Meryl flipped over the egg timer and Rosencrantz began to film on his new iPhone. (I had insisted on playback after some cheating from Ethel.) Feeling the pressure to win, I made the first thing that came into my head: a rather large bull, and running out of modelling clay, a rather tiny penis...

The room went quiet. They all looked at the penis. Then looked at Daniel. Then looked at me.

'So, this is my payback?' glared Daniel. 'Embarrassing me!'

'No! That's not yours!' I said. 'I mean...'

''Now tha's crude Coco,' said Ethel. (This is the woman who every year takes out her teeth, sticks them up the turkey's arse, and makes it talk.)

Meryl stared in horror as the tiny appendage began to wilt by the warmth of the open fire. Why did I fashion it erect? My son was there! She thumped it flat with the copy of *Chasing Diana Spencer* she was resting the scorecard on. Tony crossed his legs protectively and Rosencrantz, being Rosencrantz, continued to film it all. If it ends up on YouTube, he's dead.

I'm now hiding upstairs in bed with the bottle of Drambuie. They've all moved to the music room. Daniel is thumping out 'Good King Wenceslas' on the Steinway piano and the rest of them are singing along. I keep hearing Meryl's shrill voice saying, 'Where is Coco? We need someone to sing the descant.'

Six more days to go.

Miss you!

Coco x

Friday 26th December 23.33
TO: chris@christophercheshire.com

I'm sorry you are having such a terrible time with your family. Why do we do it every year? I suppose the threat of your parents disinheriting you is kind of a reason. Marika loves to go back to Slovakia because it's her real home. What's my reason? I've never got on with my in-laws and relations with Daniel are at an all-time low... You know what it is? I'm a cheap venue. I'm the only one with enough room for everyone. I should charge them! How much is your family paying for the villa?

When I came down this morning, Meryl was cooking bacon on the George Foreman grill Tony gave her yesterday, and Ethel was drinking the drained-off fat from a tea cup. The Christmas tree had been rotated to the silver side, even though technically it is the coloured side today. I've turned it back. It's war.

Daniel had already left for his first Boxing Day show at 10am. After lunch of sausages on the George Foreman grill, we took the Tube down to Richmond and saw the matinee. I must give him credit, he's done a brilliant job with the music, but the script is very far from the traditional *Snow White*. In this version, Postman Pat lives with a red Power Ranger next door to the seven dwarves.

We went backstage afterwards and met a girl called Sophie who played Snow White. She made us all tea, and berated Daniel for his four sugars, which was a tad overfamiliar for my liking. She looks the type who might wake up with seven men in her bed.

We made some small talk. I ignored Daniel. He ignored me. Rosencrantz quizzed him, asking him if there was a homosexual subtext to Postman Pat living with the red Power Ranger. He's studying Queer Theatre next term at his drama school and has been encouraged to investigate gay undercurrents in popular culture.

Daniel was at a loss, until Ethel saved him by saying, 'Don't be a prat Rosencrantz, everyone knows Postman Pat is married.'

On the way home in the car, Meryl said it had spoilt the magic, seeing behind the scenes. I reminded her it wasn't really that magical on stage, especially when Dame Dolly Mixture sung 'It's Raining Men' with too much hairy cleavage on show and the Power Ranger bouncing around in his Lycra.

At bedtime relations between Daniel and me were still frosty. I kept getting flashbacks of Snow White stirring his four sugars lasciviously. I tried to initiate make-up sex but the bloody Horlicks Meryl insisted on making him kicked in, and he fell asleep when his head hit the pillow.

We haven't done it since they lit the Advent crown on Blue Peter (nineteenth December). I know our sex life is less vigorous now but we usually seem to make up for it around the festive arguing.

I can't sleep so I'm just out on the landing trying to get my iPhone to synchronise with my computer. I'm not having any luck. Meryl and Tony, however, have been synchronising for the last twenty minutes. It's not very vocal, but the headboard is loud. I'd wondered why Tony declined his usual Horlicks.

Saturday 27th December 09.44
TO: rosencrantzpinchard@gmail.com

Dear Rosencrantz,

No. I won't bring you up a bacon sandwich in bed. I'm not your slave, and I don't know how to switch on the George Formby grill.

P.S. If you're coming downstairs, could you bring my reading glasses? They are on my bedside table. The papers have just arrived. I want to see if *Chasing Diana Spencer* made the Top 10.

Saturday 27th December 18.04
TO: chris@christophercheshire.com

Window Box Winemaking has stayed at number 1 in *The Times* non-fiction charts for the sixth consecutive week.

Regina Battenberg is on the cover of the *Saturday Review* with Oz Clarke. In the picture, they are on her balcony in Croydon, enjoying a glass of her Croydon Beaujolais. Regina is wearing a tiara — who does she think she is?

I had prayed that *Chasing Diana Spencer* would hit the Top 10, but no, nothing. However, my agent Dorian texted to say that I have just broken the WH Smith Fiction Top 100 — at number 100. Meryl and Rosencrantz offered to come along and see it on the shelf.

We walked round to the little WH Smith at Marylebone Station but their book chart only went up to number 50. Then Rosencrantz was contacted via Facebook via his iPhone to meet up with friends, so Meryl asked if I fancied riding the tandem to the branch in Holborn.

After overcoming the thought that people might see us as a couple of mad lesbians, I loved being the passenger. Meryl expertly steered us across London, shooting down alleyways, across parks and through little quaint streets I'd never seen before.

Meryl made me pose for a photo next to a small pile of *Chasing Diana Spencer*, and even distracted a sales assistant whilst I swapped them with a load of Ruth Rendell mysteries on the 'recommended read' shelf. Then she took me to Starbucks.

'This coffee isn't exactly all celebratory, Coco,' she said, eyeing me over the top of her Frappuccino, before arranging her features into a smile, which always makes her look a bit like Margaret Thatcher. 'You should let Daniel go and do this *Windy Whistle* show.'

'*Whistle UP the Wind*,' I said.

'You know he has issues about being breadwinner,' she said. 'And the house.'

'This. Again,' I groaned.

'Your parents left you a very nice house, Coco. He can never compete, he could never get you that himself. You know, I looked up a house like yours on the Internet. A million pounds it was selling for!'

'It's our house,' I said. 'It's always been our house.'

'All I'm saying is it must always be a knock to his... manhood.' I didn't like her knowing use of the word 'manhood'. I wanted to tell her that the tiny penis on Christmas Day did NOT represent Daniel, but it felt awkward. Meryl and myself are not exactly *Sex and the City* girls.

'Look, it was never about me not letting him do this job,' I said. 'He should do a job he loves. He just makes bad business decisions.'

Meryl excused herself and went to the loo. A minute later my phone went. It was Daniel.

'I've just heard you made the WH Smith chart,' he said. 'Congratulations!'

'Thank you,' I said suspiciously. 'So we're talking now?'

'Course we are,' he said. 'Look Cokes. You know that feeling you have about getting in the charts? That's the feeling I get at the thought of launching *Whistle Up the Wind.*'

There was a silence.

'And, Tony just texted me,' he added. 'He looked up the production company on Companies House. They've posted profits for the past six years. It's kosher.'

'Okay,' I said. 'Do the job, but promise you'll involve me next time?'

'Wouldn't have it any other way,' he said. 'I love you Cokes! You're the best.'

I got off the phone as Meryl came back. She was a bit too surprised to hear Daniel called. She'd probably phoned him from the loo. I wouldn't be surprised either if Ethel hadn't been up on the roof of Starbucks, feeding dialogue down to Meryl via an earpiece. I think they all played me like a fiddle.

Marika is incommunicado in Slovakia. She forgot to pack her phone charger. You know how I found this out? She used the last bar of her battery to text Rosencrantz, asking him to change her Facebook status to 'Snowed in, and forgot to pack my phone charger.'

It makes me think I should join Facebook. What else am I missing?

Sunday 28th December 10.14
TO: feedback@apple.com.uk

Dear Apple,

My son and I were each given one of your iPhones for Christmas, and I just have a technical query about the touch screen interface. I couldn't find the answer to my particular question on your website.

Does it matter if the screen has been sprayed with Windolene? My sister-in-law has a real thing about greasy finger marks on shiny surfaces and cleaned both of our phones when she did my patio window. They seem to be working fine, but please advise.

Coco Pinchard

Sunday 28th December 13.04
TO: chris@christophercheshire.com

The Christmas tree is currently set to coloured baubles, though it seems to change when I'm not looking. I spent the morning in the kitchen with Meryl, perched on one of the breakfast stools, smoking and watching her bake. She always insists on showing me how to make bread, even though I look far from interested.

The *Sunday Times* Rich List came out today. Meryl is beside herself that your father, Sir Richard, is 497th.

'Why didn't you tell me you were friends with royalty?' squealed Meryl.

I explained that your father isn't royalty, but was knighted for services to catering in 1999 after patenting a super-strong paper serviette. Meryl said if they had known, she and Tony would have had you on the top table at her fortieth birthday 'do'.

She asked why Daniel and I haven't had any other friends round for mince pies.

'After twenty years of marriage you must have some joint friends?'

I said we didn't, really.

'You poor thing. It's Daniel, isn't it?' said Meryl. 'He can be rather self-absorbed in his music. I'm glad I have Tony... I'm very fortunate in that respect.'

She gave me a look of such pity that I excused myself and went into the living room. I had to have a good look at Tony to remind myself how fortunate *I* am.

Relief washed over me. His flies were undone, his Christmas tie was decorated with dried egg yolk and gravy, and he was reading a well-thumbed issue of *Undertakers and Funeral Directors Digest.* He takes his job as an undertaker very seriously, as does Meryl. I'd already had it thrust in my face several times to see the 'Mortician's Tip' Meryl wrote in with, advising mixing a little baking powder in with foundation to prevent the latter clotting when it hits the embalming fluid.

Ethel was sat beside Tony, watching the Food Channel. I turned and saw Regina Battenberg, looking rather rough in high definition, plugging *Window Box Winemaking.* The wine critic, Jilly Goolden, was tasting her Croydon Beaujolais.

'Looks like pisswater,' said Ethel, through a mouthful of Quality Street.

Jilly put it more eloquently as reminding her of 'Pick 'n' mix in a bottle.'

'Why isn't that publisher, or that useless agent of yours, getting you on the box?' said Tony. 'This Battenberg woman doesn't need to sell any more books.'

He had a point, so I went and phoned Dorian. I got his assistant, Emma, who said he was too busy to take my call.

'He's in a crisis meeting,' she said breathlessly.

'Why?' I said.

'We're worried about Regina's wine being likened to pick 'n' mix. It's a sensitive time, what with Woolworth's going bankrupt.'

I heard Dorian yelling in the background and she put the phone down.

I'm up in my office again. The only place I can call my own. I want my house back, especially the kitchen, even if all I use the gas hob for is lighting fags.

Tuesday 30th December 17.09
TO: chris@christophercheshire.com

Meryl has surged through the house and cleaned it from top to bottom. She had a row with Daniel after hanging a Magic Tree air freshener in the piano, the only place she couldn't get to with the crevice tool on the hoover.

Daniel's contract has come through for *Whistle Up the Wind*. It's touring some large venues in North America, but rehearsing above a supermarket in Peckham. This hasn't allayed my fears.

Wednesday 31st December 16.47
TO: chris@christophercheshire.com

After lunch M + T went back to Milton Keynes on the tandem, and I took Ethel home. They all said thanks for a wonderful time. Did we have the same Christmas?

There is a patch of carpet worn away under the tree. I should have put my foot down on Christmas Eve and had only coloured decorations.

JANUARY 2009

Thursday 1st January 00.15
TO: chris@christophercheshire.com

Fireworks from the London Eye are bursting above my head, filling the garden with reds, yellows and blues, but I am on my own. I don't know where Daniel is. He promised he would be home by eleven.

Happy New Year x

Thursday 1st January 00.31
TO: rosencrantzpinchard@gmail.com

Thank you for the video you emailed of the cork erupting from a bottle of Champagne in slow motion. Very arty but an old-fashioned phone call would have been nice. Have you heard from Dad?

Thursday 1st January 00.38
TO: rosencrantzpinchard@gmail.com

That picture you just emailed of you dancing on a podium. Is that your father with you? Why is your father with you? What's he doing dancing on a podium?

Thursday 1st January 00.52
TO: marikarolincova@hotmail.co.uk

I was so pleased to hear from you. I wish I'd come to your party in Bratislava. Thank you for the pic of the stripper you sent. He's gorgeous.

However, your text read, 'I bought the stripper poisoned and cold!' I've been racking my brains, then realised it must be your predictive text. Did you mean to write 'I bought the stripper Smirnoff and Coke'?

Maybe it's the baby oil on your fingers... ;-)

Daniel stood me up.

Thursday 1st January 12.04
TO: chris@christophercheshire.com

Daniel turned up last night at the NYE party Rosencrantz was attending at the KOKO club in Camden. Rosencrantz was not impressed. His father had brought with him the Wicked Queen, Snow White, Dame Dolly Mixture and a couple of Dwarves – all in costume.

What was he thinking? Daniel is trying to squirm his way out of it, saying the punch at their after-show party was spiked and he got carried away. I am furious with him for standing me up. Rosencrantz is equally furious. Daniel was thrown out of KOKO after leaping off a podium and attempting to crowd surf the VIP area...

I received a phone call from Dorian. I have three book signings lined up and an interview on the seventh for the London FM Breakfast Show. It gets a million listeners!

I came off the phone excited, went up to the bedroom, and told Daniel very loudly all about it. He is in bed hungover and throwing up in a bucket.

Friday 2nd January 11.35
TO: chris@christophercheshire.com

I drove Daniel to work. On the way he asked if we could pick up Sophie (Snow White) from hospital! She spent yesterday in a ward at University College London Hospital with suspected alcohol poisoning. Which is ironic, as it was the Wicked Queen who was buying her Apple Martinis all evening.

Sophie was stood waiting outside Goodge Street Station in her Snow White costume, her lips tinged black from where they'd pumped her stomach. She seemed in a mood with Daniel and barely said thanks when I dropped them off in Richmond. Maybe it's good he is going to be off working with a more professional bunch on *Whistle Up the Wind*.

Afterwards I drove to Stansted Airport and picked up Marika. She looked so thin. She's lost nearly a stone.

The village where her mum lives has no running water. When the blizzard hit on Boxing Day, the bucket froze in the well. They had to break the ice on the deep end of the swimming pool and the chlorine gave them the runs.

When the road gritters made it through, Marika and her sister went to Bratislava for NYE. She went a bit wild and slept with a stripper in the corridor of the Best Western Hotel! They couldn't get into her room; his baby oil ended up everywhere, and neither of them could get purchase on the door handle.

I took her straight home. She has to mark two hundred and fifty of her pupils' GCSE science projects before term starts Monday.

She looked depressed when we pulled up outside her flat in Dulwich.

'Hello London, goodbye fun,' she said.

I have missed Marika, and you.

Saturday 3rd January 15.01
TO: dorianreid@reidandwright.biz

Dear Dorian,

I have been to two book signings today and both have been a disaster. I know January is a dead time for retail so I thought I might have been placed in a prominent area of the bookshop.

This morning in Bromley, I was put right at the back, in the Business section, where two people asked me if I was the old blonde woman, Margaret Mountford, from 'The Apprentice'. This afternoon I trudged out to High Barnet where I was put in the Royal Interest section and a woman asked me if I was David Starkey!

I know I have short blonde hair, and I was wearing my glasses, but it's no excuse. When I'm in Oxford Street on

Tuesday, could you please make sure they know who I am, and that I'm sat far away from the Art section? Being mistaken for Andy Warhol would send me over the edge.

Coco

Sunday 4th January 11.34
TO: chris@christophercheshire.com

The drear of January has begun. I took down the Christmas tree and put it behind the shed. Its needles had all fallen off, leaving just a brown skeleton. I put it down to decoration-related stress. Daniel is working, Rosencrantz is out doing God knows what and Marika is still marking GCSE coursework.

I got bored and I did something I thought I would never do. I Googled myself.

My good reviews from *The Independent*, *The Times* and *Marie Claire* came up, but first on the list, and in a bigger font, was an Amazon reader review I'd never seen before:

★ 1.0 out of 5 stars. (**Daphne Regis**) December 14, 2008 **This author should check her history books!**

This review is from: **Chasing Diana Spencer (Paperback Edition)**

I am a huge fan of the Monarchy of the Great British (I never miss Her Highness the Duchess Fergie-Ferguson on Oprah). However, I think in this book, *Chasing Diana Spencer*, the author

---

> Coco Pilchard has her facts wrong. She has Camilla Parker-Bowles and Prince Charles announcing their engagement in 1981? It was Lady Diana Spencer who married Prince Charles in 1981, NOT Camilla. This author should check her history books! I recommend Andrew Morton's *Diana: Her True Story*. It's all in there.

One star! Did Daphne from Ohio not realise that my book is a comedy, a work of satire? A re-imagining of history, of what would have happened if Camilla and Charles had been allowed to get it on. And Coco PILCHARD?

This is the first thing people find when they Google my name.

I also see that my ranking on Amazon UK is scraping into the top fifty thousand at number 45,870. Worse still, further investigation has me at number 400,034 on Amazon.com.

There's also Amazon Spain, Amazon France, Amazon Germany... Amazon China.

Monday 5th January 11.14
TO: chris@christophercheshire.com

Having bought two copies of my own book, I have gone up to 21,984 on Amazon UK... but down to 500,034 on Amazon.com

Do you know any French, Spanish, or German people? What about anyone from China?

Monday 5th January 16.33
TO: mrli@crouchingtigertakeaway.co.uk

Dear Mr. Li,

Hello, it's Coco Pinchard (I usually order Kung Pao Chicken with Crispy Seaweed). For many years, you have always asked, on completion of my order, if there is anything else you can do for me. I can now say, 'Yes there is!'

Would you be able — please — to look up my book *Chasing Diana Spencer* on amazon.cn (Amazon China) and tell me if it has a good ranking and/or if it has good reader reviews? I would be most grateful.

Coco Pinchard

Monday 5th January 17.01
TO: chris@christophercheshire.com

Just had this email from Dorian:

ATTACHMENT
TO: cocopinchard27@gmail.com
FROM: dorianreid@reidandwright.biz

Dear Coco,

I have just returned from an exhausting day of meetings to find twelve messages from you. I assumed something catastrophic had happened but my assistant said all these queries were about your ranking on Amazon.

Coco. I am your literary agent. Not your PA.

Amazon buys from your publisher and sells your book independently. None of us, least of all me, has any influence over your position on its chart.

At your request, I have spent considerable time on new branding for your book signings and I am happy to allay your fears that you do not look like Margaret Mountford, David Starkey or Andy Warhol.

As for how Amazon calculates rankings, it says **on its website**:

'For competitive reasons, Amazon.com generally does not publish this information to the public.'

Now, unless you have a concrete book proposal, and/or a new manuscript, please don't waste my time.

Dorian

That Dorian can be so vicious with his words, and his fonts. I didn't say I thought I looked like David Starkey, Margaret Mountford or Andy Warhol. I said I was mistaken for two of them.

Mr Li got back to me, and said that my book is ranked number 5,015,001 on Amazon.cn.

He said I should view this as a proud achievement from a population of one billion. He sent over some Kung Pao Chicken, on the house.

It says something if the only person giving you constructive feedback on your career is the owner of your local Chinese takeaway.

Monday 5th January 15.00
TO: danielpinchard@gmail.com

Your poster on the fridge says tonight you have no evening show, so do you fancy a nice takeaway? I feel I should thank Mr Li.

Rosencrantz is off to the National Theatre with some of his drama school lot.

We will have the house to ourselves.

Monday 5th January 22.11
TO: chris@christophercheshire.com

I just had a row with Daniel. I pointed out that he has some grey chest hair mixed in with the black. Which incidentally looks very sexy on him, but he flipped out and said I made him feel old. He's shut himself in our bathroom doing God knows what in the mirror, probably plucking.

I have eaten both our Chinese takeaways and I'm still hungry.

Tuesday 6th January 20.00
TO: chris@christophercheshire.com

I came back early from my book signing in Oxford Street. It was cancelled due to staff paper cuts. Three of them fell foul to a rather sharp pile of Margaret Drabbles, and due to Health and Safety, they couldn't continue working.

When I got home, I went upstairs to get changed and there was Daniel in bed with Sophie aka Snow White. They were naked. Her thin legs were wrapped around his back. Nothing was left to the imagination.

Their red grimacing faces turned to me in shock. I ran downstairs and locked myself in the pantry. I couldn't breathe. After about five minutes, there was a knock on the door. I opened it and there was Daniel, standing there dressed.

'Coco, I can explain.'

'How?' I shouted, incredulous.

'She only came for a singing lesson... I've been stupid.'

I grabbed a bag of flour to throw at him but it bent back in my hand and covered me instead.

'I'm going to go,' he said quietly and left.

I stayed in there for ages, the dough forming on my cheeks. Then I heard a knock at the door. I thought he had come back, but it was Marika. She had brought me a copy of *Amazon for Dummies*.

I told her why I was covered in flour.

'Piča! Kurva!' she shrieked, and then hugged me tight. She always swears in Slovak when it's something really bad.

She poured us whisky and we went upstairs. Sophie's youthful imprint was still spread-eagled on our bed. Like a dirty angel in the snow. Marika stripped the sheets and put everything in bin liners. I found some Valium that Meryl had left after Christmas and we split one in front of the telly. *Sliding Doors* was on BBC1 and Sky 3. It must mean something. I wish I could be the Gwyneth Paltrow who didn't come home and didn't find her husband in bed with another woman.

Wednesday 7th January 11.04
TO: marikarolincova@hotmail.co.uk

Rosencrantz hammering on the bathroom door woke me up this morning. My face was stuck to the bath mat. The last thing I could remember was sitting on the toilet, swigging brandy.

'I've been knocking for like a couple of minutes,' he said looking at me wobbling on my feet. 'There's a car like waiting downstairs to take you to some radio interview.'

'London FM!' I trilled, bolting past him.

As I got to the top of the stairs, he popped his head out of the door.

'Mum, why is there like brandy by the toilet?'

'Um, Kim and Aggie say it's great for getting lime-scale off the bowl,' I said.

He narrowed his eyes suspiciously.

'Look, I'll talk to you later,' I yelled, running a wet wipe over my face and throwing on a long coat.

Daniel obviously hasn't said a word to him. Surely, the one who has the affair should break the news?

I didn't have any time to think about it as I ran down to the car. The driver wasn't pleased at having just twenty minutes to get me to the studio in North London and we made it with only seconds to spare.

A harassed producer met me at the door.

'Have I got time for a coffee?' I said. I was still a little drunk and could feel flour in my hair.

'Sorry, no,' she said. 'You're late. Vanessa has already had to extend the weather and talk about Scotland.'

She ushered me into the brightly lit studio as I heard myself being introduced by the relieved looking host, Vanessa Pigeon.

'And talking of windswept weather on the Orkney Isles,' she said, 'our next guest has just blown into the studio.'

The interview seemed to go well. Vanessa said she loved *Chasing Diana Spencer* and that the rumour is I could be a potential contender for the Anne and Michael Brannigan Book Club on Channel Five!

On the outside, I was witty and engaging, if a little hyperactive. I hope that you couldn't tell I'd just found my husband in bed with another woman?

A place on the A & M Book Club would be an incredible ray of sunshine.

Thursday 8th January 12.01
TO: marikarolincova@hotmail.co.uk

I've just had this email from Rosencrantz:

ATTACHMENT
FROM: rosencrantzpinchard@gmail.com
TO: cocopinchard27@gmail.com

Hi Mum, I like love you. Dad like phoned me. He said you found him 'courting' Snow White! I said, 'Don't u mean like fucking?' and he told me off for like bad language.

Apart from the betrayal, she can't even like act. How can he even like her, like?

I've de-friended her on Facebook. I'm on your side.

He's staying with Nan. He like turned up at her nursing

home. She wasn't too pleased to see him. She's charging him twenty-five quid a night. Harsh.

Love, Rosencrantz x

P.S. Heard you on the radio. You were like way mad!

I'm worried about the habit he's got into of using 'like.' It has crept in since Christmas. I thought when he went to drama school, they would batter all accents and colloquialisms out of him.

Thursday 8th January 15.36
TO: chris@christophercheshire.com

I wish you had been able to hear my interview as I need your opinion on it. Marika told me it made her laugh, like when I am, 'drunk and on a roll'. As with Rosencrantz's 'mad' comment, I feel unsure.

Dorian has asked me to come in and see him tomorrow morning. It must be about the Anne and Michael Brannigan Book Club. He only wants to meet if money is coming his way. Inclusion in the club can guarantee a best seller.

Instead of coming here, do you want to meet for a coffee in Soho?

Friday 9th January 23.31
TO: marikarolincova@hotmail.co.uk

Dorian didn't say much for the first ten minutes I was in his office. He has a dark, wide, imposing desk. We sat with acres of space between us, just the Apple symbol on his iMac glowing menacingly. He let me babble on before holding his hand up. I stopped and grinned stupidly whilst he adjusted his rimless glasses.

'Coco,' he said, 'do you have a drug or alcohol addiction problem?'

'What?' I said, surprised.

'Do you have a drug or alcohol addiction problem?' he repeated, louder and slower.

'No,' I said. 'Obviously that's what an addict would say, but I really mean it!' I tried to joke.

'I'm serious, Coco,' he said. 'You seem, erratic. Last week you were convinced you were Andy Warhol.'

'No,' I said. 'I didn't want people to mistake me for him. There's a big difference.'

'Your radio interview?' He raised his eyebrows.

'It went well,' I said, trying to sound light.

'Did it?' He fixed me with a stony gaze. 'Why did you feel you had to slander Anne Brannigan?'

'What?'

'You made a crude joke alleging that the TV presenter Anne Brannigan of the Anne and Michael Book Club is an alcoholic.'

'There must be some mistake,' I said.

Dorian picked up a computer print-out. 'I have a transcript, provided by Anne Brannigan's people, and I quote, 'Anne loves a drink, slip her a case of vino collapso and she'll put anybody in her book club.' End quote.'

'Oh lord. I didn't mean it like that,' I said. 'You've taken it out of context. I was just trying to be funny. Vanessa Pigeon laughed.'

A cold feeling began to rush through me.

'Well, Vanessa Pigeon doesn't work for the people at the

Anne and Michael Book Club,' he said. 'They didn't see the funny side, and until yesterday they were seriously considering *Chasing Diana Spencer* for the shortlist.'

'They were?'

'Coco, I'm afraid...'

'It was a silly joke,' I interrupted. 'Like, Jordan's got big tits! Everyone knows about Jordan's tits and loads of comedians joke about Anne Brannigan and her wine...'

'Coco,' said Dorian.

'You remember last year's final? She dropped a Barbara Taylor Bradford on Martin Amis' foot,' I said, continuing my gabble. 'And it wasn't because she was drinking Vimto.'

Dorian held up his hand.

'This has gone to the top of your publishers at the House of Randoms. I've had senior executives on the phone. *Dismayed* they have an author who is not supporting the Anne and Michael Book Club.'

'I do support them.' I began to cry. 'It's just everything is falling down around me.'

'Coco,' he said, passing me a tissue awkwardly. 'Regina Battenberg is also my client. I cannot risk her position in the Anne and Michael Brannigan Book Club. For that reason, I am terminating our agreement.'

I sat there, stunned.

'You will hear from your publisher too,' he said. 'Sales of *Chasing Diana Spencer* have been very slow, and they're now taking van loads of returns. They're going to recall the rest. They need to distance themselves from your comments.'

'Recall them?'

'Yes,' he said. 'Then they'll be pulped.'

He pressed a buzzer on his desk and had his assistant show me out.

I stumbled into Old Compton Street in tears and truly felt like throwing myself in front of a car, but the only thing on the road was one of those bicycle rickshaw things.

I heard a whistle and Chris came bounding up, all tanned and happy.

'OMG!' he said seeing my tears. 'You're in the club! I mean, the book club?'

'No,' I said, and told him everything.

'Oh my godfathers,' he said, hailing a cab. 'We need better surroundings than Café Nero.'

We zoomed through Soho as he fumbled for some tissues. There was copious snot and chest heaving. I couldn't stop.

'It's fifty quid if she's sick,' said the driver, eyeing me in his rear-view mirror.

We pulled up at a non-descript looking doorway.

'This is Cathedral Private Members' Club,' said Chris, pulling out a gold laminated card. 'I've been on their waiting list for an age. It's discreet.'

Even in a state, I was impressed by Cathedral. A small lift spirited us down into the bowels of Soho and, with a ping, we were in a stunning bar. It actually looks like a mini-cathedral, hewn out of London's filthy subsoil and decorated, floor to ceiling, in marble. Below the beautiful domed ceiling, and where the altar should be, was a long bar.

We sat in a sleek wooden confession box (with the top half cut off) and Chris ordered Martinis from a passing cardinal.

'Screw them,' he said. 'Anne and Michael wield such power, and in my opinion — not wisely. Your book should be top of their bloody list.'

'If I'd have just chilled out during that interview,' I said. 'Am I crazy?'

'No. You are one of the best writers I have ever had the pleasure to read,' smiled Chris. 'You just have terrible luck. This and Daniel, you don't deserve... I expected more from him.'

'I'm so pleased to see you,' I said.

Chris didn't look like the holiday had relaxed him.

'It was purgatory,' he said dramatically. 'My mother still won't entertain the fact I don't like women.'

'You're forty-three,' I said. His face dropped.

'I meant, you're forty-three,' I said making my voice go up at the end. 'How can she not know by now?'

'She's in denial. I'm the son and heir to the napkin fortune,' he said. 'She invited all these awful Pandora's, Domenica's and India's over on Boxing Day, who I am sure would have got me hard as a rock if I were interested. All with lovely hair and well bred, like show dogs. Mother trotted them round the terrace but I was far keener on one of the waiters... She flew into a rage and made me sit with my sisters' children for the rest of Boxing Day lunch.'

The drinks arrived. We took a long pull on them.

There was a ping of the lift, and I saw Regina Battenberg emerge flanked by a tall, handsome young man. She was wearing a long kaftan, character turban and was carrying her mangy dog, Pippin. She looked much like you would expect Norma Desmond to look, if she ran an animal shelter.

'Look!' I hissed to Chris.

'How did she get in?' he said. 'I've been on the waiting list for three years.'

I hid behind a fake Bible, but she saw me and came over.

'Coco,' she said, pulling her pale leathery skin into a cold smile. 'What a nice surprise.'

We air-kissed. Her little boss-eyed mutt growled at me.

'This is Ricardo,' she said, gesturing to the handsome man. 'He's a model. He's just landed the new Armani campaign.'

'Well, this is Chris,' I said, 'and he's, um... rich.'

Chris glared at me.

'A nice thing to be,' said Regina, shaking his hand. 'What do you do?'

'Um... I'm between jobs,' said Chris.

'He's just come back from Christmas on his parents' private island,' I gushed, sounding horribly like Meryl. 'It's near Hawaii.'

Chris looked at me and tried to change the subject.

'It's a relief to finally get a Cathedral membership, the hoops you have to jump through with the application.'

'I didn't have to worry about all that,' she laughed. 'My friend Stephen recommended me... You know. Stephen Fry? We often meet here for a drink and a mutual Twitter.'

We all laughed falsely.

'One more thing, Coco,' she said. 'I just spoke with Dorian.'

'Really?' I said.

'Yes. Bad luck and all that, but at this crucial time, we can't have you throwing up balustrades in front of the Anne and Michael Book Club.'

'Balustrades?' I said.

The groomed young man whispered something into her ear.

'Of course, I mean bollards... The things, you know that stop...'

'I know what a bollard is,' I snapped.

'Well, don't be one then,' she said coldly. 'Good afternoon.' And with that, they were gone.

'What a bitch,' I said.
'I know,' agreed Chris. 'But what's a bollard?'
I told him.
'Ooh. She is a bitch.'
'Order more drinks,' I said.

Saturday 10th January 17.45
TO: chris@christophercheshire.com

I didn't sleep. I have just got back from helping Marika out at a car boot sale in Crystal Palace; she thought fresh air would lift my depression. It didn't. January is not a great time to be standing outside on a frozen football pitch.

Marika's stall was impressive. She has been watching a lot of *Mary Queen of Shops* on BBC2. She had her clothes rails sorted into sizes and a two-man tent as a changing room. Crowds of people who wanted to try on her old Per Una underwear mobbed us. Some didn't even bother to use the tent.

On the way home, we stopped at a McDonalds and talked about my situation.

'You write a new book and you find a new man,' said Marika, through a mouthful of French fries.

'It's not that black and white,' I said.

'Why not? You live in London, with huge amounts of opportunity. You own a house, you have talent, and you are attractive... People make the mistake of thinking things are hard. Where is Daniel?'

'Staying with Ethel. He hasn't even contacted me.'

'Doesn't his pantomime finish tomorrow?'

'Yes.'

'We're going to the after-show party,' she said. 'You need to go in there and make him, her and everyone feel uncomfortable.'

'I don't know about that,' I said.

'He brought another woman into your bed,' she said. 'You need to get him where it hurts. Right now, he is taking you for a fool. He still sees this Snow White every day, and you do nothing?'

I looked at my sad face reflected in the dark window.

'Chuck him out properly,' she said. 'His clothes. Dump them on the street.'

'No.'

'Yes,' she insisted. 'He needs to know not to screw with you, or at least not to screw other women and expect to get away with it.'

I was all psyched up to do it when Marika dropped me home. Then I opened Daniel's side of the wardrobe and stared at his clothes.

My face is still streaming with tears. How has my life ended up like this?

Sunday 11th January 17.44
TO: chris@christophercheshire.com

Well, we went to the party.

'You just have to be strong for ten minutes,' said Marika, as we pulled up behind the theatre. 'Say your piece, and we go.'

I'd managed to accommodate Daniel's clothes, after folding them, in five bin liners. As she loaded the car Marika had pulled out the lily-of-the-valley-scented drawer liner I had placed in each bag, saying, 'What are you, his dry cleaner?'

We went in through the stage door and up to the green room. Daniel was sitting with some musicians and a couple of the Dwarves. Big chunks of scenery were being carted out. The room went very quiet when we entered and his mouth fell open.

'Coco, Marika,' he said. 'What a surprise, you look...'

'She looks bloody amazing, considering. Because of you she hasn't slept,' said Marika.

'Did you have a nice Christmas, Marika?' said Daniel, attempting to change the subject.

'Piss off,' she snarled, grabbing a can of lager from a bucket on the table.

'Um...' he said, his eyes darting around. 'Shall we go and talk?'

I heard myself say, 'Okay.'

The plan had been to drop some witty line, slap him round the face, and then walk out, but it seemed ridiculous now we were here.

Marika glared at me as I followed Daniel down a murky corridor and into his small dressing room. He closed the door.

There was a picture stuck to the mirror of me, him and Rosencrantz taken last summer at Thorpe Park. We were grinning in those plastic rain ponchos after a ride on the Log Flume. The water had made them stick to our bodies, and next to Daniel and Rosencrantz I resembled a rather quirky frozen turkey.

He went to say something, but the door flung open and Snow White burst into the room.

'As promised, I'm not wearing any...'

The colour drained from her pale face when she saw me. Her bottom lip began to tremble and she put a hand up to it before running out. Daniel looked past me anxiously.

'What? What?' I shouted, shaking him. 'You want to run after her? What about ME!'

I shoved him out of the way. He followed down the corridor, shouting for me to come back. I carried on through the green room, taking Marika with me.

He emerged from the stage door as I was throwing his clothes out of Marika's car boot into the wet street.

'To think I folded these!' I screamed at him.

It wasn't the most inspired parting shot, I thought, as I slammed the boot and got in the car.

I looked back at him as we pulled away. He was trying to get his clothes out of the rain. I wanted to help him. Even after what he had done to me.

'Coco,' said Marika, stopping the car by a bus shelter. 'This is not a good situation. You have to be strong.' She wiped a tear from my cheek. 'For years my mother turned a blind eye to my father's cheating and it nearly destroyed her. You can't stay with him.'

I came home and stared at the ceiling in the spare room for hours.

Tuesday 13th January 08.48
TO: clivethenewsagent@gmail.com

Please can you cancel *BBC Music Magazine*, *BBC Proms Magazine*, and *Keyboard Companion*.

Thank you, Coco Pinchard

Wednesday 14th January 23.47
TO: chris@christophercheshire.com,
    marikarolincova@hotmail.co.uk

Daniel has been round repeatedly. I ignored his knocking. On his fourth attempt, I opened the front door on the latch. He stood in the rain unshaven, looking annoyingly handsome.

'Can I come in?' he said through the gap. I was about to say 'no', when Rosencrantz arrived home from college, and I had to open the door.

'Hello,' said Daniel, following Rosencrantz into the hall.

'Yeah, like, whatever,' muttered Rosencrantz fiddling with his iPhone

'I'm still your father!' yelled Daniel. 'And speak properly!'

'Don't you shout at Rosencrantz,' I said, stepping between them.

'I think Dad needs his passport,' said Rosencrantz, looking up from texting. A flicker slid across Daniel's face.

'Is that what you're here for?'

'Well, that. And other things,' he said. 'It's not my fault. I need it for work!'

I pushed him out, slammed the door, and locked it. Daniel stayed banging on the door for a few minutes, then it was quiet. The rain began to fall harder, pinging off the roof. Rosencrantz made coffee and lit me a cigarette.

A couple of hours later the phone went. It was Ethel, moaning about Daniel sleeping on her floor, on a Lilo.

'I know 'e's me son an' all that but 'e's so noisy, tossing and turning,' she said. 'Surely you can make it up? 'E needs that passport.'

'Ethel,' I said. 'Daniel brought another woman into our

bed and I saw them at it.'

There was a pause whilst she covered the phone, and I heard her muffled voice shout at Daniel, 'You never told me that's what yer did!'

Then the receiver began to clatter as she tried to put it down, still shouting. In all the years I've known her, she's never managed to replace her phone back on the hook in less than a minute.

I am going to eat a Peppermint Aero and go to bed.

Thursday 15th January 11.01
TO: marikarolincova@hotmail.co.uk,
        chris@christophercheshire.com

Daniel came round. I caved in and let Rosencrantz poke his passport through the letterbox. He only has ten days to get his visa. I stayed upstairs in bed. I just want to sleep. Thanks for your messages.

C x

Sunday 18th January 16.45
TO: marikarolincova@hotmail.co.uk,
        chris@christophercheshire.com

Ethel came walking into the spare room this morning and plonked down a cup of tea on the bedside table.

''Ere, get this down yer,' she said, leaning on the bedpost to catch her breath.

'How did you get in?' I asked, pulling the covers up to my chin.

'Yer son. 'E's worried about you,' she said. 'And yer neighbours are going to wonder why you've got your curtains shut in the afternoon. People talk.'

'It's not the 1950s, Ethel,' I snapped.

'If it were 1950, you and Daniel would still be man and wife,' she said. 'If I'd 'ave chucked out my Wilf whenever 'e gave some woman the glad eye, I'd never've got any shelves put up.'

I looked at her.

''Ere love, 'ave some tea,' she said pushing it up under my nose. I took a gulp and choked.

'It's got whisky in it,' she said. 'Perk yer up.'

She crossed the hall and began to run a bath.

'Danny's comin' over and I want you two to talk,' she shouted, clanking around in the bathroom.

'Just leave me alone,' I said, sinking below the covers.

Ethel came back in, wiping bath foam off her arm, and perched on the end of the bed.

''E's gutted for what 'e did,' she said. ''E's been in tears in the residents' lounge all week. One of the women told 'im to shut up during *Emmerdale*. Why throw away twenty years in 'aste?'

I agreed to have a bath and get dressed.

When Ethel had gone downstairs, I looked at myself naked in the mirror. I think I may have lost some weight, but I'm no Snow White. That girl had such smooth, taut skin. That has gone from me and I will never get it back.

When I came downstairs, Ethel was leaving on the arm of Rosencrantz.

'We're going to Soho for a coffee and a look at all the poofs,' she said, straightening her hat.

Rosencrantz gave me a hug, saying, 'You know, I think

heterosexual men are like stupid, as a race. I hope he like knows what he's throwing away.'

'Come on, stop talking shite,' said Ethel and pulled him out of the door.

When they'd gone, I perched on a stool at the breakfast bar, waited for Daniel and began to think. If this turns out to be an apology, a sincere apology, maybe it could work if he wants to try again. I thought I could make him sleep in the spare room for a few months... Maybe I haven't lost everything.

When I opened the door, he looked so good. He pecked me on the cheek, handed me a bunch of roses and we went through to the kitchen. I got this warm feeling and realised this maybe was just a horrid blip and somehow our relationship might gain strength from it.

However, he told me he'd not been happy for a long time. That we got married too young and he wants to separate. I sat there with my mouth open.

'Coco,' he said. 'I'm giving 'us' a gift if you will. We can move on to pastures new. You'll thank me one day.'

'What?' I cried, feeling my face getting redder. 'A gift? I'll give you a gift,' and I hurled the coffee pot at him.

He ducked and it burst down the kitchen wall.

'That could've killed me!' he shrieked.

'You're only here because you're scared of Ethel,' I shouted. 'You just want an easy life with her for a few days until you skip off on your crappy tour.'

'Crappy tour?' gasped Daniel.

'Yeah! Crappy tour!' I screamed. 'I've had your fucking mother telling me how upset you are, that you want to talk, and all she's done is make it easier for you to dump me!'

I started to beat him over the head with the roses.

'Don't be rude about Mum!' he shouted. 'I'm going upstairs to get my stuff.'

'You're not!' I said, pushing him.

He pushed me back and I crashed into the table. With strength I didn't know I had, I dragged him by his hair down the hall. Opening the front door with my free hand, I shoved him out, slamming it behind him.

The letterbox opened.

'You pulled some of my hair out,' he protested, shocked.

'Well, I don't want it!' I said, pulling the little wisp of black and grey hair from between my fingers and shoving it through the letterbox.

I came up to the spare room and stared at the ceiling. After a while, my rage subsided and it sunk in. I'm going to be alone.

I heard the door go and Ethel and Rosencrantz chattering, which subsided when they walked into the kitchen.

Rosencrantz came up but I pretended to be asleep.

Monday 19th January 10.07
TO: rosencrantzpinchard@gmail.com

Hi love, I just woke up and I see you've gone. I hope you don't mind me emailing. I would rather write this than have to tell you.

Your father and I are separating. I am so sorry. He's coming to get some of his stuff tonight. I'm going over to Chris's whilst he is here.

We both still love you so much. Please don't take sides.

Mum xxx

Tuesday 20th January 11.38
TO: chris@christopherchesire.com,
 marikarolincova@hotmail.co.uk

Daniel took the blender! He has moved to a Travelodge in Peckham to rehearse *Whistle Up the Wind*. What does he need a blender for in a Travelodge?

Rosencrantz is furious. He is halfway through Katie Price's juicing diet. He wants to fit into some twenty-seven-inch-waist jeans he has seen in American Apparel.

Ethel evicted Daniel from her room at the Rainbow Nursing Home now that he is an 'impending divorcee'. She says she might die of shame.

If only.

Friday 23rd January 13.34
TO: chris@christopherchesire.com

I am not ignoring you. I switched my phone off and made a nest in the spare room to watch *The Sopranos*.

Marika just came round in her lunch hour. Rosencrantz had been updating her via Facebook. He asked her to make my favourite cauliflower cheese, which she brought with her.

'This is not constructive,' said Marika, surveying the sweet wrappers and mess in the spare room.

'It is,' I said. 'It's taken my mind off things.'

She picked up *The Sopranos* box set. 'Where are you up to?'

'The fourth series,' I said.

'You've got till Monday. Then we need to get you back

out there. Me and Chris are arranging something.'

Where are you taking me? She wouldn't say. I refuse to go to an over-forties disco.

Saturday 24th January 11.33
TO: marikarolincova@hotmail.co.uk

Chris came over and watched some *Sopranos*. He admitted he was rather thrilled by Tony Soprano. I am too. He's so greasy and corpulent. It must be the power thing. Are we all that predictable?

I decided I might try to move back into my bedroom. Chris helped me cart the duvet and TV through, but I found an earring by the bed, which wasn't one of mine.

Chris, with his expert eye, identified it as from the Coleen Rooney range in Argos. It brought back images of Daniel and Snow White in a state of ecstasy. He flushed it down the toilet.

I'm staying in the spare room for now.

Sunday 25th January 20.08
TO: chris@christophercheshire.com

AAGH! I was just watching the final episode of *The Sopranos* with Rosencrantz when the screen went blank. He's ferreting around the back of the television to try to see what went wrong. I have to know how it ends. Don't tell me!

Sunday 25th January 21.34
TO: chris@christophercheshire.com

Why didn't you tell me that's how *The Sopranos* ends? After forty minutes spent faffing around with Scart plugs, I pressed 'play' on the remote control, and the screen jumped to life with the credits rolling. I'd sat on the pause button. That's how it ends, with the screen going black.

I put in so many hours with that box set, and like everything now, I feel cheated.

Rosencrantz thought it was 'like genius'.

Monday 26th January 10.30
TO: chris@christophercheshire.com

Daniel flies to Chicago at lunchtime. He phoned Rosencrantz this morning to say goodbye. Apparently, *Whistle*, as he is now calling it, is going to be a huge hit. He invited Rosencrantz to see him off at the airport but he declined. We are still without a blender and Rosencrantz hasn't made it to a twenty-seven-inch waist. I told him to get the jeans in a perfectly enviable size thirty. However, he said that thirty in indie boy terms is obese.

Marika says you are both taking me out tonight and 'no' is not an option.

Tuesday 27th January 10.43
TO: rosencrantzpinchard@gmail.com

If you do have to get drunk after your classes, please remember this is my home too. When I opened the front door to collect the milk this morning, I found a half-eaten kebab on the doorstep.

Tuesday 27th January 17.18
TO: chris@christophercheshire.com

Rosencrantz just came home from classes grinning at me. It was my kebab. He found me on the doorstep at one this morning, clinging to the boot scraper for dear life and shouting, 'The world is spinning!' I am mortified. Did we really get kebabs?

Tuesday 27th January 18.43
TO: chris@christophercheshire.com

Ah yes, we were doing Drambuie shots in the Shadow Lounge... I remember. The barman made a big show of blowing dust off the bottle, saying 'older people' only ever ask for Drambuie.

I sincerely hope none of Rosencrantz's friends were there. I remember you and Marika going up on stage to help judge the amateur male stripper contest and me dancing, no, grinding against the winner...

The only thing I should be grinding at my age is pepper.

Was fun though. Made me forget for a bit.

xxx

Wednesday 28th January 09.07
TO: rosencrantzpinchard@gmail.com

I've just had an email from your drama school with this term's reading list. Thirty-two books? That's going to be over £300! Do you really need them all? The *Complete Works of Shakespeare* (£49.99) has never been touched and ditto all of Stanislavski's scribbling's (£19.99 apiece). All I ever see you read is *Heat Magazine*.

Wednesday 28th January 11.22
TO: danielpinchard@gmail.com

Dear Daniel,
Please can you put some money into our current account? The joint account is empty. I need to buy Rosencrantz's books.
Coco

Wednesday 28th January 15.01
TO: chris@christophercheshire.com,
marikarolincova@hotmail.co.uk

This just in from Daniel:

ATTACHMENT
FROM danielpinchard@gmail.com
TO: cocopinchard27@gmail.com

Coco,

I have just deposited £100 into the joint account. That is all I can spare now. I haven't had my first *Whistle* cheque through yet. Why are we still paying the council tax and water yearly? The direct debit cleaned nearly four grand out of our joint account. That's half what I earned over Christmas, and you're asking for more. I've also had to pay yours and Rosencrantz's phone bills. His is £87 for the month! I have had a word with him about it.

Why didn't you tell me about your book? I am very sorry for you. Despite everything that has happened, I think *Chasing Diana Spencer* is a brilliant piece of writing.

As the iPhone was your Christmas present, I will pay the remainder of its contract, but you really do need to find your own money solution.

Yours, Daniel

My own money solution! Cheeky bastard, he's the one who left me!

Thursday 29th January 14.55
TO: marikarolincova@hotmail.co.uk

Have just been round to Chris's and raided his library. He had everything on Rosencrantz's list apart from the play *Shopping and Fucking*. He's boycotted it from his shelves after the writer Mark Ravenhill once pushed in front of him and bought the last packet of cheese and onion crisps during an interval at the National Theatre.

Chris has *Chasing Diana Spencer* displayed in a cabinet, on a cushion.

Do you have *Shopping and Fucking*? If not, I will look online.

Friday 30th January 15.32
TO: complaints@westlondonbooks.co.uk

Dear West London Books,

I wish to complain. This morning I logged into your website to buy a copy of *Shopping and Fucking* by Mark Ravenhill but I was logged out for using 'improper search terms'. I then phoned your help desk. I was told my language was disgusting and your agent terminated the call. Do your agents read? I wasn't just mouthing off for the sake of it. *Shopping and Fucking* is a published play! I've just been to my local charity shop where they had THREE copies on their shelves. The cashier told me that she and her friends had recently read it for their over-eighties book club, and it had generated quite a lively discussion. That's what books are all about! I look forward to reading *Shopping and Fucking* and I believe, as with all good writing, it will enrich and educate me.

Coco Pinchard (Ex-customer)

Saturday 31st January 10.56
TO: rosencrantzpinchard@gmail.com

Last night I read *Shopping and F**king* and I wish I had never picked it up. I had to have half a bottle of wine and take three Nurofen. Those poor kids all named after Take That getting involved with drugs and prostitution! One is your age. You know you can always ask me if you need extra money for shopping. I'd rather you did that than the other things.

Saturday 31st January 12.22
TO: chris@christophercheshire.com

I have just had my severance package from Dorian.

He included a letter from my publisher saying that because of 'poor sales' in a 'tough market' they have withdrawn *Chasing Diana Spencer* and will not be printing a paperback. They have allowed the rights to revert to me, but it means I don't get the last instalment of my advance. This has blown a huge hole in my budget. (I now have to rely on asking Daniel for even more money.)

The most horrifying thing is that the 3,000 remaining hardback copies of *Chasing Diana Spencer* are due to be pulped next week by a company called TBS Returns (probably stands for To Be Shredded).

They have included an email address for them in case I want to keep any copies.

Marika is here with a box of Chardonnay. You want to come over, get terribly drunk, and celebrate the end of a terrible month? I think I've reached rock bottom.

Saturday 31st January 23.56
TO: enquiries@tbsreturns.co.uk

A Pulping Poem, by Coco Pinchard
Oh, ye great soaring warehouse in Essex!
Open your hallowed doors, and let me see your lights
I will wear my bestest tights
For tis soon in the month of Feb-yur-ee
My book will travel to thee
Great TBS returns!
Where no book never burns
But with such a double negative
Is pulped, and gulped
In frenzied recycling activity
That ain't no nativity.
Nothing is born; no star is followed, when a manuscript is
man-u-ripped!
Three thousand copies I do have withdrawn
Three thousand copies maketh Coco so forlorn.
If I could have but a tenth of these for myself
To fit on my Ikea bookshelf
A happy cow I'll be
Moooooooooooo.

Ms Coco Pinchard (author, poet, and don't she know it!)

FEBRUARY

Sunday 1st February 12.33
TO: rosencrantzpinchard@gmail.com

Something's wrong. The house is shaking!

Sunday 1st February 12.37
TO: rosencrantzpinchard@gmail.com

Well, can you turn down the volume on *Star Trek: Voyager*? I thought we were having an earthquake when the *Enterprise* hit warp speed. Why did you let me sleep until nearly one?

Sunday 1st February 13.47
TO: marikarolincova@hotmail.co.uk

Did you get home okay? Chris says he woke up in his front garden an hour ago. It's all coming back now. The huge amounts we drank. Rosencrantz coming down twice to tell us to keep the noise down. My head feels like it's full of mice in spiky golf shoes.

And my poem... I have just had this email:

ATTACHMENT
FROM: iain.anderson@TBSreturns.co.uk
TO: cocopinchard27@gmail.com

Dear Ms. Pinchard,

We never normally enter into correspondence with authors or readers. Much of it is abusive due to the unfortunate nature of our work. However, your poem of late last night greatly touched our morning staff. In one instance, it made Terry who drives the forklift shed a tear. We adored its irony.

So, on this occasion we will grant your request to 'Open our hallowed doors', and tour our facility for the pulping of your book *Chasing Diana Spencer*. I have sent the three hundred copies you requested and waived the P & P. Do keep writing, out of all tragedy comes hope.

I have booked your visit for 10.30am next Saturday 7th. Due to limited number of hard hats available, we can only grant you one guest.

Yours faithfully,

Iain Anderson (Head Book Pulper) TBS Returns

I am *cringing*. Why didn't you stop me from sending that poem! It's awful, awful, awful. I went 'moooo' at the end of it.

Where am I going to put three hundred copies?

Monday 2nd February 17.56
TO: chris@christophercheshire.com

The newspaper didn't arrive this morning. I phoned Clive the newsagent and he said the bill was not paid for January. Luckily, there was nearly a tenner in change down the back of the sofa. I cleared the bill and bought *The Independent*. They have announced the shortlist for the Anne and Michael Book Club.

Anne and Michael Brannigan were on page seven, clinking wine glasses with Regina Battenberg. *Window Box Winemaking* is top of their list. Anne Brannigan was looking a little twitchy and drinking orange juice...

I have decided to go on Saturday to TBS Returns and get closure. I've never had closure before, but the way everyone bangs on about it these days, it may be my salvation. Once it has happened, I can move on. Every day I replay my literary downfall in my head. Do you want to come along? Marika has a hot date on Saturday with an even hotter Greek guy.

Monday 2nd February 19.04
TO: marikarolincova@hotmail.co.uk

A humiliating call from Daniel this morning. The pompous bastard informed me he was willing to put an 'allowance' of £300 per month into my current account. He then hung up saying he was in the middle of a *Whistle* sound check.

Tuesday 3rd February 17.01
TO: marikarolincova@hotmail.co.uk

Parcelforce woke me at midday with three hundred copies of *Chasing Diana Spencer*. They are piled up against the wall in the living room. I am pretending they are modern art. The white spines look quite good with the black writing.

Thank you for the offer to put me on your school's list of supply teachers, but I am going to try to weather the storm. I couldn't go back to being an English teacher, not after telling everyone when I left that I was going to be a writer.

Friday 6th February 16.30
TO: marikarolincova@hotmail.co.uk

What a wasted, depressing week. I just sat on the stairs this morning crying. I thought I had turned a corner. I don't know if I can go tomorrow but Chris is insisting.

P.S. Enjoy your date tomorrow.

Saturday 7th February 18.00
TO: marikarolincova@hotmail.co.uk

I was looking for my car keys this morning when the doorbell went. Chris was grinning on the doorstep in a smart suit. Parked by the old red telephone box sparkled his mother's Bentley.

A distinguished looking driver got out and opened the door.

'I thought we'd go in style,' said Chris.

'How will your mum get to Harrods?' I said, grabbing my bag.

'I told her about the Tube,' he said. 'She's going to try it with her friend India; they're very excited.'

The car barely made a sound as it slid across London. As I predicted in the poem, TBS Returns was a huge warehouse, but it lacked hallowed doors. It had those plastic strips flapping in the breeze. Once we slid through the gates, we were searched, briefed about the fire exits, and asked to sign a confidentiality agreement.

'Just remember,' said Chris as we descended in the lift, 'you're not a bad writer. One day you'll be bigger than Regina Battenberg.'

'No thanks,' I said. 'She's packing a lot under that Kaftan.'

As the lift opened, we took in the enormity of the warehouse. Books were piled floor to ceiling and forklift trucks buzzed about.

We were also confronted by the sheer damn sexiness of Iain Anderson, 'Head Book Pulper'. I had imagined some fusty old git and I blushed when he held out his hand to greet us.

'Coco Pinchard!' his voice echoed confidently. 'The writer and poet.' I guffawed like a slapper on a hen night and went red. He put his hand on the small of my back and ushered us into a nearby cherry picker. Chris hopped in after and he closed the gate.

Our bodies were packed close as we rose up over the warehouse. With his full lips, dark stubble and muscular lean body, Chris and I locked eyes in agreement. Iain was hot.

'You just made it,' said Iain, as the cherry picker slowed its climb. '*Chasing Diana Spencer* is next.'

He pointed to a forklift carrying a wooden pallet stacked high with my book and moving towards the pulping machine.

I went to say something profound but the forklift swerved and dumped them in one go. As they hit the spinning blades, the hardback covers squealed and cracked. I felt tears coming and, for some reason, buried my head in Iain's chest. It was firm and muscled and he smelt so wonderful.

I realised what I was doing and pulled away, but a big string of snot hung between my nose and his shirt pocket.

'Oh God!' I said, mortified. Chris's eyebrows shot up and he fumbled for a tissue.

There is nowhere to run in a cherry picker, and it was a long minute before all the snot was accounted for.

'We often forget how tough it is to be a writer,' said Iain, as we descended back to earth. I wasn't sure if he was changing the subject or being polite about the silvery trail of snot now drying on his shirt.

'A lot of the staff read your book this week. It's great,' he said. 'In fact, we reviewed it in our internal magazine, *Pulped Fiction*.'

'Thank you,' I said, as he helped us out.

'I'm sorry I didn't have more time to talk to you, but I've got to go. Best of luck,' he said.

And that was it, over so quickly. On the way home in the car, Chris asked if I had had the anticipated closure.

'No, but I now have a nice cringeworthy memory to add to my woes.'

'I know,' said Chris. 'If he'd have been a minger it

would've been much less embarrassing.'

'It's made me realise that if I ever go on the pull again, I'm limited to the over forties. Your youth, it goes.'

'Try being me,' said Chris. 'In gay years I'm virtually a pensioner.'

When I got home, Iain had emailed me the book review. I have attached it.

Chasing Diana Spencer By Coco Pinchard
Published by House of Randoms. **£19.99**

A sublime piece of comic fiction from first-time writer Coco Pinchard. Set in 1981 in a parallel reality, Prince Charles is to announce his engagement to Camilla Parker-Bowles. With a week to go before the official announcement, the Queen is visited by the ghost of Queen Elizabeth I, who informs her that a grave error has occurred in the order of the Universe.

If she wants to save the monarchy, and the future of humanity, Prince Charles must marry a young woman called Diana Spencer, working as a ski instructor in a sleepy corner of France. The Queen is forced to don a disguise and undertake an epic journey to find Diana before it's all too late. Full of comedy, drama, and delightful plot twists, this novel must be read before the scheduled shred. ★★★★★

Sunday 8th February 13.30
TO: chris@christophercheshire.com

Are you around for some Sunday lunch? Rosencrantz is in love, Marika is in love. I am not. Are you? You know I always wish you happiness but please don't tell me you've fallen in love since yesterday. I need a fellow ying for their loved-up yang.

Marika had a wonderful dinner with her Greek guy, Aristotle. He was chivalrous, made her laugh and the lingering kiss he gave her whilst pressed up against the gas meter was so good, she has lost the will to smoke.

'His pheromones have flooded my body, and taken away the cravings,' she said as I lit up a fag, my fifteenth of the morning.

Rosencrantz met a guy during a flash mob this morning at King's Cross Station, organised via Facebook. Three hundred strangers congregated at precisely 11.09 and all performed the Macarena. Post flash mob, when they were being herded out of the ticket hall by the police, Rosencrantz got chatting to Clive, a handsome older guy wearing Prada sunglasses.

'I'm like in love,' he said. 'The writing's on the wall.'

I presume he meant his Facebook wall.

Doesn't anyone meet in the pub anymore?

I've made Yorkshire puddings (from a packet).

xxx

Monday 9th February 10.00
TO: marikarolincova@hotmail.co.uk

At seven this morning I shuffled past my computer on the landing when it started to trill like a 1950s phone. There was a popping noise and Meryl appeared, sat in her front room with her palm tree wallpaper in the background. Her mouth was moving but there was no sound.

In my bleary state, I realised it was the new Skype account Rosencrantz downloaded to talk to the Prada sunglasses guy, Clive. I clicked on the speakers and Meryl came booming through at full blast, saying, 'Coco! It's cockcrow, and you're still in your nightie?'

I said I was recovering from a boozy lunch with Rosencrantz, Marika and Chris where we all talked about men.

'What's Rosencrantz talking about men for?'

'Because he's gay,' I said. 'You remember? He told us all over the PA system at your fortieth birthday party.'

'Yes,' said Meryl shuddering. 'But, are you *sure* he's gay. He'd make some girl very happy.'

'Look,' I said. 'I am not going to debate my son's sexuality with you. Again. The penny should have dropped years ago when you made him all those evening gowns for his Barbie dolls. Now. What can I do for you?'

'I was seeing if you wanted to come for Easter?'

'When is Easter?' I asked.

'When is Easter?' parroted Tony, popping up behind Meryl. 'You Labour voters. I bet you could tell me when Ramadan is but not Good Friday.'

'Tony, I'm talking,' said Meryl, pushing him away. 'Coco, Easter falls on April the tenth. Mum's coming. Daniel will be in the States, *Whistle Up the Wind* is doing very well... It'll be your first Easter alone.'

Meryl blinked and let it hang there. I was too tired to think of an excuse, so I agreed.

'Super, I'll send you a notelet to confirm. Must dash.'

With that there was another popping sound and the

screen went blank.

What are you doing for Easter? Could you manufacture a fake relative who could die, and invite me to the funeral? I must try to get out of it. I must also get Rosencrantz to switch the computer off when he is finished. This Skype thing is too close for comfort. Last night, I was unwittingly introduced to Clive as I walked past in a towel.

'Ooh. Isn't Mum a curvy goddess?' he crooned.

I couldn't tell if it was meant as a compliment. He still had on his Prada sunglasses, indoors, at night. Their first proper date is tomorrow evening.

Wednesday 11th February 23.18
TO: rosencrantzpinchard@gmail.com

Thank you for your message. Why can't you lie like other teenagers? I don't need to know that the date is going well and you are going back to Clive's 'for coffee'.

Chris is *here*. He just showed me the text you sent him; 'Will the sunglasses come off along with the underwear?'

Could you please not send things like that to Chris? It puts him in a position of knowing too much and then he feels he has to tell me.

I went for tea and corned beef sandwiches with your nan today, she sends you her love. There is a new resident in her home, Mrs Burbridge, who is jostling to be top dog. Last night she led a coup in the residents' lounge, which resulted in *Eastenders* not being shown. I told her to tell Mrs Braun, the manager, but I was met with a torrent of expletives culminating in, 'I ain't a grass!'

She is plotting to bring down Mrs Burbridge.

'I control what is on the box round 'ere,' she said, her eyes flashing.

I told her not to make trouble, but she said whatever she does, it won't be traced back to her. If I was Mrs Burbridge, I would be scared. I saw Ethel surreptitiously slide the key off the tin of corned beef and into her handbag.

Thursday 12th February 15.47
TO: chris@christophercheshire.com

Rosencrantz has ended it with Clive. They went on a second date yesterday to the Chamber of Horrors at Madame Tussauds. It was very dark, and for health and safety reasons a member of staff ordered him to remove his Prada sunglasses. Apparently, Clive has rather overdone it on the eye surgery. It looks like two peeled eggs are straining to evacuate his head. Rosencrantz screamed in terror and ran into the arms of a Dracula waxwork.

Saturday 14th February 13.44
TO: chris@christophercheshire.com

You got six Valentine cards? I got a gas bill. Marika has had nothing from Aristotle, even though on their last date she let him take her up the Oxo Tower.

Presents from Clive keep arriving for Rosencrantz. They were supposed to be going for a luxury Valentine's journey on The London Eye... The eye-rony!

Saturday 14th February 17.07
TO: chris@christophercheshire.com

At four thirty, after champagne, handmade Belgian chocolates and a Tiffany Silver Spork had been delivered, Clive knocked on the door.

'Don't answer it,' said Rosencrantz, leaping into the airing cupboard and closing the door.

Clive banged again and looked through the letterbox. I ran into the living room but he followed and saw me through the window. I pretended to be surprised to see him, and went to open the door.

'What can I do to win his heart?' begged Clive.

'You should find someone who wants to settle down,' I said, as nicely as I could.

Clive pulled off his sunglasses and shouted, 'Does he know how rich I am? He'll want for nothing!'

Despite being forewarned, I still took a sharp intake of breath. I don't know how his eyes were managing to stay in his head.

'Um... money isn't everything,' I said weakly.

'If you believe that then you're a fool!' he spat. 'I know you're in there Rosencrantz,' he shouted. 'I could make you a star!'

We stood there, awkwardly, as Rosencrantz remained in the airing cupboard.

'Fine!' he said, and turning on his loafers, he hailed a cab.

Rosencrantz quickly forgot about Clive. In fact, within three quarters of an hour, he had arranged a date via Facebook with a boy from his Elizabethan dance class. I couldn't forget the look of desperation on Clive's face. Will he ever find someone? Will I?

Please don't cancel your date. I am okay. Aristotle came through and is taking Marika on a romantic horse-drawn carriage ride through Hyde Park. I'm just going to have a bath and go to bed early with the Belgian chocolates. I'm going to mash them up in a bowl, and eat the lot with the Silver Spork.

Sunday 15th February 11.44
TO: chris@christophercheshire.com

No, I didn't have the best evening. I was getting ready for bed when Daniel phoned. I thought it was going to be a nice build bridges/Valentine's call, but all he wanted to know was if Ethel's spare teeth were in the filing cabinet. She had rung him in a panic. Her set has vanished from the glass beside her bed. Yesterday, Ethel stole Mrs Burbridge's wig and threw it in the tea urn, where it melted onto the filament. She thinks the missing teeth are retaliation.

The sum of my Valentine's evening was spent sterilising her spare set. I am taking them over in a minute; they have steak Diane for lunch, and the nursing home use the cheapest cuts of meat.

You want to come over later? Marika wants to tell us about her amazing night with Aristotle. She is also on at me to join up to Facebook. Which is where she found him. She thinks it would do me good to meet new people.

Monday 16th February 17.00
TO: marikarolincova@hotmail.co.uk

I am just fiddling with my new Facebook profile. What does it mean if someone pokes me? I just had an old school friend do just that. A guy called Rhydian. He was my first boyfriend. He dumped me because I threw sand at him. I was six at the time.

Tuesday 17th February 04.01
TO: marikarolincova@hotmail.co.uk

Do you remember a woman called Regan Turnbull? We taught with her when we were both at St. Duke's comprehensive. She has the most awful picture of me in one of her Facebook albums. Taken the night we got drunk in 1998 after the OFSTED inspection. Bad angle, bad haircut, bad diet. I look fifty – I was only thirty!

Tuesday 17th February 04.12
TO: marikarolincova@hotmail.co.uk

Sorry! Go back to sleep. I completely lost track of the time. I will message her and ask her to take the picture off. Rhydian's poke was platonic. He is married.

Tuesday 17th February 21.00
TO: marikarolincova@hotmail.co.uk

I now have one hundred Facebook friends. Just keeping up with all of them is exhausting. You click through their photos and profiles and you are confronted with another person you had consigned to your past.

One of them is a woman who heads an influential policy group at Chatham House, campaigning against beheadings in Saudi Arabia. The last time I saw her, we were five and I tried to steal her Cindy Doll. She ended up with the body and me with the head.

Rosencrantz had to prise my hands off the mouse this evening when dinner was ready.

'You haven't like washed today, Mum,' he said.

No response from Regan Turnbull. I keep looking at that awful picture. She never asked if she could put it out there for the entire world to see!

Wednesday 18th February 16.30
TO: marikarolincova@hotmail.co.uk

Sorry I missed your calls. I turned on the computer at nine this morning, then I looked up and it was three o'clock!

Two hundred and eleven friends and counting. I chatted to Rhydian today. He bought me a virtual cactus, which I must remember to virtually water. I bought him some virtual chocolate.

We worked out our porn names. Mine is Bambi Turner for which he sent me a super poke, and his is Kenton Fluffbag. I threw a sheep at him. He is so nice to chat to. He has a daughter the same age as Rosencrantz.

Bad news re Regan Turnbull. On further inspection, she hasn't posted on her wall or updated her status in months.

I phoned the number listed on her profile and her husband answered. He told me she ran off with another man last summer, and hasn't been heard of since. She met the man on Facebook.

I asked him if he knew her account password to remove the photo but he said, 'If I did, this affair would've been nipped in the bud.' Poor man.

Wednesday 18th February 17.03
TO: marikarolincova@hotmail.co.uk

I have now looked at the photo of me so many times that it's coming up as the first result when you Google Coco Pinchard!

Daphne from Ohio is now in second place.

To top it all, the cactus from Rhydian has died. I forgot to virtually water it. Am gutted.

Wednesday 18th February 21.47
TO: marikarolincova@hotmail.co.uk

Had my first tiff with Rhydian. My status is set to, 'Coco is currently annoyed with Rhydian'.

The reason; he bought me a virtual goldfish, to make up for the loss of my virtual cactus. What with mounting friend requests and my search for Regan, I just don't have time for pets.

Thursday 19th February 08.04
TO: marikarolincova@hotmail.co.uk

I haven't slept. Rhydian said the virtual goldfish would be low maintenance, but it was ill in the night.

I also found Sophie Snow White's profile. It is set to private so I can't view her. I don't want to friend request her.

A horrible thought... What if she is still seeing Daniel?

Thursday 19th February 09.15
TO: marikarolincova@hotmail.co.uk

I found a way around it. I set up a fake account as Karen Pritchard and friended Snow White.

There are many pictures in her photo album, mostly taken in nightclubs holding on to different men with her pink-stained tongue poking out. None of Daniel, thank God.

I am going to engage her in some online chat, and pump her for information.

Thursday 19th February 10.01
TO: marikarolincova@hotmail.co.uk

I hope you don't mind, but I used a photo of you on my fake profile. I was talking to Snow White as Karen and she wanted to know what I looked like. The only pictures I had on the hard drive were of you or Goldie Hawn, and even she's not that gullible.

Snow White is in a relationship with a guy who works as a DJ in Manchester. She said that she *was* seeing an 'older guy' but he was 'crap in bed'.

I am quite offended... Daniel is/was actually rather good. Am I terribly inexperienced? Should I get out there more? However, where is 'out there' these days?

Thursday 19th February 11.46
TO: marikarolincova@hotmail.co.uk

I have just written something on Snow White's Wall that I am not proud of.

I wrote SLAG.

As well as Daniel, she was sleeping with Prince Charming from the Pantomime!

Thursday 19th February 11.56
TO: marikarolincova@hotmail.co.uk

Oops. No, I didn't. I wrote SALG. Snow White thinks it's a 'cool word' and she has started up a new Facebook group called 'The SALGS'.

Just she and I are members so far.

Thursday 19th February 12.30
TO: marikarolincova@hotmail.co.uk

I blew my cover and told Sophie what I thought of her. She sent one word back: FREAK.

She also ordered me to leave The SALGS which now has 124 members, including Chris!

Thursday 19th February 19.00
TO: chris@christophercheshire.com

Thank you for leaving the SALGS, I appreciate your loyalty.

I just experienced an intervention when Marika came up the stairs with Rosencrantz. I hadn't noticed the door go. She took me into the bathroom and showed me my reflection in the mirror.

I was shocked. I looked ancient and unwashed with huge

dark circles under my eyes.

Rosencrantz has changed the passwords on my accounts and deactivated me. He has taken on my virtual goldfish.

They led me downstairs, poured wine, and made me eat. I thought I would be so mad with them but I felt calm. I'm not in a good place, but the Internet is a far worse place for me to be right now.

Friday 20th February 16.33
TO: marikarolincova@hotmail.co.uk

Thank you for last night. A good sleep has put things in perspective.

Ethel just phoned to see how I am doing. Apparently, she came over in the week but I didn't see or hear her.

She said if her Wilf were still alive, he too would have been addicted to the Internet.

'What with all that free porn, it would've made life easier for 'im,' she said. 'In later years 'is back was so bad 'e couldn't reach the top-shelf magazines.'

I told Ethel I wasn't looking at that kind of thing and put the phone down.

I have just had a text from Rhydian asking if I fancied a drink this evening. He says he misses me on Facebook. Should I go? It's only a drink and our Facebook relationship was platonic. Might be nice to get out... I've just sat on the stairs all morning, smoking.

Friday 20th February 20.00
TO: chris@christophercheshire.com

Why aren't you answering your phone? I need you to save me from Rhydian. Foolishly, I came out on a date with him. He is a total nut job. His wife left him last Friday. He joined Facebook to find a new partner. What's more, his daughter Lizzie is here too (and equally nuts). He thought meeting her would be a good way to integrate me into the family. He said he never should have dumped me when we were six. I am hiding in the toilets.

What am I doing?

Friday 20th February 21.44
TO: chris@christophercheshire.com

Where are you? It's packed in here. We just had food, which is difficult when people are dragging their oversized handbags over your head as they pass. Lizzie told the story of her mother's betrayal. Last week she came home from school early to find her sitting on the gardener's face. The only reply I could think of was, 'You're so lucky to have a big garden.'

Come and get me, please!

Friday 20th February 22.00
TO: chris@christophercheshire.com

No. I am in All Bar One, not The Slug and Lettuce. The windows are all steamed up so I can't see out. We are at the back. I can barely stand. I have had too much wine. Lizzie just cornered me when Rhydian was in the loo saying, 'I knew he'd find me a new mother on Facebook. You were the best out of all the others we looked at.'

What if she didn't run off with the gardener? What if they killed her?

Saturday 21st February 11.19
TO: chris@christophercheshire.com

I thought I told you it was the All Bar One in Covent Garden, sorry hun. On the upside, at least you now know where all the other All Bar Ones are in Central London? ;-)

I finally got away at midnight, lying that I had forgotten to take the anti-rejection drugs for my *heart transplant.*

'You must get them,' said Lizzie, 'and come back for us!'

Rhydian walked me outside to the pavement. We stopped by the window awkwardly. Then I heard a squeaking sound. Lizzie was at the window and was looking through a smiley face she had drawn in the condensation. She gave her dad the thumbs up and he leant in for a kiss. My stomach contracted in a panic. I pushed him away and threw up spectacularly over the bonnet of a parked Mercedes. Their faces fell in disgust.

Rhydian produced a tissue, saying, 'Well, this has been, um, lovely.'

Lizzy's face, still at the window, was now boiling with tears. I just ran for it and didn't stop until I reached Leicester Square. Maybe my vomit saved me. I haven't heard from him.

Monday 24th February 16.18
TO: rosencrantzpinchard@gmail.com

Hi love, tried to ring but you're not answering. You must be in mime class. I know they are very strict about you not speaking. Your nan has been taken to Casualty after a nasty fall. I don't know much else. I am on my way to the hospital. The key is under the wheelie bin. If you're hungry, I'm afraid all we've got is Wagon Wheels...

Monday 24th February 21.33
TO: danielpinchard@gmail.com

Answer your phone! I have left you three messages. Your mum has had to have an emergency hip replacement at The Aldgate East Hospital in Whitechapel. The surgeon says it went well. I was with her when she came round from the anaesthetic. She had a fight with Mrs Burbridge at the nursing home over who was going to call the bingo balls. It got physical and Ethel fell/was pushed off the stage. I asked her if she reported it to the manager, but she is still going on about not being a grass.

Tuesday 25th February 15.04
TO: danielpinchard@gmail.com

I took your mum some nicotine patches this morning; she said that she would prefer them to grapes. When I got there, she was very pale and in a lot more pain than yesterday. The nurses don't seem bothered. They were all huddled round a computer playing *The NHS Sims*, looking after virtual patients.

I phoned Mrs Braun at the Rainbow Nursing home, and she says Ethel will no longer be welcome as a resident when she is discharged from hospital. I asked why. Mrs Braun says when she tried to break up the fight Ethel, called her a 'potato-faced Kraut'. I said she has called me far worse, but Mrs Braun said that they have a zero-tolerance racism policy.

I then phoned Meryl. She had to bellow above the noise of her food mixer as she's knee deep in royal icing, making a four-tier wedding cake, and can't visit before the weekend. Tony can't either. He has a backlog of coffins due to a local outbreak of Legionnaires' disease.

I told her that your mother will be homeless when she gets out of hospital, but she said she had to go, and put the phone down. We need to sort this out.

Wednesday 26th February 15.01
TO: marikarolincova@hotmail.co.uk

Chris came with me to the Rainbow Nursing home. Ethel's room had been emptied. Three drab suitcases and a hatbox sat waiting in reception. There was no note or message. The teenager on the desk informed us that Mrs Braun had gone to visit her sister in Berlin.

Mrs Burbridge hasn't been evicted. We saw her through the window of the residents' lounge surrounded by pensioners. There was laughter and music playing loudly and the sun was glinting off her smooth, bald head.

Thursday 27th February 21.34
TO: marikarolincova@hotmail.co.uk

Rosencrantz came along to Whitechapel for evening visiting. I was shocked how Ethel's condition had deteriorated. They have moved her into a stinking ward full of old women moaning in the gloom. The lone nurse on duty was engrossed in a book about alternative medicine.

When we reached Ethel's bed, she was waxy and delirious. We tried to give her some water but her body tensed up and she began to shake. I shouted for the nurse, and seeing Ethel, she pressed an alarm. Within seconds, a team of doctors sped in and swished the curtains around her bed. We were asked to wait outside in the corridor. After a long hour, a consultant came and told us Ethel had had a cardiac arrest. They managed to revive her but she is unconscious and on a ventilator. I had to play twenty questions but he finally admitted that it might be the MRSA superbug, brought on by her wound not healing.

'So, nothing to do with that filthy ward?' I said.

The consultant said Ethel was being moved to intensive care and then he had to go.

Meryl and Tony are coming down early tomorrow morning and Daniel is on standby for a flight home.

Friday 28th February 03.30
TO: rosencrantzpinchard@gmail.com

I can hear music coming from your room, can't you sleep either? You fancy a hot chocolate?

Friday 28th February 10.06
TO: marikarolincova@hotmail.co.uk

I phoned the hospital at 7am. Ethel is still unconscious, but stable. At 8.30am, Meryl and Tony were on the doorstep in cycling gear with windswept hair. They had biked down in the freezing rain.

They were acting with forced gaiety. Meryl was barely through the door when the bicycle clips came off, the rubber gloves went on, and she was cleaning my oven. Tony pulled a brick out of his bum bag saying he'd brought it to drop into my cistern to save water. As he disappeared up the stairs, I lit a cigarette and watched Meryl.

'You okay?' I said.

'Yes, thank you,' she said, scrubbing furiously. 'Just a little saddle sore but apart from that...'

She burst into tears. I went over and gave her a hug.

'What will I do if...?' she sobbed.

Tony came downstairs. I signalled him to come and hug her but he went very red saying, 'Ah, I'll just um...' before scuttling into the garden.

I poured us each a large brandy, and for the first time ever, she's not cooking or cleaning. We're sat watching an episode of *Sex and The City*. I think it's cheered her up a bit, although she's had to keep asking me what a lot of things mean.

Daniel lands at nine tonight.

MARCH

Sunday 1st March 09.45
TO: chris@christophercheshire.com

Daniel knocked on the door at 10pm. He was surprised I hadn't picked him up from Heathrow. He had a tan, a small ponytail and was sporting some woven cloth bracelets around his wrist. Everything about him screamed mid-life crisis, including the faux American accent. I managed to be civil for about fifteen minutes, until he thanked me for saving him some cold fish fingers under 'ah-loo-min-um' foil.

'You're a Londoner, Daniel, from Catford.'

'But in America I can be whaddever I want,' he said.

'Can you stop being a dickhead then?' I snapped.

He slept downstairs on the sofa. Meryl tried to instigate a big jolly cooked breakfast with Daniel this morning. I stayed upstairs with a couple of Pop-Tarts and Rosencrantz stomped off to college with a cold 'hello' and a Fruit Corner.

M + T have gone on ahead to Whitechapel on the tandem. Daniel and I are waiting for a taxi. I feel like I am trapped in an Ingmar Bergman film. I'm looking out into the grey drizzle whilst Daniel plays mournfully on the piano downstairs.

Monday 2nd March 16.30
TO: rosencrantzpinchard@gmail.com

Nothing has changed. They have put even more machines around your nan's bed so now only two of us can be in her room at a time. I'm sharing shifts with Tony and your Dad is going in with Meryl. It doesn't look promising.

Tuesday 3rd March 19.00
TO: chris@christophercheshire.com,
    marikarolincova@hotmail.co.uk

I held Daniel's hand on the way home in the taxi tonight. The latest news from the consultant is bad. He doubts Ethel will ever wake up; she was starved of oxygen for twelve minutes.

They have placed electrodes on her temples but there was little sign of brain activity, not even when we put on her favourite, *The Jerry Springer Show*. The hospital has started talking about the 'option' to switch off her ventilator.

Rosencrantz has just come home from classes and lit up one of my cigarettes. I didn't say anything. Ethel would be proud, her saying has always been 'Cigarettes maketh the man'.

Meryl is mopping the kitchen floor. Again. Tony is outside in the gloom oiling the tandem and Daniel is playing some dark dramatic Rachmaninoff on the piano.

Wednesday 4th March 23.56
TO: chris@christophercheshire.com,
    marikarolincova@hotmail.co.uk

Thank you for the lilies that you both sent. Ethel would have loved them, but flowers aren't allowed in Intensive Care.

When we got back from the hospital tonight, we opened some wine and all sat in living room looking at old photos of Ethel. She was scowling in most of them, even the ones from her own wedding. The only picture we found of her looking happy was taken in 1949, when she won a ballroom dancing competition at the Catford Working Men's Club. She looked like a different person, young, beaming in a slim elegant gown next to Daniel's dad. I asked them why she never smiled.

Meryl told us Ethel had had all her teeth out in the fifties and that the false ones she was given were too big.

'Why didn't she get smaller ones?' asked Rosencrantz.

'Couldn't afford to,' said Daniel. 'Then when Dad died and left her with two small kids and no money, life was hard. I suppose she got used to not smiling.'

The hospital had been pushing us all day to make a decision about turning off Ethel's life support. After more tests, it is almost certain that she will never wake up. We opened more wine and it felt like a horrible version of jury duty, discussing the pros and cons of keeping Ethel alive. In the end it came down to the fact that she told us on many occasions, 'If I'm a vegetable, switch me orf, don't faff, and don't waste the 'lectric bill dithering.'

A cloud descended over the room as we realised, we had made the decision.

Meryl, Tony, and Rosencrantz drifted off up to bed; Daniel and I were left alone. One lamp was glowing and the fire was beginning to die down. The rain rattled on the roof. He leant over and topped up my wine glass.

'Could I get some warder?' he said.

'Oh Daniel, drop the accent,' I sighed. 'You sound like a bad Cliff Richard impersonator.'

I went into the kitchen, and when I came back with a glass of water, he was crying. He took a long drink and wiped his eyes.

'I thought Mum would live to see her fourscore and ten.'

I put my arm around him.

'You want to know why I did it? Why I cheated on you?'

'We don't need to do this now,' I said.

'I don't want to end up like my mother. Bitter, miserable and never achieving anything,' he said.

I asked him how shagging a twenty-year-old would help him achieve something.

'She needed me.'

'I didn't need you?' I said, hurt.

'Yeah, I've gone and you're fine.'

'I am not!'

'Mum said you've been living the life of Riley, out on the tiles with Chris and Marika, enjoying this house, which I could never have bought you, no matter how hard I toiled.'

I went to protest, but I realised Ethel wouldn't be able to defend herself ever again. Damn, I thought. Even on her deathbed she's getting one up on me.

'I'm just... nothing,' Daniel said, and began to sob.

I sat beside him.

'Do you know how proud I am of you?' I said. I stroked his hair and held him close. 'I need you so much.'

He pulled away, looked into my eyes, and kissed me. It

was like a switch being flipped in my stomach, flooding me with heat. Before I knew it, we were racing up the stairs, tugging off our clothes and having the most passionate sex in years. Afterwards I lay in his arms on the bare mattress of our old bed. He traced his finger slowly down my stomach.

'Coco,' he said, staring into my eyes.

'Yes,' I said breathlessly, his finger tracing lower.

'I want you to do something for me.'

'Yes?' I whispered, closing my eyes.

'Would you switch off my mother's life support machine?'

I pushed his hand away, got up, and scrambled for my clothes.

'What?' he said. 'Meryl says she can't, she won't let Tony and I couldn't... Please?'

I struggled into my jeans. 'Why did you have to ask me now?'

'Well,' he said, tapping his watch as if we were late for the theatre.

I pulled on an old t-shirt. He lit a cigarette and passed it to me.

'Please,' he said. 'I would do it for you. Please.'

I couldn't say no to his pleading face. I said I had to go and came back to the spare room. I cannot sleep. What have I done?

Thursday 5th March 14.30
TO: chris@christophercheshire.com,
    marikarolincova@hotmail.co.uk

We got to Whitechapel at eight this morning. There is nothing more depressing than a shabby Victorian-era hospital on a cold grey day.

When we arrived at Intensive Care and saw Ethel, I knew that we were making the right decision. She was dressed in a fresh gown. A nurse had just finished bathing her. He was a nice chap but he had very bony fingers. Ethel hates bony fingers, they give her the creeps.

The fluorescent light fizzed and the rhythmic sound of the ventilator sucked air in and out of her lungs. Her fringe had been combed off her forehead, which she would have hated, and without her teeth, her scowl was sunken and diminished.

'I think we should all like say something, before we do this,' said Rosencrantz.

We took it in turns. Rosencrantz went first and told her he loved her. He said that he would endeavour to sleep with Rupert Everett, like he promised her he would.

'I always thought you would live like long enough for me to like tell you all about it,' he said.

There were raised eyebrows from everyone. Tony went next, and promised her coffin would be of the best quality.

'We've got a marvellous selection in at the moment, cherry, maple, oak, all with lovely brass features. Goodbye.'

Meryl went next. She was crying so much she could barely speak, so she just kissed Ethel on the cheek. Then it was my turn.

'Ethel,' I said, 'goodbye. I know we have had our differences but I hate that this has happened to you... and in case you can hear, they asked me to press the switch. I didn't volunteer.'

I took her comb and combed her fringe back over her forehead, just how she always wore it.

Daniel went last, and if I'm honest, he did go on a bit, giving a long lament that she will never get to see him realise his full potential. I half expected Ethel to open one eye and croak, 'Pull yerself together, yer big girl's blouse.'

The consultant was getting twitchy, as this had gone on for some time. He gave me a nod, and I walked over to switch off the life support. I was confronted by a confusing array of plugs. The hospital hadn't said *exactly* what I had to do, and I didn't feel like I could ask. I took a deep breath and pressed a switch. A pedestal fan by the bed sprang to life and swirled all Ethel's get well cards off the bedside cabinet. The second switch turned on the television and the opening credits of *This Morning* boomed out.

'Excuse me,' said Meryl to the consultant, as if she were lost in Sainsbury's, 'could you direct my sister-in-law to the correct switch?'

I felt an inappropriate laugh rise up in my chest, which burst out. They all exchanged scandalised glances.

Apologising, I took a deep breath and pressed the correct switch. The ventilator filled her lungs one last time and slowly wheezed to a stop.

'Her chest is still rising!' cried Rosencrantz.

'This is sometimes normal,' said the consultant kindly. 'Many patients do carry on breathing for a few minutes.'

'So right now, she's like dying?' said Rosencrantz.

We all looked at Ethel. She had a serene scowl on her face. Meryl gave a deep sob so Tony and me took her out, and Rosencrantz and Daniel followed. We had no interest in seeing what little colour Ethel had left drain from her face.

We went down to the cafeteria, ordered coffee, and sat staring into space. I don't know how long we had been there when the consultant appeared at our table.

'It seems Mrs Pinchard is breathing unaided, and with a

stronger pulse,' he said. 'Now, this is an awkward crucial time, it could go either way, but she has shown stronger life signs in the last hour. Much stronger than we'd expected.'

We are still at the hospital. Ethel has now been breathing unaided for four hours. Meryl is in on the phone trying to get in touch with the Steakhouse we had booked for a memorial lunch. Tony had put down a deposit of fifty pounds. He is pacing up and down saying, 'I know this is an emotional time, but fifty pounds is fifty pounds.'

Friday 6th March 11.09
TO: chris@christophercheshire.com,
      marikarolincova@hotmail.co.uk

Ethel has now been breathing by herself for twenty-four hours. The thought of arranging a funeral had been bad enough, but now we are trying to prepare for what Ethel will be like if she wakes up. She could have serious brain damage.

When we got back last night, I went outside with Daniel to share a cigarette. We both squeezed onto the shed step at the end of the garden and looked out across London. It was clear and we could see for miles. Daniel pulled me into his coat.

'I'd like to try again,' he said, exhaling smoke into the glowing sky. 'I love you, and the thought of losing you like I nearly did Mum is just awful.'

'You're going away,' I said.

'Not forever,' he said looking into my eyes. 'I want to make it right. I'm sorry. I love you.'

He kissed me. We slept together again, properly, in our bed. Why is high emotion such an aphrodisiac?

Friday 6th March 17.33
TO: chris@christophercheshire.com

Marika can be so blunt sometimes. She phoned this morning to say my emails have become very 'Mills and Boon'. She said she is deeply sorry about Ethel, but that I am sleepwalking back to Daniel, who is exploiting the situation to make himself feel better, and win me back. I hung up on her.

Ethel, it seems, is tougher than we thought. At 3pm, she opened her eyes and told Meryl that she looked like she was retaining water, 'Gallons of it.' At 3.15pm, the doctors ran tests to check for brain damage. She could not remember the Prime Minister's name, but she did know who the current landlady is in *Coronation Street*. They are calling it an unprecedented recovery.

Saturday 7th March 10.14
TO: chris@christophercheshire.com

I thought *you* would be supportive of my decision. What about when you and Marika have gone back to people who, in your case, were blatantly not right for you?

Gus, the married banker? He dumped you three times and you had to pretend you were reading the gas meter when his wife caught you in their downstairs cupboard. And Marika wasted two years with John the PE teacher who destroyed her confidence and had her at his beck and call.

Despite this, I always supported you. This is my marriage of twenty years. Family is family, you love them unconditionally.

Now I have to go. That dickhead Tony has started a row about something with Rosencrantz.

Saturday 7th March 12.05
TO: rosencrantzpinchard@gmail.com

Wherever you went, you can come home. Meryl and Tony have gone.

Saturday 7th March 12.12
TO: meryl.watson@yahoo.com

In your haste to depart, you left your Carmen rollers. Coco

Saturday 7th March 13.23
TO: meryl.watson@yahoo.com

Rosencrantz, where are you? Meryl and Tony have gone. I am sorry Tony got so nasty with you, the arrogant greasy bastard. They both vanished upstairs after you stormed out. An hour later, Meryl knocked on the living room door and they came in, all packed and dressed in cycling gear.

'I think we're going to leave,' said Meryl frostily and they walked out with their Lycra shorts whistling, slamming the front door.

They'll be back; we're a free place to stay when they come to London.

Do you think you will be home soon? Dad wants to play us some songs from *Whistle Up the Wind*. It's ages since we all sat round the piano together.

Saturday 7th March 15.01
TO: rosencrantzpinchard@gmail.com

Oh God! Oh God! Oh shit! I have just sent the email slagging off Meryl I was meant to send you *to* Meryl by mistake! Damn this email invention. In the olden days (pre-1994), if you mistakenly addressed mail you had so many ways of backing out at the last minute: not writing the envelope, not licking the stamp, not going to the postbox. Where are you?

Saturday 7th March 15.54
TO: rosencrantzpinchard@gmail.com

This just arrived from your aunt. She thinks Tony won the argument.

ATTACHMENT
FROM: meryl.watson@yahoo.com
TO: cocopinchard27@gmail.com

Coco,
You sent me an email by mistake. Was it destined for Rosencrantz maybe? Not wanting to pry, I have deleted it unread. However, my eyes could not help but pick out the word 'bastard'. Why are you sending this to your *son*? Surely as a 'writer' you could afford to put your point across more elegantly?

We made it back on the tandem in two hours, fourteen minutes and twelve seconds. We did have the wind in our backs, and Tony is always a better cyclist after winning an argument.

I will be popping down to see Mum in the week. Don't worry. I won't be staying. I will get the train.

Meryl

P.S. Re the Carmen rollers, I can think of several places you could put them. You take that big house for granted! Nevertheless, if they are really in your way, send them on and I will reimburse you for the postage.

Saturday 7th March 16.30
TO: meryl.watson@yahoo.com

Dear Meryl,

I'm pleased to hear you made it back on the tandem in record time. Has Tony calmed down after his row with Rosencrantz? It was a very trivial argument, don't you think? I dug out one of my *Harry Potter* novels and looked up the house system at Hogwarts School of Witchcraft and Wizardry. The Houses are Gryffindor, Ravenclaw, Hufflepuff, and *Slytherin*, not Silvikrin as Tony insisted.

Rosencrantz was right. Silvikrin is a brand of hair shampoo designed to nourish, condition and pump up volume. Maybe whilst you are waiting for me to send your Carmen rollers you could try it. It could help you achieve the volume your hair lacks.

Keep me posted with what you find out about nursing homes. I hope that what Mrs Braun said about getting the local authority to blacklist Ethel was just in the heat of the moment.

Coco

Monday 9th March 10.43
TO: rosencrantzpinchard@gmail.com

Who is this 'friend' you are staying with? You'll be back tomorrow to say goodbye to Dad, won't you? I'm arranging a trip out to see him when his show is in Los Angeles at Easter. Would like to come?

I have always asked you not to take sides. Please can you respect that now? Your Dad loves you very much. I'm not trying to play happy families, and I have not forgotten what has happened. It just wouldn't hurt to spend some time together, the three of us. Fancy joining us for a walk around Regent's Park later?

Wednesday 11th March 23.44
TO: danielpinchard@gmail.com

How was the flight? I miss you already. The last few days were so idyllic, just talking and spending time together. Your mum was moved out of intensive care today, earlier than they had thought, and begins physiotherapy next week. So far, it's just me coming to Los Angeles for Easter.

Chris and Marika are ignoring me, so is your son.

Love Coco xxxx

Thursday 12th March 18.01
TO: rosencrantzpinchard@gmail.com

Who did you bring home last night? In future, it would be nice to be introduced, and it would be polite to be asked *before* you have overnight guests. I heard your bed going like the clappers. For my own peace of mind, I am going to assume you, and whoever, were jumping up and down on it to the music you were playing. I know you have your iPhone on, so please reply when you get this call/email.

Mum

Thursday 12th March 20.13
TO: danielpinchard@gmail.com

I have just spoken to Rosencrantz. He would like to come to Los Angeles at Easter and he wants to bring his new *boyfriend*. I asked him why I haven't been introduced. He said they haven't reached the parental introductions stage. I said it seemed serious as they are at the jumping up and down on beds stage. The chap is called Christian, and it seems he is a man of means. He is willing to pay his own airfare.

I think it's all happening rather fast. I have demanded I be introduced to him on Saturday night.

Coco x

Thursday 12th March 23.13
TO: chris@christophercheshire.com

Is five days too quick to get into a serious relationship?

Thursday 12th March 23.17
TO: chris@christophercheshire.com

I am not talking about Daniel and me. I was talking about Rosencrantz. Now I know your *real* opinion on us getting back together...

Also, how much longer is Marika going to keep ignoring me? I'm not stupid, I know what I am doing. Daniel has apologised. We are taking it slowly, but we are most definitely back together.

Friday 13th March 14.02
TO: marikarolincova@hotmail.co.uk

I am sorry. You were right. You were so right.

ATTACHMENT
FROM: danielpinchard@gmail.com
TO: cocopinchard27@gmail.com

Dear Coco,

I was awake all night after we came off the phone. I'm sorry. I can't do this. You need too much from me, but I need to get out there and achieve things, and I can't do it with you. Next to you, I am nothing. You are an incredible, generous, vibrant, amazing woman and you will always be my best friend. I am sorry.

We can make this quick and painless. I have found a link to an online divorce site: www.zippydivorces.com. It will be cheaper than going through normal solicitors and arguing over how to separate everything.

Daniel

He's telling me in an *email*? And *separating everything*? How could I be so stupid! Oh, and now I'm 'vibrant'! What the fuck does that mean?

Friday 13th March 15.44
TO: chris@christophercheshire.com

Spoke to Daniel. He didn't answer his phone until the tenth attempt. He was shocked at how angry I was, he had expected some tearful heap. He tried to convince me that the online divorce option was the best. I told him I am not separating anything.

'Well, you have to,' he said, with harshness in his voice. 'Otherwise, I'll cut you off. How much money do you have? A couple of hundred?'

He wants half the house. I asked him what has changed. He said it was him and not me. The emotion of nearly losing Ethel made him 'rash and vulnerable'.

Marika came straight over from work.

'You were right,' I said.

'I was starting to hope I was wrong,' she said, and gave me a long hug. I refuse to crumple. What a bastard he is, and how stupid I am.

Saturday 14th March 21.56
TO: marikarolincova@hotmail.co.uk

I met Rosencrantz's new boyfriend today. I wasn't going to but I refuse to let Daniel disrupt my life further. I was very impressed with Christian. Tall, blond, gorgeous and charismatic, he was dressed top to toe in theatrical high fashion, sort of Vivienne Westwood meets Elizabethan fop. He is studying at the London College of Fashion. He's only twenty but his back story is impressive; son of government diplomats, spent his childhood travelling, speaks fluent Mandarin, has volunteered for the Red Cross and last Christmas he raised £7,000 hiking up Kilimanjaro for charity. He is so mature, and so wise for his years.

After he had gone Rosencrantz told me off for talking so much.

'I didn't need to hear about you and Dad in so much ... *detail*.'

'You've hardly said 'like' all evening,' I said, surprised.

Rosencrantz told me that Christian fines him fifty pence every time he drops a random 'like' into a sentence. I had wondered why Christian was clutching a limited edition Vivienne Westwood piggy bank. Why didn't I think of that?

Sunday 15th March 15.45
TO: marikarolincova@hotmail.co.uk

Meryl rang today, the row wasn't mentioned. She gave me Ethel's new phone number/email address in hospital! She has had a 'communications module' installed next to her bed by a company called Bedside Entertainments Ltd. She can now watch television and communicate with the outside world. I asked her if it was expensive.

'Not with the NHS,' said Meryl. 'The greatest gift this country has given us is universal healthcare for all!'

She was sympathetic about Daniel, but commented how difficult it will be dividing things up.

'I would hate to lose half my Wedgwood, let alone half my house,' she said.

Afterwards I thought, why do I have to lose half?

Monday 16th March 13.43
TO: marikarolincova@hotmail.co.uk

Had coffee with Chris in Regent's Park for what he called a 'Divorce Summit'. We sat on the tables by the lake in the early spring sun. He said he had looked up three-bedroom houses similar to mine in Marylebone. One sold last week for over *a million pounds*. My granddad bought it in 1929 for £600! I'm not pretending I'm naive to think what it's worth but it's always been just our house, and the thought of selling it... Well, I did cry over my chocolate muffin. Chris has offered, as an early Christmas present, the services of his solicitor.

'You can't let Daniel get away with zippydivorces.com,' he said. 'What with that and Meryl on his side, they'll take you to the cleaners.'

He has booked me in tomorrow to see Mr Spencer, the Cheshire family's solicitor.

Tuesday 17th March 13.44
TO: chris@christophercheshire.com

I had an uplifting meeting with the dapper Mr Spencer in Chelsea. I was just getting over how I sank ankle deep into the decadent Axminster carpet in his waiting room, when he took me into his office. Is that chandelier real? And the paintings, I am sure I saw a Picasso. Even his laptop had a mahogany trim. I was only in there for twenty minutes but his soothing, clipped tones made me feel so safe and confident.

He has outlined a plan of action and explained my rights. How much is he *costing?*

Wednesday 18th March 18.09
TO: danielpinchard@gmail.com

Daniel,

Yesterday I met with a solicitor. This is what is happening. As you are the unfaithful deserter, I keep the house. I am also requesting a one-off settlement of thirty thousand pounds.

Unless you arrange for collection, your personal belongings will be packed and shipped to Meryl. Your Steinway piano will be placed in storage and you will be sent the bill. I am sure you think this unreasonable, but in the eyes of the law, it is *entirely* reasonable. My solicitor told me that, if I wanted to, I *could* pursue you for monthly spousal support for, well, ever.

Let me know the fax number for your hotel. My solicitor needs to send you some paperwork.

Wednesday 18th March 22.16
TO: chris@christophercheshire.com

Just had a phone call from Daniel. I could hear him
sweating across the Atlantic. He asked how I could afford a
divorce lawyer from Chelsea.

'You're gonna clean me out,' he said, sounding panicky.

He says if I sell the Steinway for £15,000, I can keep the
money. He will pay the other £15,000. I said I would talk to
my solicitor and put the phone down.

He's a cheeky bastard. I took out a loan to pay for that
bloody piano.

Thursday 19th March 19.12
TO: marikarolincova@hotmail.co.uk

I went to visit Ethel today in hospital. She was
surrounded by elderly patients, perched on the end of her
bed, and dotted around in wheelchairs. They were crowded
round the little screen provided by Bedside Entertainments
Ltd. As I reached the bed, an episode of *Murder She Wrote*
was finishing, so the patients excused themselves. Ethel
didn't introduce me, even though she was on first name
terms with them all.

'I've spoke to Danny,' she said when I'd sat down.
'Divorce,' she mouthed, shaking her head. 'I couldn't tell
anyone on the ward. The shame would finish me orf!'

We sat and looked at each other for a minute.

'Why do you want to take all his money, Coco? You've
got *your* house, that must be worth a few bob?'

I reminded her that Daniel wanted the divorce.

'It's up to wives to tell their 'usbands what they want,' she snapped. 'Yer too soft!'

She pursed her lips and we stared each other out again. An old woman shuffled past in a nightie covered in pictures of cats.

''Ere Dora,' shouted Ethel. 'This is me daughter-in-law. The one 'oo switched orf me life support.'

Dora looked scandalised.

'She was on a ventilator at the time!' I said, seeing the other patients start to prick up their ears. 'And it wasn't my decision.'

Dora didn't look convinced. Ethel then told me that when I'd 'pulled the plug' she'd had an out-of-body experience. Looking down from above she had seen us all around her bed. (My roots needed touching up, apparently.) With her back pressed against the polystyrene ceiling tiles, God had told her to get down, as she still had work to do.

'And 'e was right,' she said, lowering her voice. 'I need to save yer marriage.'

She leant over and fumbled around in her locker, pulling out an Ann Summers lingerie catalogue. She pushed it across the bedcovers.

'This is your solution?' I asked. 'Crotchless knickers?'

'Well, there's more flattering stuff for women yer age.'

A nurse, who came to check Ethel's chart, interrupted us.

'Did Mrs Pinchard tell you how well she's doing?' she said. 'She can get outside for a cigarette.'

'Nurse Carol 'ere got me the Zimmer frame with the ashtray welded on it,' said Ethel proudly. 'She's like a second daughter.'

I'd had enough by now and got up to go. Ethel grabbed my arm.

'Please don't do it,' she whispered. 'There's a lot to be said for a sexless marriage, I'd recommend it, just please don't *divorce*.'

I *almost* felt sorry for her, as she is always boasting about her son's big house with its en-suite bathroom. Daniel grew up with an outside toilet.

Friday 20th March 13.47
TO: chris@christophercheshire.com

Daniel has hired himself a solicitor. A guy called Derek Jacobs. The name sounded familiar and then I realised why. Derek Jacobs was the Pantomime Dame in Snow White! He used to practice law before he had a mid-life crisis and went off to drama school.

Christian has been staying here for most of the week. I did have the rule of no overnight guests but he is so easy to have around. He now lights me a cigarette whenever I come home. Also, Rosencrantz is so happy. They spend lots of time cuddling on the sofa in front of old black and white films. Christian has the Powell and Pressburger box set. We all watched *A Matter of Life and Death* last night, as the rain tink-tonked on the roof.

This morning Christian was up before all of us. I came down for breakfast to find him sat at the kitchen table with a sewing machine and bundles of fabric. He is making costumes for Rosencrantz's first year project, a short play. Christian seems like a keeper.

Saturday 21st March 14.00
TO: danielpinchard@gmail.com

This email isn't divorce related. As per every year, I am reminding you that tomorrow is Mother's Day. It is no longer my job to buy a card and forge your signature.

Rosencrantz went to see Ethel yesterday; he said she had crowds of old folks around her bed watching television. It seems a near death experience has made her more sociable.

Monday 23rd March 10.34
TO: meryl.watson@yahoo.com,
    danielpinchard@gmail.com

Daniel and Meryl,

I have just received an invoice from Bedside Entertainments Ltd. It's not an NHS service. It is a premium rate service and Ethel put my name down for billing! She has been charging the other patients to watch television. I thought it was odd she was being so sociable, but now I know why. Rosencrantz said her water jug was full to the brim with fifty pence pieces. She had told him it was for charity.

I've scanned in a copy of the bill. How can Bedside Entertainments justify their call tariffs, *and* charging £4.99 to watch *Carry on Up the Khyber*? Ridiculous. The TV/phone module has been removed until the bill is settled.

ROBERT BRYNDZA

INVOICE

FROM: Bedside Entertainments LTD, 44 The Street, Swindon, SN1 1SN
contact@bedside.ents.info

TO: Coco Pinchard, 3 Steeplejack Mews, Marylebone, London NW1 4RF

13/03/2009	Call to USA	Duration 104 minutes	£72.80
	Call to MILTON KEYNES	Duration 163 minutes	£57.50

16/03/2009	Pay-Per-View 4 episodes of 'Columbo'		

(starring Peter Falk as the unassuming cigar smoking police detective of Italian descent)

			£19.96
	Call to USA	Duration 67 minutes	£46.90

17/03/2009	Pay-Per-View 1 episode of 'Diagnosis Murder'		
	(starring Dick Van Dyke and Barry Van Dyke)		£4.99
	Call to MILTON KEYNES	Duration 134 minutes	£46.90

18/03/2009	Call to USA	Duration 100 minutes	£75.00
	Call to MILTON KEYNES	Duration 173 mins	£60.55
	Call to USA	Duration 70 minutes	£53.90
	Call to MILTON KEYNES	Duration 73 minutes	£24.50
	Pay-Per-View 2 episodes of 'Murder, She Wrote'		

(starring Angela Lansbury as writer and amateur super sleuth Jessica Fletcher) £9.98

22/03/2009	Pay-Per-VIEW FILM Carry On at Your Convenience	£4.99
	Pay-Per-VIEW FILM Carry on up the Khyber	£4.99
	Pay-Per-VIEW FILM Chippendales LIVE	£9.99
	(adult content with partial male nudity)	

SUBTOTAL =	£492.95
+ VAT @ 15 %	£73.94
TOTAL =	£566.89

PAYMENT MUST BE MADE WITHIN 7 DAYS OF RECEIPT

Bedside Entertainments LTD
"Proud to have been entertaining the sick and infirm since 2008."

Tuesday 24th March 08.40
TO: chris@christophercheshire.com

I hadn't heard a peep from Meryl or Daniel about this bill, so I went to Whitechapel in a rage. Ethel looked quite shocked.

'Where's the jug?' I said, searching her bedside locker.

'They've confiscated it,' she said, rearranging her nightgown. 'I was going to give it to charity.'

I asked her which charity.

'Um... The Little Spastics,' she said vaguely. 'It was all a mix up with the bill.'

At the back of her locker, I found her savings book. When I opened it there was only £2,000 left. £18,000 had been transferred out.

'Where's your money gone?' I said.

She looked away.

'Ethel!'

She told me she had given it to Daniel to buy his piano.

'So, you've lent *him* money to buy *his* piano?'

'He said you were selling it, against his will.'

I told her that he had suggested selling it and that it's worth only fifteen grand.

'What about the other three grand?' said Ethel, sharply.

I looked at her.

'The little bastard!' she said.

I came home to a message from Mr Spencer. Daniel's pantomime dame/solicitor has agreed the divorce paperwork, giving me the house, and a lump sum payment of £30,000, based on the difference of what the piano sells for. He is expecting me to get £15,000 for it. However, his stupid solicitor/pantomime dame failed to specify in the paperwork how much I *actually* have to sell it for.

I have been thinking about how I can pay you back for Mr Spencer's services. You have always talked about having a piano in your library. How about I sell it to you for, say, 1p? You get a lovely old piano and Daniel has to cough up £29,999.99p! It will teach him a lesson, and the best thing is — it's legal.

Wednesday 25th March 15.44
TO: marikarolincova@hotmail.co.uk

I officially filed for divorce today. Chris has invited us over tonight for drinks around his new piano to celebrate. He has given me a shiny penny mounted in a tiny frame. Under it he has written: *Here's to the future.*

Thursday 26th March 09.02
TO: chris@christophercheshire.com

Daniel received the paperwork from Mr Spencer, which included the invoice for the 1p piano! He rang up screaming, 'Divorce won't come quick enough, you bitch!' before slamming down the phone.

Then I went to visit Ethel. She's not happy with Daniel either. She phoned him after I left the other day, and 'Put the fear of God up 'im.' He wired the money back to her within the hour.

'I didn't think you had it in you,' she said.

There was a hint of admiration in her voice. She said it might have lasted if I had been a cow from day one.

'I was a cow to my Wilf, and we 'ad an 'appy marriage —
until he got himself squashed by a bus.'

Due to an administrative error, her phone bill has been
paid by the NHS trust. A copy of the bill was mixed up with
her medical notes and they thought Bedside Entertainments
was a new kind of rehabilitation therapy. The jug of money
was confiscated by Nurse Carol and donated to charity.

'Guess 'oo the fat bitch give it to?' said Ethel, lowering
her voice. 'Miss Tiggywinkle's bloody Hedgehog Hospital.
What are those prickly little bastards gonna do with it?'

At that point, Nurse Carol came up to take her blood
pressure and Ethel said, ''Ello love! It's me favourite nurse!'

Saturday 28th March 10.47
TO: rosencrantzpinchard@gmail.com

I was woken at seven this morning by a phone call from
the hospital. They said to come and collect your nan, as she
had been discharged! When I arrived an hour later, she was
sat in the reception in her big fur coat with a scowl.

She has been declared fit enough to be an outpatient and
was thus a 'bed blocker'. She has to go for rehabilitation
three times a week for the next couple of months. She can't
manage the stairs to the loo, so she is in the living room on a
camp bed with one of my lovely never-been-used Jamie
Oliver pans. I know I never cook but it hurts me to think of
the first, or second thing that pan will contain.

Are you home tonight? She's looking forward to seeing
you.

Saturday 28th March 12.01
TO: marikarolincova@hotmail.co.uk

I came out of the bathroom naked this morning as the computer was ringing and Meryl and Tony appeared via Skype.

'Tony, look away!' ordered Meryl from the screen.

I screamed and ran into the bedroom. When I came back in a dressing gown, I could hear Meryl yelling at Tony to go and have a cold shower.

I sat down and tried to compose myself.

'Coco,' she said. 'Do you always walk around naked?'

'Only when I'm alone,' I said, vowing to tell Rosencrantz to switch off the computer when he is finished.

'Large bosoms always put Tony at sixes and sevens,' she said, as if it were my fault he saw.

'You got my messages then?' I said, trying to change the subject.

'Yes,' she said. 'The hospital *did* phone me this morning but I said you were the closest kin, for her outpatient appointments.'

'What about nursing homes? Both Ethel and I would rather she is in a nice home.'

Meryl then told me that Mrs Braun has gone ahead and written to the local authority, effectively blacklisting Ethel in the London area.

'I can't be a full-time carer,' I said. 'I need to start thinking about working again.'

'Oh Coco!' she said. 'If you were an Indian you wouldn't think twice about caring for *family*.'

'Well, um,' I said, momentarily thrown off.

'Look,' she said, flashing her Margaret Thatcher smile.

'You need to acclimatise yourself to the day, and put your bra on. Let's just agree what I have said on principle and we can talk more. It's just short term; that's what family does, well, at least whilst you still *are* family.'

With that, the screen went blank.

I will find Ethel a home if it kills me. Otherwise, I will kill her.

Saturday 28th March 16.45
TO: marikarolincova@hotmail.co.uk

The cheapest private nursing home is seven hundred pounds a week!

'I'm not forking out that,' said Ethel.

'Me either,' I agreed.

She then waved a copy of Rosencrantz's *The Stage* newspaper, with an article about a new council-funded nursing home for retired theatricals. I am going to write a suitably dramatic email and hope it will land her a place.

Sunday 29th March 09.00
TO: jeanie@williamshakespeareresthome.co.uk

Dear Miss Jeanie Lavelle,

I have just seen your article in this week's edition of *The Stage*. Your nursing home for retired theatrical artistes looks marvellous. I am seeking suitable accommodation for my mother-in-law, Mrs Ethel Pinchard.

Ethel doesn't have an Equity card, or any TV/theatre/film/radio experience but I think she would fit in well in the world of elderly show biz. She is very outgoing, opinionated, and prone to over-excitement. As far as her theatrical pedigree is concerned, she was a formidable player on the Catford Karaoke circuit in the late nineties, often winning first prize singing 'I'm a Pink Toothbrush, You're a Blue Toothbrush'. She was recently forced to leave her nursing home of five years when it collapsed due to subsidence, losing many of her beloved possessions, and her local authority medical records.

With best wishes,

Coco Pinchard

Sunday 29th March 14.48

TO: rosencrantzpinchard@gmail.com

I didn't know you had given Christian a key! Nan was dozing in the living room, when he let himself in the front door. He woke her up as he was stuffing your iPod and some CDs into his bag. She thought he was an intruder and whacked him over the head with a Jamie Oliver milk pan full of wee.

He's lying down wrapped in a sheepskin rug. His suit is dry clean only, and, being a fashion expert, he has refused all of your father's clothes. The living room is a no-go area so your nan is draped across a beanbag in the music room. She is kicking off because the portable TV in there doesn't have Sky. Could you come home please?

Monday 30th March 12.03
TO: chris@christophercheshire.com

There are further ructions between my new house guests. Christian offered to do some Reiki healing on Ethel's new hip, as an apology. Halfway through, lying face down on the sofa, she broke wind so violently that Christian, who has a hyper-sensitive sense of smell, was taken ill. He is still retching in the bathroom. Rosencrantz is furious.

Ethel is still laughing and I must admit I had to struggle to keep a straight face. She keeps saying, 'It was a ripper, I'll give him that.'

Monday 30th March 13.45
TO: clivethenewsagent@gmail.com

Please can I put in an order for *The Socialist Worker* newspaper. My mother-in-law appears to be staying here now.

Also, could I stop my order for *Nuts*, *Loaded*, and *Zoo*. Rosencrantz came out over a year ago and I never got round to cancelling them.

Thanks,
Coco Pinchard

Tuesday 31st March 10.00
TO: rosencrantzpinchard@gmail.com

Dear Rosencrantz,
I know you are under pressure with your play starting on

Friday but it doesn't mean that you can be disrespectful to your nan. Ignoring her this morning was rude. She adores you.

I am going to ask the doctor about her noxious emissions when I take her for physiotherapy this week. Luckily, it's sunny and warm outside, so I've put her on a chair in the garden. Christian needs the kitchen to finish your costumes.

Mum

APRIL

Wednesday 1st April 11.01
TO: chris@christophercheshire.com

Ethel just came into the kitchen with an article from *The Daily Mail*. Apparently, scientists have engineered a silent crisp, which makes no noise when eaten.

'It'll be a boon,' she said excitedly.

She asked me to hot foot it to the Tesco Metro on Baker Street and get some for Rosencrantz, as his noisy mouth-manipulation of crisps drives her mad.

I pointed out that today is April Fool's day, and that it's probably a joke article but she refused to believe me saying, 'The *Daily Mail* don't lie!'

Then I had a phone call. A strangulated Margaret Thatcher-style voice came on the line. She congratulated me on reaching the top of the waiting list for a local allotment, with three sacks of manure as a welcome gift.

'Ha ha, Rosencrantz,' I said. 'You won't April Fool me with that stupid voice.' There was silence. Then the voice said it was no joke, that her name was Agatha Balfour, and she was calling from the Augustine and Redhill Allotment Association.

'You and your husband put your name down for a local

Allotment in 1991,' she said. 'You've just reached the top of the list.'

I babbled around, apologising and said that I couldn't even keep a virtual cactus alive on Facebook. She advised me to take it. Allotments are like gold dust and she has been bribed by all and sundry to jiggle the list.

'Just this morning I turned down tickets to see Leonard Cohen at the O2,' she said. 'And I do love Leonard…'

I asked how much it was.

'Fifteen pounds.'

'Is that per week?'

'No, Mrs Pinchard, *per year.*' She went on to say that it has unparalleled views of London and a well-equipped shed with furniture. I had a vision of writing in the shed and gazing out at the view. I said I would take it, and apologised for thinking she was an April Fool.

'Not to worry Mrs Pinchard,' she said. 'My son is the same, I've spent the morning pulling cling film from all my lavatory pans,' then she rang off.

She must have a big house.

Ethel snorted when she heard.

'You? Gardening? Them poor earth worms.'

You and Marika can come and help dig in your wellies and I can start writing again. I need to do something apart from drive Ethel to and from the hospital.

Thursday 2nd April 13.44
TO: marikarolincova@hotmail.co.uk

This afternoon, I took Ethel to see a room in The William Shakespeare Rest Home. The manager, Miss Jeanie Lavelle, had replied enthusiastically, saying a space for Ethel had come available. The far from Shakespearean home is in a yellowing Victorian terrace, on a dirty street in Penge.

Miss Jeanie, as she asked us to call her, is what you would term a frustrated actress. At the back end of her fifties, heavily made up, dressed in a mini skirt and a tight flowery top with a plunging neckline, which looked as if it was slowly regurgitating her enormous crinkled bosom.

She greeted us like old friends and led us down a hallway, filled with the smell of old school dinners and disinfectant. We passed pictures of Miss Jeanie showing her acting achievements; posters for long forgotten plays and several stills of her in television shows *Prime Suspect, Cracker,* and *Silent Witness.* In all she was pictured on the mortuary slab.

"Guess what my casting type is?' she said.

'Old floozy?' said Ethel, giving her the once over.

There was an awkward pause, and Miss Jeanie showed us through to the 'dayroom'.

Six elderly actors and actresses were sat in a dingy lounge in high-backed chairs staring listlessly at a television. A film with Oliver Reed and Vanessa Redgrave was playing. If I remember correctly, the film is called *The Devils* and has been banned since the 1970s due to its story of sex-crazed nuns in seventeenth-century France. Daniel took me to a special BFI screening of it at the Barbican a few years back; for the art, of course, nothing to do with the huge amount of nudity.

'The residents are enjoying one of my performances,' said Miss Jeanie, 'I played sex-crazed nun number four.'

Most of the residents were snoring. An elderly gent called out for a commode.

'Ooh! We're just in time!' said Miss Jeanie, ignoring him.

She turned up the volume as a scene began, with nuns ripping off their habits and engaging in an orgy around a statue of Christ. A shiny-faced ginger-haired nun (and you could see she had been an authentic ginger) romped past the camera.

'There! That's me!' cried Miss Jeanie grabbing the remote and rewinding. Her pendulous bosoms swung backwards slowly then leapt back to life.

'Oliver Reed was wonderful,' she said.

'Have you got Sky?' asked Ethel, disgusted.

'No, but we have a lovely big box of videocassettes which you would be free to rummage around in,' she said, as if Ethel were five. 'Let's go and see your new home!'

'They're all bloody out of it,' hissed Ethel as we went up in a lift.

The free bed was in a shared room. Miss Jeanie barged into without knocking. A sad-looking old lady was sat in a wheelchair. Miss Jeanie seemed annoyed to find her there, and pushed her out into the corridor.

'There, now you can see,' she said, closing the door.

It was a squash for the three of us between the single beds and it stunk of urine. A small window overlooked a square of concrete, which had once been the garden.

'I would need you to write me a cheque today, for six months in advance,' said Miss Jeanie hopefully. 'There is a queue of people wanting the room.'

Ethel's face crumpled. I couldn't leave her there.

Friday 3rd April 10.31
TO: chris@christophercheshire.com

I came down this morning to find the kitchen awash with shoes and material. Christian and Rosencrantz are frantically finishing the costumes for Rosencrantz's play, which opens tonight.

As I put the kettle on, I noticed Christian sticking a Swastika onto a jacket with his hot glue gun. I realised that with everything that has been going on, I know nothing about this play.

I asked if Ethel would enjoy it, as she wants to come along too.

'Course!' said Rosencrantz. 'It's all about stuff in the Second World War.'

I left them to it. After the shock of seeing Miss Jeanie's wotsit on television, Ethel will enjoy a wartime story. Do you want to come? Marika has parents evening.

Friday 3rd April 23.36
TO: marikarolincova@hotmail.co.uk

Just back from Rosencrantz's play. I say play, it was called *Anne Frank: Reloaded*. What a shocker. Rosencrantz played Anne Frank! For a story set during World War II, there were an awful lot of disco tracks. Ethel looked very confused. She had been looking forward to singing along to 'Roll Out the Barrel'. I watched most of it through my fingers.

It *was* fairly faithful to historical fact until the wall behind the wardrobe slid open, a huge disco-ball descended from the ceiling and lots of male Nazis burst out with their tops off. Then Anne and the rest of the Franks escaped in a giant glittery roller skate, made from a shopping trolley, which rolled into Berlin and squashed Hitler.

I had made a big thing about wanting to come backstage and say hello afterwards. It hadn't entered my mind that the play might be awful. We waded through the throng in the student bar and found Rosencrantz amongst some fawning luvvies. Everyone was telling him what an amazing piece of theatre it was, and most vocal in his praise was the drama school principal, Artemis Wise. He was red in the face and obviously pissed.

When he saw me, he slammed down his Campari shouting, 'It's Mum! What did you think, Mum? Don't keep mum, Mum!'

I didn't know what to say. I said it was a spectacle.

'You mean specta-cu-lar,' he laughed, flashing the bits of crisps in his fillings. 'Your son is going to be a huge star!'

Christian saw my face and I gave him an awkward smile. Artemis leant forward to ruffle Rosencrantz's hair, but slipped off his bar stool. The students rushed to help him up, and I used the diversion to leave. Luckily, I had the excuse of taking Ethel home. She'd had a bit of a turn. I think being pinged in the eye by a G-string emblazoned with a Swastika did it. The last time she saw Rosencrantz act was in 1986 when he was a chick in *Mother Goose*. All he did then was pop out of a papier-mâché egg and do a little dance.

We drove home. Chris had stayed on to chat to the actors (mainly the ones in the G-strings). I made Ethel a cup of Bovril to steady her nerves, and then Rosencrantz and Christian came home to pick up some wine for their first-night party.

'What did you think, Mum?' he said excitedly. 'I wrote the script.'

I asked him why he had picked such a controversial subject. He said I had inspired him to reimagine historical events with *Chasing Diana Spencer*.

'I've read your mum's book,' said Ethel putting ice on her eye. '*She* told a good story... I've not seen such a load of crap since the BBC put *Eldorado* on... And that Chris, 'e won't need to buy a dirty mag for at least a fortnight!'

'It wasn't that bad,' I said, seeing Rosencrantz's face drop.

'Oh,' he said. 'Not that bad?'

There was a horrible pause. I looked at Christian for help but he looked away. I thought, should I treat him as an adult and tell him the truth? On the other hand, lie and tell him it was wonderful? I decided to be honest.

'You were very good in it,' I said, 'but I thought it was, well... cheap, sensationalism.'

Rosencrantz's eyes filled up.

'Well, *we've* sold out!' he said. 'I bet *you* couldn't do that!'

He straightened his Anne Frank wig and stormed out. Christian followed, stopping to hug me and saying, 'I told him that the G-strings were too much, but he wouldn't listen.'

'You need to nip this acting lark in the bud before he ends up in the gutter,' said Ethel. 'Stripper Nazis! If you'd walloped 'im once in a while, I'd never 'ave 'ad to sit through two hours of stripper Nazis.'

I went into the garden for a cigarette. I wish Daniel were here. Being a parent is a two-man job.

Saturday 4th April 21.00
TO: rosencrantzpinchard@gmail.com

Did you stay at Christian's? I feel very upset about last night. I decided to tell you the truth because I want to respect you as a fellow artist, but I should have worded it differently. It's partly my fault. I came along in the same frame of mind as I used to with your primary school nativity plays.

I thought there was some very strong dialogue and I am proud of you. And remember, it's the first thing you have written. If I think back to the first thing I ever wrote, it wasn't nearly as good as *Anne Frank: Reloaded.*

Now, this next bit is from your nan, it's all her words, typed herself with one finger. **She missed *Britain's Got Talent* to write this.**

all right boy,

If bein close to death nots never taught me nothing its that you dont get a second chance, I dont want to spend any more time fallen out with you. When I was a lass, I didn't have half the things you have. At your age I had to go out and wok. If Id ave told my old mum I wanted to be an actress she would ave walloped me and sent me down the clap clinic.

I'm sorry I ad a go at you. I was just shocked my little Rosencrantz could be in such a blue play. But i has to realise the world as changed and you were only doing whats the fashion these days, to be a bit blue. if you do another play. You should watch Dads Army, they never said nothing rude and still had us rolling in the isles.

Your granddad wasnt a looker like you. He could ave eaten an apple through a picket fence, but I loved the old git. did you know when he died wed had a row that morning? he stormed out, and that afternoon a bus squashed him. Id give anything to ave made up with im before he died. Come home, look both ways when you cross the road, and I will give you a big hug.

Yer Nan xx

Saturday 4th April 22.33
TO: chris@christophercheshire.com

Rosencrantz came home after his show with a big bunch of flowers for me, and some pork scratchings for Ethel. They had a standing ovation for the performance tonight, led by the principal. He is thrilled with the play. A member of the Arts Council is coming to see it and they are hoping for an increase in funding for the school.

Sunday 5th April 15.46
TO: chris@christophercheshire.com

Christian was making us pancakes this morning when Ethel clacked in on her walking frame with a copy of *The Mail on Sunday* between her teeth. She showed us a small article tucked away on page thirty-seven called 'Wicked Whispers', where they dish dirt on people in the public eye. It read:

Rumour has it that despite a million-pound Arts Council cash injection, North London-based drama school, The Dramatic Movement Conservatoire, is in financial trouble. However, help could be at hand from the student body, in particular the muscled torso of theatrically named Rosencrantz Pinchard, writer and star of Anne Frank: Reloaded. *Sir Ian McKellen and Graham Norton, both financial donors in the past, are said to be attending tonight's performance with pockets bulging.*

At Wicked Whispers, we wonder where Rosencrantz did his Second World War research. Maybe from his mother, the author Coco Pinchard? Her debut novel, Chasing Diana Spencer, *went down like a V2 bomb!*

Ethel was the only one who laughed at the V2 bomb reference. Rosencrantz gave me a hug and Christian put a lot of Grand Marnier on my pancakes.

Monday 6th April 15.44
TO: chris@christophercheshire.com

Ian McKellen and Graham Norton didn't show up. Apparently, the principal went very pale when he saw the empty seats. I asked Rosencrantz how the school could be having financial difficulties. There are three hundred students all paying eight grand per year.

Since *the Daily Mail* mentioned *Anne Frank: Reloaded,* Ethel has changed her opinion, calling it 'a masterpiece' and 'better than *Cats*'. I reminded her she has never seen *Cats*.

'Well, I saw Elaine Paige sing 'Memory' for a girl in a wheelchair on Cilla Black's *Surprise Surprise,*' she huffed. 'I got the gist.'

Wednesday 8th April 22.44
TO: marikarolincova@hotmail.co.uk

At eight this morning a journalist called Eva Castle knocked on the door. She said she was from *The Daily Mail*. She said she had nothing to do with the 'Wicked Whispers' piece the other day and that she wants to do a nice fun piece on up-and-coming faces, and having a mother and son angle would be a great story.

We chatted for twenty minutes, then she asked if she could come back later with a photographer for a proper interview. Good job because at 8am my face was hardly up and coming.

I spent all day thinking about what to wear and what to say. Rosencrantz rushed home from classes at six, but Eva Castle hasn't come back or phoned. I hope she hasn't been run over. The junction at the end of the road is very dicey.

Thursday 9th April 10.09
TO: chris@christophercheshire.com

I wish Eva Castle had been run over. On page seventeen of The *Daily Mail*, there is a big article about Rosencrantz's drama school. It seems the principal, Artemis Wise, has embezzled five hundred thousand pounds! There is a sidepiece about how star pupil Rosencrantz Pinchard tried to save the school with his own self-penned play, and how he has risen above hardship despite his 'broken home'.

The broken home part is expanded on in another section, devoted to my literary downfall. There are quotes from Regina Battenberg who says I am 'unpredictable'. And Dorian, who says he had to let me go because I am a 'loose cannon'. Anne Brannigan was 'unavailable for comment', stupid cow. They have used an awful picture, taken yesterday morning of me, eyes half-closed in my dressing gown with a cigarette. Someone must have been loitering in the bushes with a zoom lens when Eva Castle and I were talking.

Rosencrantz was turned away this morning. The Dramatic Movement Conservatoire has closed a day early for Easter due to 'an internal investigation'. Artemis Wise has gone missing.

Thursday 9th April 15.56
TO: marikarolincova@hotmail.co.uk

Yes, it was me. I was set up. Chris has been here answering the phone. People I haven't spoken to in years have been ringing saying they recognise me. This is offensive, considering the picture. Even Regan Turnbull rang! She gets *The Daily Mail* in Spain. One positive thing is that she has taken the awful picture of me off her Facebook profile.

Rosencrantz just asked where I've put his suitcase. I forgot he and Christian are off to see Daniel tomorrow in Los Angeles. Meryl also phoned to arrange the collection of Ethel for Easter. Tony hates driving into London, so has asked if we can meet at Junction 23 of the M25 for the handover. She didn't mention the article; she only gets *The Daily Mail* for the Sudoku, which she does whilst her egg boils in the morning.

Friday 10th April 21.24
TO: chris@christophercheshire.com

I dropped off Rosencrantz and Christian this morning at Heathrow. When they were queuing up for check-in, a group of pensioners in front started to whisper and nudge and a little wizened old man came shuffling over.

'Yes, it was me in *The Daily Mail*,' I said irritably.

However, he pulled a copy of *Chasing Diana Spencer* out of his coat and asked me to sign it. I blushed and apologised, scrawling my name, but my happiness was short-lived. When he tottered back to the group, I heard him say, 'See, I told you it wasn't Margaret from *The Apprentice*.'

I must get rid of these glasses, it happens every time I forget to put on makeup.

'Enjoy yourself with Dad,' I said, as I gave Rosencrantz a goodbye hug.

'We're just going for the free accommodation!' said

Rosencrantz cheekily. He kissed me and skipped off to security.

'I'll look after him,' promised Christian and he hugged me goodbye.

I drove home then came straight out again with Ethel. She didn't want to go. It is, apparently, more fun at my house. At Meryl's, there is no Sky but there are strict bedtimes and meals have to be eaten at the table. Her face went white when Tony pulled up at the motorway services. He had brought the hearse. He said Meryl hadn't come with him, as the only way they can legally carry a third passenger in a hearse is if they are lying in the coffin. Ethel was relieved. She has been put in the coffin on previous journeys, and even with the lid off it's not comfortable.

The house feels so empty. I cannot believe I am saying this, but I think I miss Ethel, just a little bit. I'm watching a repeat of *The Apprentice*. I look nothing like Margaret Mountford. It must be the glasses.

Friday 10th April 23.00
TO: chris@christophercheshire.com,
     marikarolincova@hotmail.co.uk

I came out of the shower to a missed call. A literary agent called Angie Langford from the BMX Literary Agency had left a message. She saw *The Daily Mail* article, which prompted her to read *Chasing Diana Spencer*. She would like to meet after Easter for a chat about representation! I just Googled the agency; they are HUGE. They don't call today Good Friday for nothing.

Sunday 12th April 10.47
TO: rosencrantzpinchard@gmail.com

Happy Easter love. I am pleased you are having a nice
time with Dad, and that LA is hot. I think you needed a bit
of time together after all that's happened.

I haven't done much since you left. Chris and Marika
came over for a pizza last night and we watched *Britain's
Got Talent*. We had quite a heated debate about one of the
contestants, Susan Boyle. Marika believes that Simon
Cowell, Piers Morgan and Amanda Holden must have
known that she could sing beforehand, but Chris said they
all looked genuinely shocked.

I was inclined to agree with him. I remember watching
Amanda Holden in *Cutting It*, and acting was never her
strong point.

I have a meeting with a literary agent on Tuesday!

Tuesday 14th April 12.43
TO: chris@christophercheshire.com,
    marikarolincova@hotmail.co.uk

I went to the BMX Literary Agency this morning. Angie
Langford has an office with an amazing view over
Shaftesbury Avenue. The Palace Theatre dominates the
window behind her desk, so when Angie was sat in her chair,
the big white stiletto for *Priscilla Queen of The Desert*
looked like it was balancing on top of her head. She is very
short, very tough and dresses head to toe in designer suits.

The first thing she did was offer me a cigarette. When I
took one and lit up, she looked delighted. She said that she

only works with smokers, and she cannot be friends with non-smokers either.

'What's your brand?' she said.

I told her Marlboro Lights. This seemed to delight her even more as her brand is Marlboro Red.

'That's good, you won't be nicking my fags when we're at award ceremonies. What's your emergency brand?'

'I'm sorry?' I said.

'What do you buy when you're skint?'

'Raffles, Richmond, occasionally a John Player Special.'

'Good,' she said. 'We can help each other out then. There's nothing worse than no spare change and no bloody fags.'

I think I passed her test. She sat back and put her feet on the desk. She was wearing the tiniest pair of Jimmy Choos. Then we spoke about *Chasing Diana Spencer*.

'I loved it,' she said. 'Genius. Ignore those bastards at the Anne and Michael Book Club. She *is* an alcoholic.'

I said I was shocked to hear this.

'They had to scrape her off the floor with a fucking snow shovel at the end of last year's Costa Coffee Book Awards ... and it wasn't cos she was drinking Costa coffee.'

I asked why everyone was so protective over her.

'Anne and Michael are the Mafia of the book world,' she said. 'No popular fiction or non-fiction becomes a best seller without his or her say so. You're lucky all you lost is a book deal...'

I had visions of Anne and Michael Brannigan creeping into my house with a torch and putting a book about horses in my bed.

'So,' she said. 'You got another book in you?'

I said I had, and I opened a folder I had brought full of ideas.

'Put it away,' said Angie. 'Let's have a glass of champagne to celebrate. You can deliver me an outline in three weeks... I'll tout it around and get us a nice fat advance.'

As the cork popped, I felt shocked. Should it be that easy? I have an agent! I must get cracking on the new proposal.

Friday 17th April 17.45
TO: rosencrantzpinchard@gmail.com

Thank you for your postcard. I was amazed you put pen to paper, how retro! Your nan didn't have a fun Easter. Tony slipped a disc helping her up the stairs on Good Friday, and was laid out on a plank for the rest of the week. This meant she was stranded upstairs.

They had a funeral on Easter Monday and with all the staff on holiday, Meryl had to take over embalming the body, as well as basting the turkey for lunch, which apparently tasted horrible.

Meryl only stayed for ten minutes, she and Ethel were sick of each other, and she'd left Tony on his plank with only a bowl of soup with a long straw to keep him going. She has offered to pay for the hire of a stair lift for Ethel whilst she stays here.

Tuesday 21st April 12.43
TO: admin@stairlifts2heaven.co.uk

Dear Stair Lifts 2 Heaven,
I am furious! Furious! FURIOUS! Firstly, why do you have no helpline? Aren't the majority of your customers elderly?

How many old biddies are online? I had an engineer appraise my staircase on Monday, who promised to try to get me a cancellation appointment, which he duly did for 10am today.

I had to take my mother-in-law (for whom the stair lift is intended) to her rehabilitation so I let your engineer in, trusting him to complete the work. I said, 'We're off now, the kitchen is through there. Help yourself.' Meaning he could make himself a cup of tea, if he wanted.

I came home to find, not a stair lift up to the second floor, but a stair lift installed from a door in the kitchen, which leads six steps down to the cellar. Your engineer had left, no card, no note.

Did he leave his brain at home? Does he regularly install stair lifts for elderly serial killers who need an easy access option to their victims in the basement?

I would like your assurances this will be dealt with urgently, and corrected TODAY!!!

Wednesday 22nd April 15.46
TO: Pc.damian.scudders@met.police.uk

Dear PC Scudders,

Just to inform you that further to your visit this morning, I can confirm the new stair lift has been installed and the **incorrectly installed stair lift** has been removed.

If you need further proof that a vulnerable old lady is not being kept in the cellar, you can come over today at your convenience and see my mother-in-law quite merrily riding up and down on said stair lift, whilst listening to her grandson's iPod.

I also have a written apology from the engineer at Stairlifts2heaven, who initially contacted you.

Yours truly,

Coco Pinchard

Thursday 23rd April 16.19
TO: chris@christophercheshire.com

I have writer's block. I am trying not to worry about it. Well, it's not so much writer's block, but I have been doing everything I can to avoid getting down to business and writing this book proposal. The house is spotless, the washing basket is empty. I even had a bash at baking. As Ethel was chucking away her piece of flapjack, she asked if I was okay. I told her I was blocked and couldn't do anything. She disappeared and came back with a laxative sachet.

''Ere love,' she said. 'Mix that with a cup of water and you'll be doing something every fifteen minutes.'

I told her I was blocked *creatively.*

'What a load of rubbish!' she said, plonking me down with paper, pen and a coffee. 'The only blockage that ever stopped me from working was when I cleaned the bogs up the police station. All you need do is put one word in front of the other!'

That was just after lunch. I am still staring at the empty paper.

Friday 24th April 12.19
TO: chris@christophercheshire.com

I got my contract through this morning from the BMX Literary Agency, which has ramped up the pressure. Angie included a packet of Marlboro Lights in the envelope and I went out in to the garden and smoked a couple in a row. I can feel spring in the air. Everything is starting to burst into bud. Rosencrantz is back tomorrow. He has asked if Christian can move in! It looks as if things are getting serious. Should I say yes? I do love his company and he has transformed Rosencrantz from a morose teenager into a pleasant young man.

Rosencrantz has bought you and Marika each a souvenir Cher fridge magnet, from Las Vegas. Did you know Cher is only nine years older than Ethel? I told her this at breakfast,

'Yeah, but she's twenty-two years older than you,' said Ethel. 'That makes us both old trouts who've aged badly.'

Saturday 25th April 18.04
TO: rosencrantzpinchard@gmail.com

Is your phone on? I have just tried to ring you. I am at the Pick-Up Point by Terminal 2. Marika and Chris came over for a beauty evening and I have left them with Ethel. They are perming her hair. With her hair plastered to her head and all the hair grips sticking up out of the curlers she looks a bit like Pinhead from *Hellraiser*.

P.S. Christian can move in! We will discuss the house rules, looking forward to seeing you both. x

Saturday 25th April 19.17
TO: rosencrantzpinchard@gmail.com

Love, when you get this, can you call me? Chris just phoned, he says it's showing on Teletext that your flight landed nearly an hour ago, is the baggage slow?

Saturday 25th April 19.55
TO: rosencrantzpinchard@gmail.com

I keep ringing you. It's over two hours since your flight landed. Where are you? I am worried.

Saturday 25th April 20.57
TO: danielpinchard@gmail.com

Are you still in LA? I am at Heathrow. Rosencrantz didn't get on the flight to London. I came into the arrivals hall to see Christian leaving with a very smart, severe-looking couple, whom I assume were his parents. They whisked him past and he just mouthed 'Sorry.' I rushed after them, but they got into a waiting car and sped off.

Virgin Atlantic is saying that Homeland Security at LAX Airport detained Rosencrantz. He was arrested for drug possession.

Saturday 25th April 22.47
TO: meryl.watson@yahoo.com

Dear Meryl,

There's a problem with Rosencrantz getting home from America and I have to fly out to him tonight. Daniel has only just boarded a plane to his next city for *Whistle Up the Wind,* and won't land for several hours. Could you take Ethel to yours tomorrow morning? Chris and Marika will be with her tonight. I am at Heathrow trying to buy shoes. I drove here in slippers.

Saturday 25th April 23.11
TO: meryl.watson@yahoo.com

Thank you so much, and thank you for the offer of 45,000 Nectar points. I am not sure they are quite the same as air miles and I've already booked my flight. Give my best to Tony.

Saturday 25th April 23.45
TO: chris@christophercheshire.com

I am on a plane. It's a miracle I still had my passport in my handbag from our weekend away last year. It was a choice between a flight now, or wait three days. Ironically, I have been upgraded to First Class, as Economy was overbooked. I'm standing out in my old pink tracksuit and no makeup. I bought shoes from the only place still open. Well, I say place, it was a dodgy guy with a holdall full of jelly shoes.

I'm trying to keep it together. Questions are whirring round my brain. Why did he have drugs? Did Christian know? Why Rosencrantz and not him? Where were the drugs? Did some dog sniff them out? It hardly bears thinking. I thought I knew my son. I have to go, we are taking off. I will keep in touch, and thank you again.

Sunday 26th April 01.15
TO: marikarolincova@hotmail.co.uk

I have no idea about the weather or what LA looks like. I am still in LAX Airport. Getting through customs took two hours. It seems everyone has difficulty getting in, even the Americans. I got talking to a woman from LA. She told me not to joke with Homeland Security.

'They've got the power to do *anything*,' she whispered. 'My late husband, a joker, was cute with one of them and they did a full cavity search. And I mean *full*, they had him in there for half an hour.'

'Oh dear,' I said.

She asked if I was on vacation. I said I was meeting my son.

'Me too, honey,' she said. 'Maybe we can share a ride downtown?'

Luckily, I was called to the desk before I could answer. I was electronically fingerprinted by an intimidating woman and asked why I wanted to enter the United States. I leaned forward, mindful of the queue behind, and whispered, 'My son is in custody here. Rosencrantz Pinchard?'

She leaned into a microphone and shouted, 'Primary caregiver of drug suspect 4463 is here.'

The woman behind took a step back. A tall, thin man in

a grey uniform appeared and took me off into a dingy side room. When he closed the door, the background noise stopped, like a radio being switched off.

I sat at a table. He clicked on a single lamp, and lit from below, his features seemed to elongate. Slowly he shuffled through some paperwork.

He asked what I did for a living and, being nervous, I launched into the plot of my book. After a few minutes, he held up his hand.

'Your son is being held until we charge him,' he intoned.

He sounded a lot like one of those Speak and Spell computers Rosencrantz had as a child.

'Can I see him?' I asked, feeling the tears begin to prick my eyes.

'Ma'am,' he said. 'We have a ninety-two-hour turnaround. Please be patient.'

He stamped my passport and opened a door opposite to the one I had come through. The noise from the arrival's hall broke the silence.

'What do I do now?' I said as he spirited me out.

'You wait,' he said, closing the door behind me.

So, that is what I am doing. Waiting... It's weird having no luggage, no hotel to go to, and no excitement about being away.

Sunday 26th April 03.50
TO: chris@christophercheshire.com,
marikarolincova@hotmail.co.uk

It's been nearly three hours and no one has been to see me. The crowds have thinned out to just the weirdos. In my pink tracksuit and jelly shoes, I am blending in.

I tried to get back through to the border people but the shutters were down. I have wandered through to the Tom Bradley International Terminal. It's colossal. The lights are dimmed and a sea of travellers is sleeping under blankets. I have curled up by the British Airways check in desk, which feels strangely comforting.

The cash machine won't take my card. A nice couple of British backpackers came to my rescue and swapped me $10 for the fiver I had in my purse. America really is the land of plenty; there were four different kinds of Snickers to choose from in the vending machine.

I hope Rosencrantz isn't scared. Knowing he is somewhere here and I cannot help him is killing me.

Sunday 26th April 13.48
TO: chris@christophercheshire.com,
    marikarolincova@hotmail.co.uk

I felt drool down the side of my face and a hand shaking my shoulder. I opened my eyes and it was light. A young all-American girl in a business suit and trainers was stood over me carrying a briefcase and a pair of high heels.

'Mrs Pine-chard?' she said.

The busy Terminal came into focus. The travellers sleeping under blankets had gone and I was the only person left lying in full view of a queue by the BA desk. She held her hand out and introduced herself as Tammy Oppenheimer from a company called Bond-a-Bail.

'Where's my son?' I said, pulling a crumpled newspaper off me and shaking her hand.

She said we should go somewhere private, and took me

to a nearby coffee shop.

'Now Mrs Pine-chard,' she said, unloading papers from her briefcase. 'I'm here from a Bail Bond company. I can tell you that Rosencrantz was charged at four-thirty this morning.'

'Charged?' I said. 'With what?'

Tammy shuffled her papers, 'Charged with possessing a small amount of marijuana.'

'Oh! Thank God for that,' I said. 'I thought it might be heroin.'

Tammy looked at me with disapproval, and explained that the State of California is very strict with *all* drug offences.

'How strict?' I gulped, holding onto my coffee cup.

She said that jail time is mandatory, but the good news was that Rosencrantz had been granted full bail. *Until he goes to trial.* I put my head in my hands.

'How much is bail? 'I said.

She said it was sixty thousand dollars.

'Sixty thousand dollars!' I shrilled. 'That's good news? That's nearly forty thousand pounds!'

'Have you heard of bail bonds?' said Tammy.

I said I hadn't. She explained that her company would post bail for us, in return for a ten percent deposit.

'So, in your case, six thousand dollars,' she said.

I sipped my coffee and wiped away fresh tears. Then my phone went. It was Daniel saying he was in the Delta Airlines Terminal.

'Good timing,' said Tammy. 'We have to scoot. LA Men's Jail is an hour away, and the freeway is hell at this time of day.'

I found Daniel and we went down to the car park. He

looked as bad as I did. His face got paler as I explained what had happened.

'Can I say something?' he said. 'Now don't freak out, but wouldn't it be... character building for him to spend some time, you know thinking about what he's done?'

'What?' I said. 'Leave our son in with rapists and murderers! Who knows what will happen to him with his good skin and good looks? He's our son!'

'Where's the money going to come from then?' he said. 'I've got your solicitor breathing down my neck for thirty thousand pounds.'

I said I would put it on my credit card, the one for emergencies. And if not, I would happily forfeit the money so that Rosencrantz's life isn't destroyed.

We got into the back of Tammy's huge four-wheel-drive Porsche, and screeched through the underground car park, emerging from the dank fluorescent lighting into blazing sunshine. My stomach lurched as she accelerated down a ramp and joined the freeway. Tammy seemed immune to the speed, zipping across four lanes and putting her foot down when we reached the outside lane next to a central reservation. We jolted forward and sped past the slower cars.

'Car pool lane,' she said, as Daniel and I grabbed the armrest.

Los Angeles stretched out into a haze of yellow smog. It rippled where it met the blue horizon, making me think of piss stains. In the distance, I could just make out the Hollywood Sign, but we were moving in the opposite direction toward a cluster of skyscrapers and even danker smog. I caught Tammy's eye in her rear-view mirror.

'You do know Rosencrantz is not a drug addict,' I said.

'I don't mean this to sound rude,' she said, 'but in the eyes of the State of California he is a drug addict and the sooner he admits it, the better it is for his liberties.'

My stomach leapt as Tammy took an exit. Within seconds, we were amongst the dusty slum boulevards. Endless dirty squat houses slid past, punctuated by the occasional 7-11 and fast-food joints. A tram crossed our path.

'He's an idiot,' said Daniel. 'Did you ever imagine we would be doing this?'

We passed what could only be described as a mega church, a huge warehouse with a giant mural of Jesus holding his arms out, then hit the area known as Downtown. High rises slid up out of the road and we squeezed through them until we approached a wide silver building called Men's Central Jail. *Men's jail*, I thought. Rosencrantz is still a boy. I felt cold and sick with fear.

We were waved through a checkpoint and pulled in to the car park. I went to get out but Tammy said it would be quicker if she went alone. She took a Visa card reader machine from her glove compartment and plugged it into the cigarette lighter.

'This is the document for bail,' she said. I signed at the bottom. 'And your credit card charge for six thousand dollars.'

I handed it over, she swiped it, and handed it back.

'Okay,' she said, applying red lipstick. 'Let's get Guildenstern.'

'It's Rosencrantz,' I said.

'Sorry honey,' she said. 'One character from William Shakespeare's *Hamlet* is as good as the next,' and she skipped off with her high heels clacking on the shimmering tarmac.

'Why did she have to say *William Shakespeare's Hamlet*?' said Daniel. 'As if we didn't know who wrote it?'

'Cos that's the problem right now.'

'I don't like her,' he said.

'You're a cock,' I said, and got out of the car for a cigarette. Daniel stayed inside, sweating defiantly.

After an hour, Tammy came out with Rosencrantz in tow. He looked pale, with greasy hair, wearing skinny jeans and a Cher T-shirt. He ran to me and I hugged him, checking he was intact. I wasn't sure if it was him or me who stank. Daniel just glared through the window.

We got in the car, and pulled away. We sat in silence for several miles. We took a different route, which led to the freeway along the beach. I opened the window and the sea air whipped away a little of my fear and I closed my eyes against the sun. I asked Rosencrantz if he had had a decent breakfast. He looked at me disdainfully. Then I asked him if he was a drug addict.

'No!' he said.

'But you are an idiot, are you not?' said Daniel.

'Takes one to know one,' said Rosencrantz.

'Okay. Time-out people,' said Tammy.

She passed back a document, which told us Rosencrantz couldn't leave the State of California until he gets a court date.

'I wanna get you in to see a lawyer friend of mine, he's the best,' said Tammy.

'What time?' I said.

'Honey, I haven't got the appointment yet. I am just going to drop you... here.'

The ocean stretched along one side of the road, with hotels, and restaurants the other. I asked Tammy what we should do.

'Find a motel and sit tight. I have your cell. I will call you when I know more. Stay out of trouble.'

I think she was talking to all of us. As she roared away, we stood awkwardly on the street corner. It was like we had been dropped into an episode of *Banged Up Abroad*. Only Rosencrantz was, thankfully, for the time being not banged up.

'Right,' said Daniel. 'I have to go.'

'What? You're just leaving us?' I said.

He said he had to fly back to Cleveland because he was due on stage tonight.

'Aren't you more in front of the stage?' said Rosencrantz.

Daniel took a step towards him.

'In a hole, in fact,' said Rosencrantz, looking at him.

Daniel stared back.

'I think it's called the orchestra pit,' I said, sliding myself between them. They continued to stare each other out as Daniel hailed a cab.

'Find a motel, sort this out,' he said.

With that, he jumped in the cab, and it sped off.

We have made our way down to the beach. It turns out we are in Santa Monica. Rosencrantz recognised it from *Baywatch*. He has gone to get us ice cream. I am sitting in the sand, watching surfers in the clear blue water. I have no clue what to do next.

Sunday 26th April 21.08
TO: chris@christophercheshire.com,
      marikarolincova@hotmail.co.uk

We found a cheap motel. Santa Monica is rather posh, so we walked along the sand to Venice Beach. It's rather like the Margate of California, only the weather is better, and instead of little flowerbeds full of Busy Lizzies, there are huge palm trees.

Ironically, our motel is above a tattoo parlour which sells 'medical marijuana'; I can hear the crowds walking and rollerblading along the prom below.

We spent the afternoon on the beach and Rosencrantz told me what happened. It was Christian's idea to buy some weed, when they were in Las Vegas. They only bought a small amount, enough for a few joints, which they smoked in a nightclub. Christian dropped one of their joints when he was dancing, and neither of them realised it had fallen into the turn-up of Rosencrantz's jeans (what are the chances)? Three days later when security looked through the clothes in their suitcase at LAX Airport, the joint fell out. He burst into tears when he told me that Christian let him take the blame. Apparently, he just mouthed, 'I have to go,' and carried on through security. I asked him why Christian would do that.

'He's desperate to work in America, in fashion,' said Rosencrantz. 'If he has a criminal record, he can't get a work permit.'

'What about you?' I said. 'I thought you two were, well, I thought he was the one?'

'Me too,' said Rosencrantz softly.

'I was going to say yes, about Christian moving in with us.'

'Don't Mum,' said Rosencrantz. 'I don't want to talk about him anymore.'

He is now lying on one of the twin beds in our poky motel room with his face to the wall. I feel betrayed too. I liked Christian, almost as much as Rosencrantz did.

Tammy phoned an hour ago. She has got us a meeting

tomorrow morning with a lawyer at a firm called Gregory Kaplan Associates. I need to buy some clothes.

Monday 27th April 12.00
TO: chris@christophercheshire.com,
        marikarolincova@hotmail.co.uk

I woke up at five this morning in a cold sweat, and looked across at Rosencrantz sleeping. The thought of having to fly home without him filled me with an icy trickling dread. Not even the sweet smell of weed from the bong shop below could get me back to sleep, so I went down onto the beach and sat up against a palm tree with a fag. It was warm, and buzzing with joggers and dog walkers. I was enjoying the sun when I heard the woo-woo of a siren. I looked up and racing over the sand was a policeman on a quad bike. He pulled to a stop near me and I looked around to see who he was going to speak to. I was surprised when I realised it was me.

'Morning, ma'am,' he said.

'Hello,' I said puffing away.

He just stared at me. 'Are you aware you are in violation of code 4631 which prohibits smoking on State Beaches?'

'Oh bugger, I mean sorry,' I said stubbing it out in the sand.

'If you could watch your mouth please, ma'am,' he said. 'Are you aware it's also an offence under code 4521 to leave garbage on the beaches?'

I apologised, scooped up the cigarette butt, and popped it back in the packet. I grinned at him hopefully, but he removed his helmet and got slowly off his bike. He fined me one hundred dollars! He also lectured me on the dangers of smoking and gave me a leaflet for a support group.

I made sure I disposed of the leaflet properly, then went to a shop on the promenade and bought a cheap Teflon suit to wear at our meeting. It makes me look a bit like a Hillary Clinton impersonator.

Monday 27th April 15.30
TO: chris@christophercheshire.com,
    marikarolincova@hotmail.co.uk

We just met with our lawyer, Gregory Kaplan. He is tanned, in his fifties and perfectly coiffed from head to toe in a suit so sharp it could have cut him. I presume we are low priority clients, as we didn't meet in his office but in a long corridor he calls his 'walkthrough'.

We waited for an hour before he burst out of a door and we scuttled along beside him as he talked. He thinks he can get Rosencrantz off with an infraction, which is a fancy way of saying, *I know I did it so you don't need to give me a sentence because I have already learnt my lesson.* We will also have to pay a fine and it's recommended we donate to a drug rehabilitation charity.

At the end of the corridor, he shook my hand saying, 'Give me three days and I think I can get a court date.'

The ninety-seconds we were with him cost $400.

Tuesday 28th April 17.45
TO: marikarolincova@hotmail.co.uk,
    chris@christophercheshire.com

This afternoon we took the bus to Manhattan Beach, which was divine. The houses were all painted wood and shutters. The beach was teeming with surfers and their fashionably tousled girlfriends. We walked a long way in the surf, carrying our shoes. There was a van with the Paramount Pictures logo parked on the sand and a camera crew was filming a scene with some gorgeous young twenty-something actors playing a game of volleyball.

'That'll be you one day,' I said to Rosencrantz.

'Yeah right,' he said. 'Like they're going to let me back into the country after this.'

We spent the rest of the day in silence.

Wednesday 29th April 14.46
TO: chris@christophercheshire.com,
    marikarolincova@hotmail.co.uk

Gregory Kaplan's secretary phoned this morning.

'Coco Pinchard, can you please hold for Gregory Kaplan,' she said.

I was in the middle of making sandcastles with Rosencrantz out of empty McDonald's cartons, so I dusted off my hands and waited. Five minutes passed before he came on the line. He sounded like he was in a helicopter.

'I got us into a court on Friday,' he said. '10am, it should be smooth sailing, honey. Judge Walsh is on the case and he leans well to the left. I can pretty much guarantee we'll be home free.'

'Brilliant,' I said. 'Let's hope he doesn't lean too far and fall off his chair!'

However, Gregory had already hung up. I came off the phone to see an elderly lady with a little dog giving Rosencrantz ten dollars for our collection of sandcastles.

'It's very *Bladerunner*,' she drawled. 'And I love the Hillary Clinton impersonator, nice touch.'

I realised she must have thought we were some kind of street entertainers. I told Rosencrantz to collect our things and we left.

Thursday 30th April 10.22
TO: chris@christophercheshire.com,
      marikarolincova@hotmail.co.uk

I am freaking out. Gregory just called and shouted down the phone about why we hadn't declared Rosencrantz's 'priors'. I hadn't a clue what he was talking about, but it seems in his preparations for tomorrow's case he found that Rosencrantz was arrested when he was fifteen for being drunk in Leicester Square.

'Honey, you gotta be straight with me,' said Gregory. 'Now we have drug *and* alcohol issues. You told me this kid was clean as a whistle.'

'I thought he was... he is!' I said.

'Well, find out!' he snarled. 'You don't fuck with this judge.'

He slammed down the phone. I confronted Rosencrantz, lying on his bed clutching a photo of Christian. He told me that in 2005, he had been to watch *Phantom of the Opera* with a friend. Before hitting the West End, they had topped up their Coke cans from a bottle of Tia Maria in the sideboard. A policeman found them throwing up in Leicester Square and took them to Charing Cross Police Station, where they were cautioned.

'Is there anything else I don't know about?'

Rosencrantz said there wasn't. It's hardly shocking stuff, two tipsy teenagers doing a Euan Blair whilst singing show tunes.

Thursday 30th April 18.56
TO: chris@christophercheshire.com,
      marikarolincova@hotmail.co.uk

Another terrifying phone call from Gregory. I was on hold for ten minutes before he told me that the hearing has been put back a week.

'It's gonna be tough,' he said. 'Your kid isn't looking good now, with a prior.'

I tried to explain that *Phantom of The Opera* had been involved, as I know how the Americans love Lloyd-Webber, but he hung up. I called him back, but the line was busy. Then I tried to call Daniel. We have only forty dollars left and I haven't paid for our motel room tonight.

MAY

TO: chris@christophercheshire.com,
    marikarolincova@hotmail.co.uk

Daniel is trying to work out how to wire me money. I have to keep the credit card free for legal fees. For the time being, we have moved to a cheaper motel at fifteen dollars a night. It's further back from the beach on a rundown boulevard. Yesterday afternoon we were watching an old cowboy film on TV when there was a power cut. Only the gunshots continued from the car park out front. No one died but the paramedics knocked on the door afterwards, looking for an ear.

I was woken up at one and two by cars roaring up and down. At three I went outside with a cigarette in my mouth and walked slap bang into the tallest and most beautiful black drag queen I have ever seen.

'Oh, my lordy, honey,' she said in an accent from the Deep South. 'Could I bum a light? And fire? There's no smoke without fire,' she said, winking.

I offered up one of my Marlboro Lights.

'How's business?' she said, exhaling.

I said it wasn't too brisk.

'Nawt too breesk,' she said, imitating my accent. 'I love the way you people talk. I'm Shaquille.'

She offered a powerful hand with bright red nails.

'Coco,' I said, shaking it.

'Mmm, Coco,' she said. 'I *like* that. Most British women I meet are Sue, Janet, or Marge. Is that what they call your drag queens over there?'

I said I didn't know and, for some reason, told her about the first time I met Daniel at university. How he gave me the nickname Coco when I won a bottle of Chanel No. 5 in a raffle.

'Love at first sight?' asked Shaquille.

'It was. We're separated now.'

We smoked in silence for a bit.

'Can I ask you something, honey?' she said. 'Why is a nice girl, named after a very nice perfume, staying *here*?'

I told her, and began to cry.

'Oh my! These tears are real!' she shrieked, hugging me against her padded bra. 'I never seen real tears in years. In LA, you wave your acrylic nails in front of your face, and you try... But this! This is real, British, bad-dentistry tears!'

'Everyone's teeth here are really white and straight,' I agreed.

'Even the whores,' she said, flashing her own perfect teeth.

I didn't know what to say to that so I offered her another cigarette.

'Your son at school?'

I told her Rosencrantz wants to be an actor.

'I did too,' she said wistfully. 'But don't you worry. He gonna be just peachy with a momma like you.'

A BMW came roaring into the car park and tooted its horn.

'I gotta run,' she said, checking her huge beehive in a tiny mirror. 'Thanks for the smokes, Cokes.'

'That's what my friends call me,' I said. We hugged.

Then she was gone, running admirably down the stairs in six-inch heels and into the car. I never saw who was inside. The windows were blacked out.

Friday 1st May 13.03
TO: marikarolincova@hotmail.co.uk

There was a knock on our door at nine this morning. I thought it would be the Mandarin cleaner turfing us out. She had been banging on doors and pulling drunks out since seven. When I opened the door, stood on the communal walkway, zipped up in his finest daywear, was Chris!

I screamed and launched myself on him in a big hug. He glanced over my shoulder at an old guy in a cowboy hat sleeping in the next doorway.

'I have a cab with the engine running, let's get you out of here.'

It took us about three seconds to pack. In the cab, Rosencrantz just stared out of the window bleakly, but I couldn't contain myself.

'How did you find us?' I said, hugging him again.

He told me he had spoken to Tammy, from the bail bond company.

'You're both to stop worrying,' he said. 'I think I have a way to get us all out of the country safely.'

'I can't believe you're here,' I said. 'I won't forget this.'

'I had air miles... and my life needs some excitement,' he said, embarrassed.

I jabbered away, not taking much notice as our surroundings changed, until I saw the taxi approach the Chateau Marmont Hotel. It looked like a fairy-tale castle, or chateau; whiter than the whitest American teeth, with little turrets and arched windows.

'No way,' said Rosencrantz. 'This is like the coolest hotel in Hollywood!'

'My mother had an old voucher she didn't need,' said Chris.

'My mother used to give me Green Shield stamps,' I said.

'I see it as compensation. You've met my monster of a mother.'

It was so wonderful to be in a clean room after days of smelly motels. Rosencrantz and I had a twin; Chris had booked himself the room next to ours, with an interconnecting door. He buzzed around, tipping the bellboy, who only really had my Teflon suit to bring up, and ordered us breakfast. Rosencrantz didn't take much notice of our surroundings and just sat on the bed and clicked on the television.

'You fancy going for a look round?' said Chris to Rosencrantz, handing him twenty dollars.

'Um, like okay,' said Rosencrantz, and slunk out of the door.

Chris poured us both vodka from the mini bar.

'That was the most he has spoken in days,' I said. 'He's been listless. Well, you know from all my emails.'

'I've got a plan,' he said

Monday 4th May 11.56
TO: marikarolincova@hotmail.co.uk

Sorry hun. My phone battery died as I was writing my last email. It's all over. We are in the Virgin Lounge at LAX waiting for our flight home. They have lent me a phone charger.

This is what happened. As you know, Chris is Rosencrantz's godfather. What you wouldn't have known, along with me, is that every godchild in Chris's family is left *fifty thousand pounds* in the godparent's will. He explained that it's Cheshire family policy, mainly to assist in tax avoidance. His father actively encourages Chris and his siblings to be godparents.

'Not that I did it for that,' Chris added.

He went on to say that he had looked into our lawyer, Gregory Kaplan, and that he is a big charity giver, especially when his clients need to get off drug charges, and all donations are put through Gregory Kaplan Associates. It's legal, but it makes him look like he runs a highly philanthropic firm.

'This is good for him because he is planning to run as a Senator next year,' finished Chris, sitting back triumphantly with his vodka.

'I don't get it,' I said.

'Gregory Kaplan will be keen to make sure Rosencrantz's case is steered toward a sympathetic judge,' said Chris, 'when he hears that Rosencrantz is donating seventy-five thousand dollars to a drugs rehab charity.'

'Seventy-five thousand dollars!'

'Yes,' said Chris. 'We tell Gregory that if he *doesn't* get the hearing scheduled a.s.a.p, well, some other lawyer gets the case... And the donation.'

He looked at my face.

'Coco, this money goes to Rosencrantz, whatever. Instead of waiting until I die, why not put it to use now? If he gets sent to jail, it could destroy his life.'

It didn't take me long to agree. Chris picked up the phone and dialled Gregory Kaplan Associates. Within seconds, Gregory was on the phone and within seconds, he was gone.

'What did he say?'

'He said he'll 'make it happen'.'

We had barely topped up our quivering vodkas when Gregory rang back. He had scheduled a hearing for nine on Monday morning.

We spent the rest of Saturday and Sunday relaxing, as much as we could. The Chateau Marmont is very low key, old Hollywood/film noir. Lots of leather armchairs, wooden floors, and ceiling fans. We lay by the pool, drank cocktails, and ate some truly delicious food, but none of us slept soundly and it all went by with a feeling of dread. The court case could have technically gone either way.

However, this morning we were barely in the courtroom for ten minutes. A stern but disinterested female judge heard the case and ordered that Rosencrantz pay $75,000 to the Winding Pathways Drug Treatment Center, $2,000 to the State of California and that he had to leave American soil by 6pm.

We shook hands with Gregory on our way out; an entourage of assistants, mostly young women of attributes, surrounded his blindingly white smile, and he presented us with our bill for $5,000.

I paid it and we got into a cab. I was glad to leave. It all felt very, very grubby. What about the poor kids who don't have money?

I am relieved, but I don't know how to deal with Rosencrantz? Do I need to dole out some punishment? He looks like he has suffered enough. I was caught smoking weed when I was fifteen behind our shop by my dad. I was lucky enough just to be walloped with his slipper.

We're about to board. Cannot wait to be home. Looking forward to seeing you.

Coco xxx

Tuesday 5th May 02.14
TO: marikarolincova@hotmail.co.uk

Just sorted through a pile of post and found my Decree nisi. I am divorced.

Tuesday 5th May 17.56
TO: marikarolincova@hotmail.co.uk

I was asleep on the downstairs sofa, when the bell woke me. I staggered up and opened the front door. Meryl was standing there with Ethel.

'Oh, there you are, Coco,' she said, as if she'd been searching the doorstep for hours. 'As you haven't answered any of my messages, I thought I would bring Mohammed to the mountain. Not that you look like a mountain,' she added quickly.

'Looks like she's lost a bit of weight,' said Ethel, peering at me with a surprised look on her face.

Meryl pushed past, clutching her driving gloves, with Ethel in tow. I was left to bring in her suitcase.

I followed them into the living room where Meryl was poking around the wilted potted plants and Ethel was sitting on the sofa, trying to make the television work.

'What are you doing?' I asked.

'I *told* Christopher to come over every day and water,' said Meryl, yanking the head off a dead Amaryllis. 'How was America?' she breezed, as if I'd been on holiday. 'Daniel told me all about Rosencrantz, what a scamp!'

'Why 'int yer Sky box plugged in?' said Ethel, jabbing at the buttons with a dismayed face. 'You've wiped everything!'

'Oh Coco,' said Meryl, 'she's been looking forward to *Celebrity Wife Swap* all week.'

I asked why she'd brought Ethel back.

'Now come on Coco, be fair,' said Meryl in a condescending tone. 'We've all got to pull our weight.'

I explained, as nicely as I could, that I am barely home myself, and I've already pulled my weight, looking after her for two months.

''*Er?*' said Ethel, looking up from the leads at the back of the television. 'What am I? Chopped liver?'

'Look,' said Meryl, grabbing Ethel and planting her back on the sofa. 'She's settled here.'

'No,' I said, helping Ethel up. 'She's been settled at *yours* for two weeks.'

'Exactly,' said Meryl, pushing Ethel back down. 'Coco, you have a responsibility too. We've driven all this way.'

'And an 'ole series of *Watercolour Challenge* has gone down the tubes too,' said Ethel, jabbing the remote again.

They both looked at me as if I had done something terrible.

'GET OUT! GET OUT! GET OUT!' I shouted.

Meryl's mouth opened and closed, Ethel looked at me for a moment and then tried to get the batteries out of the remote. Rosencrantz stumbled in wearing his pyjamas and with his hair on end.

'Is everything all right?' he said. 'I like heard some fucking mad woman screaming.'

'Could we watch the toilet language, thank you Rosencrantz,' said Meryl. 'Come on,' she said, prising the remote out of Ethel's grip. 'I don't think Coco's very well.'

'I'm fine!' I said, catching sight of my mad hair and knackered face in the mirror. 'I just object to... I'm tired and, Meryl, if you were Indian, you wouldn't object to caring for your own mother.'

'I've never heard anything so silly,' said Meryl. 'I think you need some rest.'

She strode out of the door pulling along Ethel and the suitcase. I sat on the sofa as I heard the engine rev up and the hearse pull away.

Rosencrantz sat down and asked if I was okay. I shrugged.

'I just like played the answer-phone messages,' he said. 'There were five from Auntie Meryl, and one from your new agent, Angie. She's reminding you about some deadline tomorrow.'

My book outline is due tomorrow and I had completely forgotten about it! The reason we have no television is that the electricity has been cut off. Daniel has stopped all our direct debits. Chris, ever the saviour, has come to the rescue again and offered me bed and motherboard. I am tapping away frantically on my laptop in his spare room.

Wednesday 6th May 09.01
TO: marikarolincova@hotmail.co.uk

Just home. Just sent outline to Angie. I am worried. I did rather pull it out of my arse at the last minute, well 4.15 this morning. Got side-tracked watching *Battlestar Galactica* with Chris, hence it ended up having a science fiction theme.

Rosencrantz has paid the electricity bill from his own money and left me a lovely note saying how he wants to make me proud and he is turning over a new leaf.

I'm off to bed. Love you.

Wednesday 6th May 17.46
TO: marikarolincova@hotmail.co.uk

Was up at 2pm woken by the doorbell, I had fallen asleep on the sofa in my coat and shoes. Outside was a horsey woman in her sixties wearing dungarees.

'Ah, you're ready,' she said. 'Good girl. Come on.'

I stared at her for a moment.

'Come along,' she said. 'I haven't got all afternoon.'

I followed her out shutting the door behind me. I am not sure why. Luckily, I twigged halfway down the road that this was the meeting I had arranged in April about having an allotment, and the woman must be Agatha Balfour of the Augustine and Redhill Allotment Association.

Did you know that, hidden away from the bustle of London, there is a whole group of little allotments, just past the outer circle of Regent's Park? Thirty long plots surrounded by tall trees and populated by a load of wild-haired old men digging in trousers held up by string. I couldn't work out where they'd come from. I had never seen them before. The streets around here are full of tourists, businessmen, and alpha mothers power-pramming.

As Agatha strode ahead up the hill, I struggled to keep up. My heels kept sinking in the soft earth. A few of the old men stopped gardening to stare at me in my floor-length fake cowhide coat, and a couple made mooing noises. I caught up with Agatha standing on the brow of the hill. The land sloped away, showing off a wonderful view over Regent's Park, the lake, and metropolis beyond.

'Wow,' I said out of breath.

'Yes,' she said, 'and your patch looks over it.'

She indicated an overgrown strip of soil with a yellow shed at the end.

'Right. Tea,' she said, bustling toward the shed, pulling a key out of her overalls, and inserting it in the lock.

Inside it has been beautifully kept, with neat wooden shelves. In one corner were two fading deck chairs and a little table. On the workbench in front of the window sat an old paraffin stove and lots of clay flowerpots.

'Now,' said Agatha, handing me a little kettle. 'Water.' I looked for a tap but she rolled her eyes. 'Water butt, outside.'

Whilst I filled the kettle, I looked at the allotment next door. It was well tended with a smart shed, but the best feature was its scarecrow. A dressmaker's mannequin was buried in the earth up to its knees. Stuck on its head was a black beehive wig and glued underneath was a cut-out of Amy Winehouse's face.

When I came back, Agatha had lit the stove and there was a warm smell of paraffin and used matches.

'I like the scarecrow next door,' I said.

Agatha produced milk and digestive biscuits out of her dungaree pockets.

'Yes, terrifies the birds nicely,' she said.

I said it really captured Amy Winehouse.

'Who?' said Agatha.

I explained who Amy Winehouse was. Agatha's face clouded over.

'That doesn't sound very appropriate,' she snorted.

'Well, you didn't know who she was until just now,' I said. 'It's funny, ironic.'

'Hmm,' she said.

There was a pause. Agatha gulped her tea and took out some paperwork. It was a contract, which she asked me to sign.

'I'm very glad this patch is going to someone younger,' she said. 'Old Mr Bevan found it all too much in the end.'

'Was he ill for long before he died?' I said.

'No, it was all quite sudden,' she said. 'He'd only just been saying to me, that morning, that he was trying to get on top of the weeds, and ironically, he did. Keeled over just beside the shed. You can still see that little flat patch where they found him, still clutching his hoe.'

I looked through the window and saw where the long grass was bent round in a small body shape.

'Right,' said Agatha. 'That's us done.' She gathered up the milk and biscuits, and handed me the key. 'Happy gardening.'

I only stayed for ten minutes after she had gone. I don't have a clue about gardening and I was so jet-lagged that my mind began to play tricks. Amy Winehouse was being buffeted by the wind and she looked like she was eyeballing me, and the thought of Mr Bevan lying dead outside gave me the shivers. What will I do with an allotment?

When I got home, I had a text from Angie at BMX. It just said;

Pls cum 2 my office 4 meet tmrw @ 9am.
I am looking back over my proposal. What was I thinking?

Wednesday 6th May 23.48
TO: chris@christophercheshire.com

I can't sleep, it's dark and a little cold, but my body is still on LA time and ready to eat a nice lunch. Marika came over tonight, she is very unhappy. She has just been turned down for a Key Worker Mortgage because she has never taken UK citizenship, even though she has paid fifteen years of income tax and national insurance here. She wants to buy her flat in Dulwich from her landlord, who is selling.

'I'm going to have to bite the bullet and move further out,' she said with a shudder.

I offered her a room here, but to get to Dulwich by 7.45am she would have to deal with the Tube/overland and a bus five days a week. It's a shame, as I used to love it when she was our lodger.

In other news... Rosencrantz went back to The Dramatic Movement Conservatoire today, and found that no one had really noticed his absence. Artemis Wise was picked up in Calais trying to board a ferry and is now in custody. There is a witch-hunt on as to who knew about his embezzlement. Rosencrantz quite innocently asked his singing teacher if she could give him an update on what he has missed (in class) but she got very flustered and dropped a metronome on her foot.

Anyway, you are probably fast asleep. I should have taken some of those Melatonin pills you offered to get my body clock back on track.

Thursday 7th May 11.04
TO: chris@christophercheshire.com

After only an hour of sleep, I had to get up for my meeting with Angie. When I arrived at her office, she was on the phone and motioned me to sit.

'Listen,' she said. 'You shouldn't have signed the bloody contract if you knew he had commitments with the Cub Scouts!'

She slammed the phone down.

'Bad day?' I said.

'What's that phrase?' she said, leaning forward to light my cigarette. 'Never work with children or animals? It should be never work with parents. One of my new authors, who's seven, is writing a book on higher mathematics ... Autistic as hell, but a nice kid, however the mother. Ugh... Anyway, we're here to talk about your book proposal; *Greg-O-Byte: Some Androids Are Different.'*

She looked at me and raised her eyebrows.

I explained that it might be a little radical, especially as a children's book.

'I know you wanted literary fiction,' I said. 'However, I thought it would be good if kids could read about being gay, under the euphemism of being a robot, not fitting in. My son is gay and I think, well, I am proud of my reaction to him telling me,' I gabbled. 'I'm sorry if it's not marketable.'

'Not marketable? You're kidding?' she said, her face lighting up. 'It's fucking brilliant. We love it. Fresh, funny, fucking great.'

'Really?' I said.

Angie pressed a button on her desk,

'Celia, tell Coco what you thought of her idea.'

'Fucking brilliant,' came the voice through the intercom.

'See,' said Angie.

'But it's a kid's book?'

'Kids is a great market to tap, all those little fuckers with pocket money and pester power. Do you know how much the Tooth Fairy pays these days?'

I said I didn't.

'A fucking fiver for a tooth! That's a paperback... David Walliams wrote *The Boy in A Dress* book which was a huge hit, and Geri Halliwell's got her *Eugenia Labia*.'

'It's Lavender, Eugenia Lavender,' I said.

'Yeah, they've made kids' books *cool* again. I think Greg-O-Byte could be huge.'

'Great,' I smiled, feeling relieved.

Angie explained that they have had a meeting and they want to pitch it as a series of ten books!

'Wow. I didn't really intend to write a series.'

'I know, fate innit,' she said. 'I didn't think I'd end up divorced with three kids and a bucket fanny, but there you go.'

I laughed, despite my reservations. Angie then opened champagne and bombarded me with ideas for her pitch for *Greg-O-Byte: Some Androids are Different.* She wants to approach the major publishing houses over the next few days.

Her enthusiasm was contagious, but not quite enough. On the train journey home, I just couldn't feel excited.

I don't know if it is the exhaustion or too much champagne. I spent two years researching and writing *Chasing Diana Spencer* and it died on its arse. I knocked this idea out in a jet-lagged few hours, and she is talking a series of books? I think I am simply being very ungrateful, am going to try to sleep. I have to write a treatment for the first three books for next week.

Sunday 10th May 12.43
TO: chris@christophercheshire.com

I finally slept a full night. Angie called yesterday morning. A publisher came back about the proposal, and as well as the outlines for the first three, has asked for a treatment of all ten books! I decided to come up to my allotment; there are fewer distractions... or so I thought.

I had not noticed before that a large part of my patch is covered in an old moulding royal blue Axminster carpet. I stuck my fag in my mouth and lifted the corner. Underneath was compacted dry soil and scores of wood lice teaming over the woven backing. I recoiled with a yelp and my lit cigarette fell on the carpet.

A handsome guy came out of the shed next door and watched me chasing my lit cigarette being blown across the carpet. He said, 'Hello.' I retrieved my fag and, on closer inspection, saw he was *very* handsome, I guessed late thirties.

'Got it!' I said going red, and he laughed. I hope *with* me.

'It's for the weeds,' he said.

'What is?'

'The carpet,' he said. 'Keeps the weeds down.'

'Ah,' I said, noticing Amy Winehouse had disappeared. 'Where's your scarecrow gone?'

He said he'd had a letter from the Allotment Association saying it is a bad role model for the kids who come up here.

'Oh,' I said. 'Did you tell them she's the first scarecrow to win five Grammy awards?'

He laughed. I expected him to introduce himself, but he just started to dig. Maybe he knows I talked to Agatha Balfour about his scarecrow. I smiled and went into my shed, sat down and got the stove going. As it spluttered to life, I looked at him through the window. He had on baggy blue jeans and a tight black jumper. His tall athletic frame wore them very well.

A mad thought popped into my head. I realised that if he turned round and asked me to sleep with him, I could do (not that he would). It was the first time I had thought about being legally single.

I have forgotten about sex, new exciting sex, I mean. The sex with Daniel was always good, but I began to think about peeling this guy's clothes off, and what he would look like. He looked like a guy who worked out and ate right, tight behind, muscular thighs, lovely pecs, and a square jaw...

I didn't know I had been staring at him for so long until the kettle started to scream loudly. He turned and saw me. I looked away and grabbed for the milk bottle, but I couldn't get hold of it properly and I did one of those juggling acts before dropping it with a crash. I grinned stupidly at him and bent down to clear it up. By the time I'd finished, he had gone.

It feels rather comfortable sitting here in a shed. I wonder how often Mr Bevan sat here. He probably never thought he would keel over by the water butt.

Sunday 17th May 10.47
TO: chris@christophercheshire.com,
    marikarolincova@hotmail.co.uk

Sorry for my lack of contact but I had banned my iPhone from the writing proceedings. It was just too tempting to tap away. Especially as you two got so excited about the Handsome Man. (I still don't know his name.) He has been here a few times, but all we've done is wave.

My shed has been a great place to work. I brought up some cushions and throws and an oil lamp but it hasn't endeared me to the Allotment Association. This morning an old man called Len banged on the door with his walking stick and shouted, 'You gonna grow anything?'

I said that I was planning a row of carrots but hadn't had the time and resources yet to implement it. This didn't go down well.

'Talk English,' he barked. 'You've bloody well sat up here for a week using it as an office. Read yer contract. We'll take it off yer if you don't turn over some soil in the next week!'

The last part of his sentence was particularly loud, which disturbed a dozen or so blackbirds and made the heads of a few old gits pop up above their fruit bushes.

When he had gone, I took my contract out of the drawer. It states that I have to keep at least 75% of it for growing fruit and vegetables and weed the other 25%. Right now, I have 100% weeds.

I gathered up my things and walked out in my heels and long coat, looking every inch the allotment abuser.

Wednesday 20th May 14.56
TO: marikarolincova@hotmail.co.uk

I went to Homebase with Chris to celebrate completion of the book treatments. I am planning to make my allotment shed a permanent writing space, and if I have to do a bit of gardening, so be it.

I was happily queuing up at the till with four bags of manure, waiting for Chris to fetch some solar lights for his garden, when the people behind started to get fidgety. The woman at the checkout said, 'Will your husband be much longer?'

What should have been a silly mistaken comment hit me like a truck. *I have no husband, I am a lonely middle-aged, single woman buying horse shit.*

A cold trickling sensation began inside my chest and I started to see stars. They multiplied and I heard myself say, 'I'm going to faint...'

My legs buckled under me and everything went black.

When I woke up, I was lying over my bags of manure and the checkout lady was spritzing me with a plant spray. Chris was kneeling beside me, clutching his cheek. She had slapped him round the face for being hysterical. I'd been unconscious for five minutes. They wanted to call an ambulance but I said I was fine, and left clutching my manure with Chris clutching his face.

'I'm single,' I said.

'And fabulous,' said Chris, but it came out as 'thabulous.'

Friday 22nd May 13.37
TO: chris@christophercheshire.com

Has your bruising gone down? I wouldn't sue the woman at Homebase. She looked very old school; in her day, you did slap someone round the face if they were hysterical. It's just a pity she had to do it three times...

I started on my allotment today. I borrowed a Strimmer from Mr Cohen next door. He was very glad to oblige when I rang his bell but I heard Mrs Cohen moaning in the background, 'Can't she afford to buy one? She's been in the papers lately.'

Mr Cohen quickly shut the door, and came out to his shed.

'We haven't seen Daniel around much,' he said.

'Yeah, um, we're divorcing. I am on my own now,' I said awkwardly.

'I've forgotten what that feels like,' he said wistfully. Mrs Cohen was watching us suspiciously from the living room window.

Maybe being single won't be all that bad. The Cohens used to be such a colourful, glamorous couple, but years of grating on each other seems to have worn them down to beige. Maybe Daniel and I were just on the cusp of beige, and fate intervened to save us from it? Maybe this is the next colourful chapter of my life?

I thanked Mr Cohen for the Strimmer, and walked up to the allotment. Len appeared, leaning on his stick.

'That won't get the weeds,' he said, tapping the Strimmer. 'It'll just chop the 'eads off. You need to dig 'em out.'

'This is just to make a start,' I said. 'Do you know where the nearest power socket is?'

'Yeah,' he laughed. 'My lounge.'

He pointed out that the Strimmer was petrol powered. I blushed and pulled the starter. After twenty minutes, it roared into life.

It took ages to raze the whole plot of weeds. Strimming is not as easy as it looks. When I switched off the motor, the silence twanged around. I hadn't seen the handsome guy arrive. He waved and came over.

'Hi, I'm Adam,' he said holding out a dark, wedding-ring-free hand. 'I realise I've never introduced myself.'

'Oh, didn't you?' I said, feigning nonchalance, 'I'm Coco.' I said, pulling off a glove and shaking his hand. 'Sorry about the noise, but I've been threatened with eviction for not digging.'

'I've put in an application for a Marilyn Manson scarecrow,' he said. 'But I don't think it'll be approved.'

I laughed a bit too hard, then scrambled for something to say.

'I'm a writer,' I said. 'That's why I've been in the shed a lot staring at you, well not staring *at* you but facing your direction... you know. Thinking, stuff.'

He asked what I wrote. As I started to tell him his phone rang.

'Sorry, I have to take this,' he said.

I stood there whilst he walked off to his shed. Several minutes went by and I began to feel stupid. He had seen me finish what I was doing, so we both knew I was waiting for him. I felt like a love-struck teenager. After a couple more minutes he was still chatting, so I waved at him, and shouted, 'Um, got to go.' He nodded and turned back to his call.

I slung the Strimmer a little butchly over my shoulder and trudged back home.

He is younger than me, and completely out of my league, yet I want to go back and talk to him again. What if he is gay? You fancy coming to help me dig tomorrow, and use your gaydar on Adam?

Friday 22nd May 18.09
TO: marikarolincova@hotmail.co.uk

I spent all day up at the allotment, but no Adam. Good job, as Chris and I got filthy digging up weeds and spreading manure. I stink of it.

At lunchtime, Len came past and eyeballed Chris, who had brought some very fancy cloth deckchairs and a hamper of Waitrose goodies. He leaned in and took a deep inhale.

'Lovely... 'oss shit,' he said.

Chris panicked and offered Len a slice of quiche.

''Oss shit!' said Len.

'Excuse me?' said Chris.

''Osssss SHIT! Good fer yer lungs!' shouted Len, spraying Chris with spittle.

Chris just looked at him. Len muttered under his breath something about yuppies and staggered off tapping his stick.

'Who in God's name was that?' he asked.

'Len, the Don of the Allotment,' I said. 'It's teeming with old gits.'

Then I realised how good this was. There didn't appear to be any other women my age or, God forbid, younger. I could flirt with the lovely Adam unheeded.

'You should be back out dating,' said Chris. 'Play the field. When did you last have sex?'

'February.'

'February?' he shrieked, sounding scandalised. 'You MUST have sex!'

Is he right? Must I? I am only just psyching myself up to a bit of mild flirtation. Since the divorce papers arrived, I have started to glance at men I see in the street, but I get the same feeling about sex as I would about a bungee jump: I can't imagine myself doing it.

Saturday 23rd May 08.34
TO: marikarolincova@hotmail.co.uk

Just had a call from Daniel where he ticked me off for inappropriate behaviour towards his sister and mother. He said I had broken the vow he had made to Ethel that our home is her home, etc. He reminded me that the house is not being signed over until our decree absolute in three weeks so it is still half *his* house. I asked him why he didn't say this before.

He told me Ethel is coming to stay until Tuesday whilst Tony and Meryl 'Get some R & R in Devon.'

Meryl has obviously got to him. He was always more scared of her than me. They are arriving in four hours. So, lots of notice. Great...

Saturday 23rd May 13.55
TO: marikarolincova@hotmail.co.uk

Meryl and Ethel arrived on time in the hearse, which always draws a few looks. My outburst, and throwing them out, wasn't mentioned. Meryl stuck to safe topics. The weather; 'Clement.' The M1; 'A carve-up.' And Susan Boyle; 'Women in my church group can sing *far* better.'

After twenty minutes of small talk, Meryl bade Ethel farewell and asked if I would walk her out to the hearse. She got in and rolled down the window with a stern look on her face. I thought, 'Here it is, the talking to.' Instead, she said, 'Coco, as you know, me and Tony are going away, alone... I wanted to see if I could borrow that television programme you have? Um...'

I looked at her blankly. '*Walking with Dinosaurs?*'

'No,' she said, going red and flustered. 'You know the thing we watched, together, when Mum was poorly?'

'Oh...You mean *Sex and The City?*'

'Shhh. Yes. That. Could I borrow that?'

'Sure, take the box set,' I said, and went and grabbed it. 'I've put the one we watched inside, on the top,' I smiled, handing it through the hearse window.

'Thank you!' she trilled, and drove off, her face a deep crimson.

When I came back in Ethel had opened a bottle of Lambrusco Bianco and sent Rosencrantz off to the shop for a packet of my cigarettes. She offered me a glass, and for the second time in the space of an hour, Daniel's in-laws surprised me.

She raised her glass to toast *me!* She said that despite being posh, I had been a 'fairly good' daughter-in-law and she hopes we keep in touch. We clinked and I went to make a little speech of thanks, but she launched into a tirade about Daniel.

He is in a *relationship*.

'She's twenty-five,' said Ethel, sitting back and pursing her lips for effect. 'She's religious and she's *American!*'

'Oh,' I said.

I was more surprised by how little I felt. Lots of things have happened lately, and I think I may be getting over Daniel.

It seems now I am no longer with him, I have ceased to be her enemy. The glass of lukewarm wine seemed to be an entry into Ethel's circle of slagging off. I joined in with the tirade, just a little bit, as I figured it would make the weekend go a bit easier. Daniel's new girlfriend is called Kendal.

'Why would you name your kid after a mint cake?' said Ethel, incredulous, '*Americans!*'

When Rosencrantz returned with the fags, I let him hear all about it and went for a peaceful smoke.

I keep thinking about Adam.

Sunday 24th May 19.43
TO: marikarolincova@hotmail.co.uk

I was up early this morning and read the papers with coffee and several cigarettes in the garden. Ethel came clicking out on her frame about eleven saying, 'What you doin' out 'ere?'

'Relaxing.'

'You've got a son in 'ere in tears,' she said.

I jumped up and followed her to find Rosencrantz huddled over a bowl of cereal, crying.

'Don't cry, boy,' said Ethel, rubbing his arm.

'What's wrong?' I said, putting my arm round him.

'Just everything, everything's gone,' he sobbed.

Instinctively I looked around the room.

''E's not talking about the bloody furniture,' said Ethel. ''E means 'is life!'

I didn't know what to do, and looked on, helpless.

''Ere, let yer Nan spark up for yer,' said Ethel.

She took a cigarette from a packet on the table and lit it, pressing it between his lips. He inhaled and exhaled.

'Better?'

Rosencrantz nodded.

'I need a number two,' announced Ethel, indicating I should talk to him as she shuffled out.

I sat down and we had a long chat. I have been so absorbed since we got back from America that I hadn't thought, or hadn't realised, he was going through things too. He'd appeared so resilient, slotting back into life.

He still feels deeply betrayed by Christian, who seems to have vanished off the face of the earth. His phone number is not working and he has mysteriously left his course at the London School of Fashion.

'And Dad hates me,' he added.

'No, he doesn't,' I said. 'He's just a ...' I nearly said something I shouldn't. 'He's just having a mid-life crisis.'

'Well, he didn't seem to want me around when we stayed with him... and that Kendal girl.'

'He was with her then?' I said, sharply.

'Yeah. Dad said we had to be careful around her, because she was from a very religious family and didn't approve of gays... I didn't want to tell you. I knew you would be upset.'

I hugged him tight. He has been working to protect me, but all I have been doing lately is thinking about myself.

I spent the rest of the day with him and Ethel, talking, and we all went for a walk in Regent's Park and had ice cream by the boating lake. He's still not right. It's something

I can't put my finger on, still something he is not telling me.

I never thought much about parental responsibility when I was with Daniel; we shared it very well, and it just seemed to happen. Suddenly being on my own with him is hard.

Monday 26th May 14.47
TO: chris@christophercheshire.com,
    marikarolincova@hotmail.co.uk

I took Ethel up to see the allotment this morning. I proudly showed her my clean, freshly dug-over soil.

'Shame yours is just muck compared to all the others,' she said and went to put the kettle on.

Adam came out of his shed, dressed in faded jeans and a tight white t-shirt. He looked great.

'Morning,' he said. He began to water a row of sweetcorn.

'Looking good,' I said. 'I mean, your plants.'

He smiled. His lips, I thought, are beautiful and full, and his teeth are so white... then I realised he had said something to me.

'What?'

'You've been digging,' he repeated, louder.

'Yes, I've been digging...' I said.

I didn't know what else to say. I heard Ethel clear her throat and she was standing in the shed doorway with a box of PG Tips.

'You want me to save the tea bags for yer eye bags?' she said, loudly, looking between Adam and me.

'Adam, this is Ethel, my mother-in-law,' I said.

As soon as it came out of my mouth, I saw him trying to work me out. Had he been thinking I was single?

'Hello,' he said.

'Yes, hello,' said Ethel, putting on her posh voice, 'she's div-horcing my son. The marriage dis-hintegrated. He's taken up with an American girl half this one's age.'

I gave her a look, and we all stood in silence for a moment.

'Well,' he said, 'I have to get on. Nice to see you.'

And with that, he shook his empty watering can and disappeared into his shed. I lit up a fag and said to Ethel that I didn't want tea and that we should go. It seems every conversation I have with him is a public relations disaster.

When we got home, Ethel looked fit to burst with her piece of fresh gossip. Rosencrantz had just come down from the shower and was rooting around in the fridge. She hoisted herself onto one of the breakfast stools and announced, 'Yer Mum 'as a new friend.'

'Oh,' said Rosencrantz, from inside the fridge.

When he stood up, he saw her gleeful face.

'Oh, that kind of friend,' he said. 'Cool.'

''E's black yer know,' she said, looking for a reaction.

'So?' shrugged Rosencrantz.

'Yer mum and a black man? The 'ole street'll be talking.'

'That's enough, Ethel,' I said.

Rosencrantz busied himself making toast.

'Rosencrantz,' I said. 'I'm not like your father, I'm not jumping into having a relationship. He, Adam, is a very handsome man I have talked to across my allotment a couple of times... Maybe it's a flirtation, but so mild that it was pretty much imperceptible. That really is it.'

'It's cool,' said Rosencrantz, buttering his toast.

'Yer dad's with a yank, and yer mum with a black man!' said Ethel trying to stir. 'At this rate you could go on *Jerry Springer*!'

'Stop it!' I said angrily.

I went upstairs, red in the face, and left Rosencrantz to lecture her about tolerance. What must he think of me, now he has been led to believe I have a boyfriend? After all the talks we had about Daniel copping off with some yank, I mean, American.

Tuesday 27th May 10.45
TO: chris@christophercheshire.com,
marikarolincova@hotmail.co.uk

I wasn't sad to see Meryl and Tony collect Ethel. After mining me for information about my life, and fixating on Adam, I'd had enough of her.

They looked very rosy and relaxed when they arrived from their weekend away. In fact, Tony was so relaxed he was willing to break their 'maximum two people in the hearse' rule, and let Ethel sit in the front between them. I nearly told him to bung her in the coffin and nail it shut.

Meryl waited until Tony was outside putting Ethel's case in before giving back the *Sex and The City* box set. She slid it across the table, wrapped in a Pashmina.

'I'll collect the scarf next time,' she said hastily, when I went to unwrap it.

She didn't say anything else about their weekend, but Ethel had told us all the gossip over dinner the previous night.

Meryl and Tony have been trying for a baby! Meryl met the wife of a fertility expert in one of her cookery chat-rooms (as you do), and invited them over for dinner. One thing led to another and Meryl has been paying a fortune for hormone injections. He recommended they get away to relax and try to get pregnant.

'I just 'ope they don't do what that Dave Beckham did,' said Ethel, 'an' name it after the place what they bonked in. Chagford Watson would be a very cruel name.'

I never knew how much they wanted a child. Apparently, they have been trying to conceive for years. Meryl had always scoffed at the subject of children, saying they would play havoc with her carpets.

Thursday 29th May 15.43
TO: chris@christophercheshire.com

I've spent the last couple of days at the allotment with Rosencrantz and Marika. Rosencrantz is on his reading week and Marika had some free days because her students are on exam leave.

I wish you would come too. I will keep Len away from you. We are planting raspberry canes and blackcurrant bushes.

Rosencrantz left the allotment early tonight to begin a new job, working in a bar on the High Street. He keeps saying he needs to start paying his way. I have told him that he doesn't need to and should concentrate on drama school, but he won't listen. He is still not right and I don't know what to do. Marika says I should give him time and space.

Adam wasn't at the allotments.

Sunday 31st May 17.33
TO: chris@christophercheshire.com

Adam showed up today as I was packing away. My obsession with wanting to see him has built up over the past few days, so when I opened my mouth to say hello, a barrage of thoughts came tumbling out.

'My mother-in-law is my ex-mother-in-law because my husband cheated on me after Christmas.' I blurted. 'It was me who left him. I'm divorced.'

'Oh,' he said. 'Okay.'

There was a pause.

'Do you smoke?' I asked, offering him a cigarette.

'No,' he said. 'My mother died of cancer.'

'Mine too!' I said, a little over-enthusiastically. 'I mean, mine too,' I repeated, in a more serious tone. 'I need to stop, smoking that is.'

'Well, there's the pub. I'm off for a drink, that's non-smoking,' he said.

'Yes, it is,' I said.

He grinned.

Then, realising, I said, 'I'd love to come to the pub.'

You would think I had never spoken to a man before.

I said I would lock up and dashed into the shed and scrabbled around for a teaspoon. I didn't have a mirror. As far as I could see, I didn't have any manure on my face.

I straightened myself up and came back out, locking the door. A beautiful, pale young girl, who can't have been more than late twenties, was standing with Adam. I stopped in my tracks. She was tall and dressed in that wonderfully tousled Boho style. Her long dark hair was fashionably messy. She held a small branch covered in light pink blossom.

'Smell this,' she was saying, holding the blossom up to Adam's nose, and leaning on his broad shoulder.

'Mmmm,' he said, 'cherry.' The 'mmm' sound he made was so deep, and expressed so much pleasure in him. The rumble of his voice went through my stomach, and made me tingle.

'Where did you get this? I hope you haven't been scrumping,' he scolded, playfully. He looked up and saw me. The girl followed his gaze and gave me a warm, perfect smile. The bitch.

'Ah, Coco,' he said. 'This is Holly, my...'

'I just remembered. I have to get home to my cat,' I blurted out, feeling ugly and out of my depth. I hurried away up the hill waving and gurning.

'Okay, maybe another time,' he called after me.

I turned back and gave him another flapping wave, which was just as silly as the half-walk half-run I was doing.

He has this calmness, which throws me. He's so laid back and sexy and *of course* he is dating a hot model in her twenties... Of course he is. I'm a naive idiot. Like *he* is going to be single!

And what about this fake cat I suddenly have to run home to? I must remember I have a fake cat if he asks me again. If he even speaks to me again. On the corner of Baker Street, my phone went, and it was Meryl.

'I've got some super news,' she said breathlessly.

I thought she would announce she is expecting twins through IVF called Torquay and Bude but she said, 'Tony and I have put down a deposit on a sheltered housing unit for Mother. It's in Catford!'

'Sheltered housing?' I said.

'Yes,' she trilled. 'We've been looking at accommodation

options. Obviously, you said no, and Daniel has had to sacrifice his home... So, we thought we would invest some of our hard-earned shekels. Mother won't own it, but she can stay there for as long as she lives.'

'Great,' I said. 'But I never said no, and Daniel hasn't sacrificed his...'

'We thought Mum should be back where she feels happy, in South London,' she said ignoring me. 'I'll keep you posted with the details, byeee.'

I will be the closest one to Ethel again, the one who she phones if she can't get the lid off something, or if she has a fall.

Fuck.

JUNE

Monday 1st June 10.19
TO: chris@christophercheshire.com

After one phone call, the world seems golden. The publisher who is extremely interested in *Greg-O-Byte: Some Androids Are Different* wants to meet with Angie and me at Cathedral Members Club tomorrow morning! She loves the book treatments I've written. Angie says it is very important that I arrive half an hour early, so she can brief me on a few things.

This time tomorrow I could be a children's author with a publishing deal! Now what should I wear? I am just Googling pictures of JK Rowling for inspiration.

Tuesday 2nd June 13.44
TO: chris@christophercheshire.com

Rosencrantz helped me pick out what to wear. I tried to emulate JK Rowling with a plain trouser suit. She always manages to combine looking stylish, intelligent, aloof, yet wise with a twinkle in her eye, which hints it could really be worth getting to know her.

Try as I might, I found myself looking as far away from JK Rowling as I could; Margaret Mountford's younger sister. I must have my hair cut. I haven't done a thing with it since Daniel departed.

I spent so long over what I should look like that I was very late. I emerged from the sauna-like conditions of the Northern Line with hair plastered to head, and when my iPhone had a signal, frantic messages from Angie came pinging through. It took an age to hail a black cab.

When I reached Cathedral, she was smoking furiously outside the tiny entrance down to the bar.

'Pinchard? What the fuck? I told you nine forty-five!' she said, grinding the stub of her cigarette into the pavement with the point of her tiny Louboutin.

I apologised, she looked me up and down, and then dragged me by the arm into one of the lifts. She jabbed a finger on BAR and the doors closed.

'I needed to talk to you,' said Angie carefully, her face tense.

The lift began its descent.

'I'm sorry. It was the Tube, then an age to wait for a...'

'Quiet,' she said. 'This is important. Your name is Kathy Trent, and I need you to not mention *Chasing Diana Spencer*. Ok?'

'What?'

The lift slowed to a ping. The doors opened into the bar. A friendly mid-twenties blonde sat waiting in a confession-box booth. She waved.

'Please, just trust me,' pleaded Angie. 'There's no time.'

She pulled her face into a smile and led us over to the blonde, who introduced herself as Louise Mulholland from Mulholland Avenue Press. I went along with Angie and introduced myself as Kathy...

'Trent,' said Angie, sliding into the booth and throwing me a look.

We ordered iced tea and got chatting.

Louise was there to make an offer for a Greg-O-Byte novel, and four other Greg-O-Byte stories to form a series. Angie seemed to relax until a tall, overly-tanned man holding a huge cardboard cut-out emerged from the back of the bar, where Cathedral has private dining rooms for its VIP members. The man clocked Angie, who was trying desperately not to be seen, and came over.

It was Michael Brannigan.

The life-size cardboard cut-out tucked sideways under his arm was of Anne Brannigan, presumably promotional material for The Anne and Michael Brannigan Book Club.

'Ange!' he drawled. 'How's tricks?'

Louise sat up enthusiastically and introduced herself. Michael then turned his attention to me. I felt sweat prickle across my forehead and between my shoulder blades.

'I know you,' he frowned.

I could see it coming in slow motion. Angle's mouth flapped soundlessly.

'Coco. Pinchard,' he said angrily. The cut-out of Anne Brannigan grinned maniacally.

'No, this is Kathy,' said Louise, looking between us. 'Kathy Trent, she's written a wonderful MS.'

'No. This woman is Coco Pinchard,' he announced, a little like the reveal in an episode of *Poirot*.

Louise looked confused.

'Is business *that bad* Ange?' said Michael.

He shot me one last look and walked away.

'Am I missing something here?' said Louise.

I glared at Angie, who was still trying to think up a lie. The silence stretched on until I offered her my hand.

'I'm sorry. I am Coco Pinchard,' I said.

Why? Why did I reintroduce myself? Louise closed her laptop.

'I need to see if I can catch Michael Brannigan,' she said coldly, and gathering up her things, she left.

'Wait! Louise!' shouted Angie. 'Coco I'll... see you,' she said and ran off, just catching the lift carrying Louise and Michael.

I was left to pay the bill.

Wednesday 3rd June 18.36
TO: chris@christophercheshire.com

What time is it? I have been in bed all day. I thought Angie would ring and then I thought I might ring Angie, but neither materialised. Either way, it's all a mess, my career... my life. Yes, I would love to go over to Marika's with you. Let's do the train, and then we can both drink.

Wednesday 3rd June 22.02
TO: rosencrantzpinchard@gmail.com

I didn't know you had the night off work, which is good, you should take a few more nights off. I would have made you something to heat up if I had known. I have been over to see Marika with Chris, I should be home soon. We just boarded the train back to Charing Cross. If you like, I could pick you up something to eat from the Tesco Metro on Baker Street?

Mum xx

Wednesday 3rd June 22.36
TO: rosencrantzpinchard@gmail.com

I think the Tesco will be closed by the time I get there. Our train ground to a halt half an hour ago. We are stuck on the tracks beside some disused office blocks and scaffolding. I have no clue why. Other trains seem to be scooting past us with no probs.

Wednesday 3rd June 23.12
TO: marikarolincova@hotmail.co.uk

We are still on the train. It broke down just before New Cross, we think. There have been no announcements and the lights have gone out. I have been and banged on the door to the driver's compartment, but no one is answering.

Thursday 4th June 00.00
TO: rosencrantzpinchard@gmail.com

Love, we are stuck, the whole train seems to have powered down and the last train out of London has gone past, packed with people on its way south. We have tried to call National Rail Enquiries but it is ringing out. Is there anything on the news? Bomb scare, person under a train, wrong kind of leaves on the track, etc.

Thursday 4th June 00.40
TO: marikarolincova@hotmail.co.uk

Chris has got us scared. He thinks the driver is dead.
Why would we stop for so long? We have walked the length
of the train and, spookily, there is no one else on board. It's
dark, and in the wind, the carriage is making creaking
sounds. I drank too much wine at yours and there is no toilet
on the train. I am eyeing a Burger King cup, which someone
left behind on a seat. If we are stuck much longer, I might
have to use it. Chris is going to phone his father, who plays
golf with someone on the board of SouthWest Trains.

Thursday 4th June 01.12
TO: rosencrantzpinchard@gmail.com

Sorry I didn't let you know what is happening, but my
phone is about to die. We are still in the same place. I have
my key, so you can lock the front door. When we get to
Charing Cross, we will have to find a taxi so I have no idea
when I will be back.

Thursday 4th June 11.36
TO: marikarolincova@hotmail.co.uk

We spent the whole night on the train! Can you believe
that nobody came to our rescue? We couldn't prise the doors
open and our phones died. What if there had been a fire?
We moved into First Class, thinking the seats might be more
comfortable but the only difference seemed to be that each

seat had a little white napkin headrest.

The sun came up at four, and, glinting off the office blocks, was surprisingly beautiful. I managed to hold on until almost 5am but then I cracked and had to use the Burger King cup. I made Chris move out of First Class and, concealing myself in the foot well between a set of four seats, went about the awkward task of peeing into the cup. Thankfully it was Burger King Tower Menu size. Mid-stream, the lights flickered on in the carriage, the train lurched forward and the bing bong automated announcement came to life saying that, 'We will shortly be arriving at New Cross.' I screamed and had to hastily finish, as the platform came into view with several bleary-eyed commuters.

We thought there might be a news crew from the national or, at the very least, regional news waiting to document our plight but everyone assumed we were two scruff bags that had caught the first train.

When we pulled in at Charing Cross, I was furious. Chris went to find the station manager, but I thought of someone better to take out my anger on. I walked along Charing Cross road to Angle's building.

I barged past her assistant and into her office without knocking. Angie was sitting with her back to the door, staring out at the tourists teeming up Shaftesbury Avenue.

'Coco,' she said, turning round. 'Fucking hell, what happened to you?'

She pulled a bottle of Glenmorangie out of a desk drawer, and poured us each a measure into cups from the water cooler. She caught me off guard.

'I know. You hate me,' she said, pushing the cork back into the bottle.

'You made me look ridiculous,' I said.

'If you had turned up on time, I could have explained.'

'Okay. Explain.'

Angie sat down. She took a deep breath.

'I can't sell a book by Coco Pinchard. You are effectively blacklisted. Your old agent Dorian, your publishing house and Michael Brannigan have seen to that.'

'Seriously?'

'Yeah.'

'Why did you take me on?'

'I like a challenge. I thought I could get you a deal under a pen name.'

'A pen name!' I spat.

'And your reaction just proved how much you hate that idea,' she said lighting a cigarette. 'But it may have worked. I have no doubt the Greg-O-Byte series would have been a huge hit. Eventually we could have said who they were really written by. You know how the press loves a comeback.'

I drank my whisky.

'So, this is it?'

'Coco. I cannot sell anything you write at the moment. Maybe I can do something with the rights to *Chasing Diana Spencer*, in a year or two. I hate to say this but you should find something else.'

Angie pulled a business card out of her pocket and passed it across her desk.

'My friend is the headmistress of a shit hot independent school in Kensington... Give her a call, they need an English teacher.'

I walked home. I couldn't face getting back on a train.

Friday 5th June 14.46
TO: marikarolincova@hotmail.co.uk

Chris's father spoke to the director of SouthWest Trains. They launched an investigation into why we were stranded and found that the driver was at fault. Like me, he'd needed to pee, and thinking that the train was empty, halted by a thicket of trees and jumped out to relieve himself. However, he got lost in the dark and the trees, finally emerging in Grove Park this morning, suffering from shock after a night spent lost in the woods around Greater London.

As an apology, the managing director has sent over to Chris several cases of vintage wine and a hamper of artisan breads and cheeses. Half of me is disgusted. If we were ordinary customers, we would have barely been refunded our tickets. The other half is really looking forward to some free wine and cheese, you fancy joining? How about a late-night picnic up at my allotment? It's very warm and the view over London is beautiful.

Saturday 6th June 11.11
TO: agatha@augustine.redhillallotments.co.uk

Dear Agatha,
Last night I fear I sparked an incident, which I am sure will be relayed back to you. I wanted to pre-empt this by sending an email.

Just after 1am this morning, I was at the allotment with a couple of friends and we encountered Len with several other gentlemen. My friend Christopher was bundled into a headlock after picking and eating a raspberry. Despite efforts to explain who we were, and that the raspberry was mine, Len would not let go and, in self-defence, was hit over the head with a clutch bag.

As far as I know, I am allowed to utilise my allotment twenty-four hours a day, and I wasn't aware you'd commissioned an elderly task force to protect the fruit crops at night. It's lucky no one was killed.

Yours faithfully,

Coco Pinchard (Allotment 17)

Monday 8th June 11.33
TO: marikarolincova@hotmail.co.uk

I don't think Len will press charges for you hand bagging him, but I received a stern email from Agatha Balfour, summoning me to attend a meeting of the Allotment Association on Friday.

In other news, I went to see Mr Spencer this morning. Neither Daniel nor I have objected to wanting to divorce, so I will get my decree absolute and be officially single this time next week.

Tuesday 9th June 08.33
TO: chris@christophercheshire.com

Meryl was on the phone asking what I would like for my birthday next week.

'Goodness,' she said. 'You'll be fifty before you know it, doesn't time fly?'

I asked for a voucher and put the phone down. She knows I am only going to be forty-two.

Wednesday 10th June 15.06
TO: danielpinchard@gmail.com

I know our legal representatives have advised us against communicating, but I am concerned about Rosencrantz. He has been behaving very oddly. He took me out for an early birthday lunch today, and it wasn't just any old lunch; he took me to La Relais De Venise L'Entrecote, the incredible steak restaurant on Marylebone Lane. He pulled out my chair for me, he paid the bill, and when an old lady walked slap bang into the plate glass window of the restaurant, he didn't, as I would expect him to, point and laugh but he ran to help. I am worried about this behaviour. Has he said anything to you?

Thursday 11th June 10.14
TO: chris@christophercheshire.com

Do you want to go to Slovakia next week? Marika is on half term and she has invited us to stay at her mother's house in the country. I did ask if it's the same house where she was snowed in at Christmas, and had diarrhoea from drinking the swimming pool water. She said yes, but the weather is hitting thirty-eight degrees so the pool will be much more enjoyable. Can you come?

She has invited Rosencrantz too, as he is on another reading week, but he has said he wants to stay and work at the bar.

Thursday 11th June 18.16
TO: marikarolincova@hotmail.co.uk

I had my hair cut this morning. I went to the really posh place on the posh end of the high street, near the button shop. I saw the senior stylist. (In my experience the only time I have ever known a gay guy to revel in the title 'senior'.) He gave me a completely different look, a cut that is wonderful but low maintenance and a warmer blonde colour, which does, as he promised, take years off me.

I have also lost 7lbs. Maybe it's all the work at the allotment. I try not to buy into all this size rubbish, but I managed to get a beautiful green Per Una skirt from Marks, in a size twelve. I don't know how it can have happened. I have been borderline fourteen/sixteen for years. A fifteen you might say.

Chris can't come to Slovakia. He has been ordered by his mother to attend his grandmother's surprise ninety-seventh birthday. Which begs the question; isn't Chris old enough to do what he wants? Moreover, isn't a surprise party for a ninety-seven-year-old a bit risky?

We are booked on a flight out on Saturday morning at five-thirty.

Friday 12th June 22.00
TO: chris@christophercheshire.com

I decided to wear the new skirt with a tight black top for the Allotment Association meeting. I also attempted to recreate what the hairdresser did with my hair which kind of worked. I figured the Association members would all be in gardening gear, and it would give me a little status to look polished.

Agatha has one of those lovely old mews houses by the park; four storeys, black railings and a brown plaque on the brickwork, announcing that in 1812 some anthropologist was born there.

I arrived as the meeting was starting. There were twenty old gits squashed on sofas and dining chairs in Agatha's knick-knack laden living room, and also Len and Adam! I hadn't expected to see him. He is the secretary, and was sitting in on the meeting, taking notes. He mouthed 'Hello'. He was dressed beautifully in dark jeans and a white jumper. The jeans were designer skinny and, on his muscly legs and with a Dolce & Gabbana silver belt, they looked great. His thin white jumper was ever so slightly see-through. His dark muscles under the white were striking.

Then the penny dropped. Adam is gay. He must be! He's so good looking, clean and tidy. That girl up the allotment could have been his fag hag, and Allotment Association Secretary? Must be gay. I was lost in this revelation when I realised Agatha was talking to me.

'Pardon?' I said.

'It has come to our attention that you may be abusing your right to an allotment,' she said, looking over the top of her owl glasses. 'Why were you in your shed at one in the morning last Saturday?'

'She was boozing with 'er poncy mates,' said Len, who was still dressed in his outdoor clothes. 'I caught one of 'em squatting down doing a piss on the path! Then she coshed me over me 'ead with 'er bag!'

'I wasn't the one with the bag,' I added quickly, as Adam was scribbling all this down.

'Mrs Pinchard,' said Agatha screwing up her face. 'Drunkenness, violence and public urination are a dreadful habit of the young in this country. You're obviously not young, so, pray, what is your explanation?'

I gulped and looked at Adam who was still writing.

'I understand you are a writer, Mrs Pinchard,' said Agatha. There were several smirks amongst the association members. 'How would you creatively describe this night-time jaunt?'

I got to my feet, determined to give Adam something positive to write, and wipe their smirks away.

'In my capacity as a writer,' I said, 'I have just received a grant from the Arts Council.'

Adam looked up. Agatha adjusted her glasses expectantly.

'A performance grant,' I added, clueless of where this was going. 'What you witnessed was a rehearsal for a piece of street theatre, called *Fruit Picking.*'

'Fruit Picking?' echoed Agatha.

I cursed myself. Why didn't I just admit that we were all pissed?

'Yes,' plunged on. '*Fruit Picking in The Moonlight.*'

'And the Arts Council funded this, because...?'

'Its focus on eating local produce, and that this is one of the finest kept group of allotments in London.'

'What about the girl pissing?' said Len.

'Well, I may have to cut that scene. Thank you for your feedback,' I said.

Len snorted. There was a silence. Agatha's old grandfather clock ticked and Adam's pen made a scratching sound as he wrote. The old gits looked as if I was bindweed, something I know they all despise.

Agatha looked around with a smirk on her face,

'Well. You certainly are... theatrical. Tonight is an official oral warning, Mrs Pinchard. Of course, we are all excited to see this wonderful play. You will have to tell us when the premiere is... Now,' she said, 'Alan wants to discuss potato blight.'

I excused myself, feeling like a supreme idiot. Everyone ignored me, apart from Adam who gave me a wink. He gets me. He must be gay! As I left, I caught sight of his writing – beautiful, flowy, and definitely gay.

It was still warm when I got home, so I opened some wine and sat in the garden. I was on my third glass when the phone went.

A voice said, 'Hi, it's Adam.'

I sat up in my deckchair, surprised.

'Sorry if this is a bit naughty,' he said, 'I got your number from the contact sheet.'

I asked if I had left something at Agatha's. He said no. There was a silence.

He cleared his throat and said, 'If you're free Monday, do you want to come and see *La Cage Aux Folles*? In the West End.'

'You *are* gay. I knew I'd worked it out tonight,' I said. 'It was the jeans that did it.'

I poured some more wine. The line went quiet.

'Er,' he said, 'I'm not gay.'

'You're not?' I gulped. 'So, who was that girl, Holly?'

'My daughter,' he said.

'But you're... and she's...'

'Yes, I'm black and she's not.'

He explained that his ex-wife is Irish and they'd had Holly when they were fifteen. I asked him why he didn't say this.

'Would you go into that much detail with someone you'd only just met? Besides, you didn't give me the chance. You ran off to feed your cat,' he said. 'What's it called?'

'My cat?' I said, scrabbling round for a name. 'Um. Coco.'

'You named your cat after yourself?'

'No,' I said, cringing. 'He's Coco Pops, like the cereal, and I'm Coco Pinchard.'

I could tell he thought I was barmy.

'*Right,*' he said. 'These tickets, for Monday...'

'I'd love to go out on Monday,' I squeaked.

'What time?'

He said he would pick me up at seven. I suddenly remembered.

'Monday? I can't. I'm going to Slovakia for my birthday.'

'Slovakia?' he said, confused.

'Well, it used to be Czechoslovakia then it divided, so maybe that's why you haven't heard of it. It's only been around for a few years.'

'No, I've heard of it,' he said.

There was another silence.

'Well, maybe another time,' I said, now wanting to die.

'Yeah, maybe.' He sounded like he really wanted to get off the phone. He wished me a good trip and hung up.

I actually had to chew on the cushion. How utterly, utterly mortifying, and annoying. He is straight and he fancied me.

I don't even know who I am these days. All these lies, I keep digging myself deeper. So much of the time Daniel used to drive me mad, but I realise now how he grounded me. I miss coming home and having someone to talk to about all the craziness in my head. Now I am on my own, it's seeping out, into my life.

Sunday 14th June 12.33
TO: chris@christophercheshire.com

Can you do me a favour and check on Rosencrantz whilst
I'm away. He is working himself into the ground with classes
and his job. Just give him a buzz and remind him to eat and
sleep. Thank you.

Monday 15th June 23.45
TO: chris@christophercheshire.com

It's official. I love Slovakia. Why did no one tell me about
it? You hear about Poland and Croatia, but not Slovakia. We
boarded our Ryanair flight in the grey at London Luton and,
two hours later, we landed in tropical heat.

Bratislava Airport is so people-friendly. We walked off
the flight, through a tiny arrivals hall and out, no endless
miles of corridors or park 'n' rides.

Marika's sister, Adrianna, was waiting for us and took us
back in her Jeep. We zoomed along a quiet motorway
framed by blue and purple mountains, past fields of corn
and sunflowers – so many sunflowers. Adrianna put the roof
down and drove fast. With the wind in our faces, I felt a
weight lift from me. I don't know why Marika ever left this
place.

Adrianna speaks English almost as well as Marika. She is
just as beautiful as Marika, but with a mass of long, black
curly hair.

The village is very different from the barren hellhole I
imagined last Christmas. It's a row of seven little cottages,
each with a lush garden full of fruit trees; plums, apricots,

pears and grapes, all well on the way to ripeness. The surrounding fields are full of giant sunflowers swaying against the perfect blue sky. Across the road, shimmering in the heat, is a derelict old mill and a little stream.

We turned into a long wide, driveway running down the side of the house. At the end was the garden with a swimming pool and a large outhouse where I could hear chickens squawking. A huge woman in her early sixties emerged from the doorway carrying a flapping hen by its feet, and placed it on a tree stump. She wore a voluminous flowery dress and had a short bob of tight black curly hair. I thought she was raising one of her huge arms in greeting, and then I noticed she was holding an axe, which she brought down on the hen. There was silence and she held up the headless bird, pulling out its feathers with her free hand.

'Why does she have to do that now?' asked Marika, embarrassed. 'She must have heard the car.'

The woman was Marika's mother. She wiped her hands and came towards us, grinning widely.

'Moja Zlata!' she shouted and grasped Marika's face and kissed her.

'Maminko!' Marika shouted, grabbing her mother's hands away from her face and hugging her. I noticed Marika's arms didn't quite make it all the way round.

'This is my mother, Blazena,' said Marika.

Blazena grinned and gave me a gut-busting hug.

'Dobry Den,' I said.

I had been practising the Slovak for hello in the car all the way. Blazena looked delighted and began jabbering away to Marika. Adrianna translated.

'Mum says she is the only farmer's wife for miles yet she gives birth to Marika, the vegetarian. She says she has saved

Marika some acorns from last year's harvest.'

I laughed, but Marika was already giving it back to Blazena, something to do with killing the bird.

Adrianna suggested we take the bags inside, as they could be here for a while. She took me to my room, which, like the rest of the cottage, is full of dark, carved wooden furniture and lots of lace. When I had unpacked, I went into the kitchen where Blazena was pouring shots of something called Slivovica, a plum brandy.

We clinked and the three of them downed in one. I took a smaller sip and it instantly filled my chest with a smooth warmth. Blazena had gutted the chicken and was pounding out the meat with a mallet. Within minutes, she had wafer thin pieces of chicken, which she expertly dusted in breadcrumbs before dropping them in oil.

'Those schnitzels, they're so thin!' I said.

'She always imagines my father's face when she makes them,' said Marika.

I laughed.

'In England you have marriage guidance counsellors, in Slovakia we pound schnitzel,' grinned Adrianna.

I thought I might have to try it.

We sat by the pool for a lunch of schnitzel, salad, potatoes and beer which was just about the most delicious thing I have ever tasted, and then with the temperature threatening forty degrees, Marika said we should sleep.

Three hammocks were hung in the shade by the pool, and after some persuading, I agreed to give it a whirl. I didn't think I'd be able to nod off, but once I had climbed in, and over the feeling of being like a suet pudding in a drawstring bag, I dropped off easily.

We must have been tired because we slept for six hours.

I woke up to the soft splash of Marika leaping into the pool. The sun had sunk down behind the cottage but, even in the burnt orange, it was still hot. Adrianna brought cold beer and we watched Marika swim.

'Is she okay?' said Adrianna.

'Yes, and no. Life in London seems to be getting harder and more expensive.'

'I wish she'd come back,' said Adrianna, 'but she has the city in her blood and coming back here would be...'

'This place is wonderful.'

'We have everything and nothing... Life is hard and you can't live on a view,' said Adrianna.

We stared out at the range of mountains, topped with snow and vanishing in the haze. Blazena came out with more beers and heaved herself into a hammock. She asked if I swam but I said I didn't want to put on a swimming costume.

'She thinks you are an attractive woman,' said Marika translating. 'She says you need to believe you are beautiful.'

'Oh,' I said blushing. 'She's only being polite.'

'She's not,' said Marika, treading water in the shallow end. 'Mother doesn't lie. She was the only one who told her sister she looked fat on her wedding day.'

Blazena nodded.

'She told her she looked like a pregnant pig,' translated Adrianna.

I didn't know what to say to that, and luckily a car pulled up in the driveway. It was Adrianna's husband, Stevko. He is dark-skinned, works in construction, and has the body to show for it.

'Famous author Coco Pinchard,' he said, jumping out of the car and kissing me on both cheeks.

'Oh, I don't know about that,' I said, flushing red.

'I'm not going to translate anything negative you say about yourself,' warned Marika.

Stevko lit a barbecue and we sat drinking Slivovica as the sun went down. It didn't take long for Marika to tell them that, as of tonight, I had become a single, forty-two-year-old woman.

'We should make you a party,' said Stevko.

They all jabbered in Slovak, then Marika said excitedly, 'We'll do it tomorrow night. They're going to invite Zobor!'

'Is that a man or a woman?'

'A band,' said Marika. 'They're huge in Slovakia, the lead singer lives in one of the cottages two doors away. It'll be a great party!'

We stayed up chatting and planning. Just before midnight, Marika checked her watch and said something to Adrianna, who disappeared and came back with a big firework. She put it at the end of the pool, lit it, and ran back to us. Coloured jets began to fire up into the sky.

'You're officially single,' said Marika. 'And it's your birthday!'

Blazena poured more Slivovica and we drank as fireworks shot into the black sky.

'To happiness and the future,' said Marika and we clinked our Slivovica glasses.

I told them the story of the past few months. They all agreed that Daniel is an idiot. Blazena marvelled at how restrained I had been when I found Daniel with Snow White. She told me that when she caught Marika's father with another woman, she pushed him into the well, and sat on the lid for the whole night!

We didn't end up coming to bed until three. I can't sleep. I have tried counting doilies. I reached one hundred and three, and was still wide-awake. So, I am emailing you from the only place I can get a signal, the outside toilet. From my vantage point, I have the most stunning view across the mountains. The field of sunflowers is slowly swaying in the moonlight, which is both beautiful, and a bit scary.

I so wish you were here with us, Chris.

Tuesday 16th June 14.01
TO: chris@christophercheshire.com

I woke up an hour ago drenched in sweat. The room was stifling. Marika poked her head around the door and saw my red face.

'Morning,' she said, and then her head disappeared.

Minutes later she returned with Adrianna and Stevko, grinning. They yanked back the covers, lifted me up, and carried me out to the pool.

I screamed but they swung me three times over the water and let go. I landed with a huge splash. It is a family tradition to throw people in the pool when it's their birthday. Good job my birthday is in the summer.

'It's like a baptism,' said Marika over the cheering, 'you're a single woman!'

When I got out, I went and looked in the mirror. I didn't look very different. My hair was plastered to my head, I looked thinner, and was a little tanned. I grinned at myself and went to open my presents.

They gave me a copy of Zobor's latest CD. In their album sleeve photos, the band wears an awful lot of black leather and blacker eyeliner. They are going to boil if they wear this get up tonight, it's forty-two degrees here.

Rosencrantz got me an iPod Nano. Meryl and Tony gave me a £5 Debenhams gift voucher, which was from the two of them, plus Ethel and Daniel. I think Meryl had put his name in to soften the blow if Daniel didn't send anything. And he didn't.

I am on my second glass of Slovak wine (excellent) and lying by the pool. Bliss. They are going shopping. I am staying here to work on my tan.

Tuesday 16th June 17.30
TO: rosencrantzpinchard@gmail.com

Thank you for the iPod Nano, but can you afford it, love? Are you at work now? I couldn't answer before because I fell asleep in the sun. I am now bright red and look every inch the Brit abroad.

I am lying indoors, slathered in natural yoghurt, which apparently should ease the pain. Speak to you later.

A very red Mum x

Wednesday 17th June 05.30
TO: chris@christophercheshire.com

Wow. I have had the most wonderful night. Adrianna lent me a gorgeous long, floaty dress which covered my red sunburn.

Marika and I were laying out the plates before the party when she commented on how great I looked.

'We needed you to look your best for tonight,' she said.

I asked her why. Marika stopped and smiled.

'Look, I know you don't like to be set up,' she said.

'Set up?'

'You see, already you've gone shrill.'

'You mean, set up with a man?'

Marika grinned again.

'Who? Who else is coming tonight? Who are you setting me up with?' I said, following her into the kitchen.

Marika picked up the Zobor CD and waved it under my nose.

'The whole band?' I said. 'Your sister's been hospitable, but she doesn't have to be *that* hospitable.'

We heard the gate creak as the band arrived. They skipped in, all young and trendy, carrying boxes of beer.

'He's nice, isn't he?' said Marika pointing at the youngest, who I recognised as Marek, the guitarist from the album sleeve.

'You're winding me up,' I said.

'No. He loves older women,' said Marika. 'He was dating the Slovakian equivalent of Cilla Black.'

'Cilla Black,' I said, 'is sixty!'

'Sorry,' said Marika. 'Bad translation, this woman is a lot younger than Cilla.'

They were all making a beeline towards us and I began to panic. Marek looked only a few years older than Rosencrantz.

'It won't happen,' I said.

'Go on.' She pushed me forward. I grabbed a shot of Slivovica and smiled.

The band was a hunky bunch: Patrick the drummer, Julius the lead singer, Jozef the bassist and Marek a dreamy, dark young slip of a lad. We spent a long time in a big group, talking. Their English was very good. Then we ate great sizzling hunks of barbequed chicken and pork, sweetcorn and salad washed down with even more beer and Slivovica.

Every time I looked at Marek, he would grin at me, showing his cute dimples. The more drunk I became, the less scared I felt about what I could see was happening.

When it got dark, Marek took me by the hand and led me out of the driveway into the fields for a walk. We paddled through the cool stream, which led to a moonlit field. He stopped and turned to me. I went to say something but he put his soft lips on mine. He was very attentive, attentive to the point that the alcohol and his gorgeous body led me, Coco Pinchard, after only one day of singledom, into having rather wild and wonderful sex in the moonlight by the stream! His skin was just so ripe and firm. He had one of those lean hot bodies, creamy smooth skin, and beautiful caramel eyes.

His English wasn't as good as his bandmates. He kept saying, 'You like the naughty, bad lady?' but he was so sexy that it didn't matter.

I figured that I wasn't just another slutty groupie as I have never listened to their CD!

I don't know what time it was when we walked back. He invited me to the house the band was staying in, but I said no. I didn't want to wake up sober with him in the daylight so we kissed one last time by the gate, and I came back.

I am now just in bed. I had to write this down to prove it wasn't all a dream. I feel like a beautiful, floaty goddess!

Thursday 18th June 07.37
TO: chris@christophercheshire.com

Ow, ow, ow. Sunburn. Grass burn. Torn dress. Mud in hair. Hung-over. Feel like a slut.

Thursday 18th June 14.13
TO: chris@christophercheshire.com

Marika had a huge row with Blazena this morning when she walked in to Marika's room, and found Patrick the drummer asleep beside her. Blazena is a staunch Catholic, and we all woke up to her roar of disapproval. Myself, Adrianna and Stevko came out into the kitchen rubbing our eyes as Marika was stood in a long t-shirt with Patrick scooting out of the front door in just his leather trousers.

Adrianna translated as Blazena accused Marika of behaving like a 'whore of Babylon' and ordered her to get married and have children. She said that Marika's bedroom was like Sodom and Gomorrah and slapped her round the face. Marika retaliated and threw a pan of (thankfully cold) goulash over Blazena, and most of the kitchen.

With a shout that could have wakened a sleeping bear, Blazena grabbed a rolling pin, chased Marika round the table and out of the front door. They reappeared through the window, Marika running across the field with Blazena in hot pursuit.

'Do you want coffee?' asked Adrianna, as if nothing out of the ordinary had happened.

I asked if Marika would be okay.

'Hopefully, but even though Mum is the size of an elephant, she can run just as fast as one.'

They came back a couple of hours later, laughing, and dripping wet. They had been swimming in the nearby lake.

I asked Marika how she had sorted it out.

'I promised her I would go to confession,' she grinned. 'The ultimate get-out clause for Catholics.'

Part of me felt sorry for Marika, getting all this grief, but it had looked kind of fun being able to have it out. I remember dealings with my own mother were a minefield of sly digs and passive aggressive behaviour, whilst always pretending everything was wonderful.

I am packing. We are going to have a look round the shops in Bratislava before our flight.

Looking forward to seeing you.

Friday 19th June 12.33
TO: marikarolincova@hotmail.co.uk

Thank you for an amazing time. London feels so cold, grey and uptight compared to Slovakia. I came home to find my decree absolute. I am officially a 'Miss', the house is in my name, and I have money in the bank. It is a real sense of anti-climax.

Saturday 20th June 08.31
TO: chris@christophercheshire.com

Meryl just phoned, and I was telling her about your grandmother's 97th party, and, how you did all the decorating. She wants you to help her pick out all the furniture for Ethel's new flat. I am sorry. I tried to come up with an excuse that I had lost your phone number, but she is looking you up in the phone book, so expect a call.

Sunday 21st June 18.55
TO: marikarolincova@hotmail.co.uk

I'm sorry, I won't make it for dinner, but if you still want
to come over Rosencrantz has made curry and he would love
to see you. Chris and myself were roped into a trip to IKEA
in Croydon to buy furniture for Ethel's new flat.

I never want to go IKEA again, well, not with Meryl and
Ethel. They couldn't agree on *anything*. Ethel doesn't like
'modern poncy stuff'. Which begged the question why we
were in IKEA?

The only redeeming feature of the day was that we
bumped into Adam in the bathroom department.

'Looks like you've been busy,' he said, indicating our
trolleys piled high. I had almost forgotten about him since
Slovakia. Meryl stepped forward.

'Hello, I'm Meryl Watson, I'm Coco's ex-sister-in-law.
This is my mother, Ethel.'

'Yes, hello. We have met,' said Ethel, going posh again.

'This is Christopher Cheshire, he is helping us with our
interior design options,' said Meryl, adding, 'his father has a
knighthood, you know.'

'Hi,' said Chris, going red.

I gave Meryl a look, and she trilled, 'Come along, toilet
plungers!' and shepherded them all away.

'Sorry about that,' I said.

He asked how Slovakia was. I said it was great. We
nodded at each other.

'Look,' I said. 'About your phone call, about the gay stuff.'

'Ahh,' he said, holding up his hands to his face,
embarrassed. He looked so cute and, for a brief moment, I
almost knew what he was thinking.

'I'm just divorced,' I said. 'You're a lovely, handsome man with good dress sense, my maths was wrong. I'm sorry.'

'Thank you. The invite to see a musical may have given you the gay idea.' He explained that his friend works for a box office company dealing with West End shows.

'So, you're not a West End Wendy?'

'No,' he said. 'Well, saying that, I do have two tickets to go and see the *Thriller* musical on Friday. It's a bit more butch.'

'Okay,' I said.

He gave me his email address.

'You'd better get back to your group, they're dying to know what's happened.'

I could just see Ethel's head poking up above a display of toilet seats.

'Happy shopping,' he said.

'Oh, it's not,' I grinned.

When I joined the others, they were all smiling.

'What a dish,' said Meryl.

I told them I was going on a date.

'She dun't waste no time,' said Ethel. 'Out on the tiles within a week of divorcing.'

'And the rest,' said Chris, grinning.

Adam turned and waved goodbye. God, he is gorgeous.

'He looks just as good from the back,' said Meryl, surprising us.

We are waiting in an endless queue with our seven trollies. We have a bed, two sofas, two easy chairs, a dining table with four chairs, two pouffes, three sets of shelves, three plants (yucca, palm and cactus), covers for chairs, sofas and pouffes, two wardrobes, one bed, two sets of drawers, a bedside table, four plates, four cups, cutlery for four, utensils, a draining board, tea towels, towels, bedding, coat hangers, a fruit bowl, a shower curtain, a bathmat, loo roll, toilet plunger and a loo brush.

Poor Chris. Meryl ignored every one of his style suggestions and all he got for lunch was a 39p hot dog.

Monday 22nd June 09.14
TO: chris@christophercheshire.com

I am composing an email to Adam. This is what I have:

Dear Adam,
Lovely to see you in IKEA. You gave me a nice surprise in the toilet department.
Here is my address, for the date we talked about;
Three Steeplejack Mews, Marylebone, London NW1 4RF
Looking forward to it.
Coco P. xxx

Monday 22nd June 10.03
TO: chris@christophercheshire.com

Yes, you're right. The toilet line is open for misinterpretation and the kisses are too familiar.

Monday 22nd June 10.14
TO: adam.rickard@gov.co.uk

Hi Adam,

It was lovely to run into you in IKEA.

My son says *Thriller: Live!* is a great show, lots of dancing, pyrotechnic bombs going off, etc. I can't wait!

My address is:

Three Steeplejack Mews, Marylebone, London NW1 4RF

Coco P.

PS I just noticed that your email address is a government one... Are you a secret agent? ;-)

Wednesday 24th June 10.33
TO: chris@christophercheshire.com

Nothing from Adam!

Thursday 25th June 09.00
TO: chris@christophercheshire.com

Still nothing. Couldn't sleep so was up at five. Have been checking my phone *constantly*. Rosencrantz was up at six, waiting for the post. He has been up early for the last few mornings. It arrived as he was leaving for classes; he grabbed it off the doormat and rifled through it before chucking it down. He won't tell me what he is looking for.

Thursday 25th June 22.00
TO: chris@christophercheshire.com

Should I phone Adam? I have been constantly checking my email. Maybe he thought he didn't have to reply. However, I asked him a question at the end, 'Are you a secret agent?' What if he really is a secret agent?

I know he can't tell me if he is, but he could at least tell me that he can't tell me, don't you think? Moreover, if he can't even say that he can't say he is not a secret agent, he could at least confirm our date.

Thursday 25th June 22.34
TO: chris@christophercheshire.com

Sorry, I will shut up and go to bed.
C x

Friday 26th June 09.10
TO: chris@christophercheshire.com

I came downstairs this morning to see a pale and wan Rosencrantz, still wearing his uniform from the bar, sat on the sofa watching the BBC News Channel.

'Michael Jackson died last night,' he said.

By the look of the newsreader, she had been up as long as Rosencrantz. As dreadful as the news was, my first thought was that my date tonight is at the Michael Jackson musical. What if they cancel it?

As the screen counted down to the eight o'clock

headlines, Rosencrantz turned with tears in his eyes and said, 'I can't believe he's gone.'

Now call me a heartless cow, but the histrionics seemed out of proportion. I can't remember him ever listening to a Michael Jackson song.

'How about some breakfast? Maybe a Pop-Tart?'

'No!' snapped Rosencrantz, as if Pop-Tarts were the most inappropriate food for the occasion.

'Have they said anything about his concerts at the O2? Or *Thriller: Live*?'

'No,' he said, 'and I can't believe that all you can think about is your date.'

I was about to protest when the phone went. It was Meryl. She too sounded upset saying, 'Oh Coco, it's all too much.'

'So, you've heard?' I said.

'Heard what?'

'Michael Jackson. Dead.'

'No,' she said. 'It's not that. I'm still at Mum's, trying to put her IKEA furniture together, it's driven me out of my mind. Have you got a quarter-inch Allen key I could borrow?'

I said I didn't and she rung off.

Whilst I was on the phone, Rosencrantz had gulped down a whole pot of coffee and was leaving the house with bloodshot eyes and a silver left hand. He had hacked the end off one of my long silver evening gloves. Not that I can see myself ever wearing them again, unless I am transported back to the eighties, but he could have asked.

Could Adam be grief-stricken like Rosencrantz? Will he still want to go on a date? You can't tell with people these days. I remember Ethel's histrionics when Diana died, and she is a Republican.

Would it seem insensitive to phone and check if the musical is on? If not, is your friend still in *The Lion King*? Could he wangle some back-up tickets?

Friday 26th June 09.33
TO: rosencrantzpinchard@gmail.com

Are you okay? Your reaction to the death of Michael Jackson seems to be out of proportion to how it really affects your life. Is this because I am going on a date? Or are you working too much? You haven't been yourself for ages. Please, let's have a chat later.

Mum x

Saturday 27th June 11.36
TO: chris@christophercheshire.com

Are you *still* asleep? You're not answering your phone. Marika is here and has heard all the gossip.

Adam phoned after lunch on Friday. He is not a secret agent; he works in health and safety for the civil service. He only received my email on Friday morning. The civil service's anti-terrorist screening software had intercepted it, because I had written the word 'bomb' to describe the special effects in *Thriller: Live!*

It just goes to show, the government is right. Terrorism affects society as a whole, even arranging a date.

Thriller: Live! was going ahead so he suggested we met for a drink before.

I was beyond nervous. We met half an hour before the

show at the Gin Bar near Embankment tube station. I dressed in black to be safe, but instantly regretted it. Adam had his work suit on and was nervous too. I kept asking him questions when there was a silence, so it felt like I was interviewing him for a job.

I did find out that he is also divorced. He married Holly's mother when they were sixteen, but he found her in bed with another woman, so we do have something in common. It's just a shame we spent what little time we had filling each other in on the baggage of our previous relationships.

The theatre was manic when we arrived. Hysterical Michael Jackson fans with candles and pictures of the King of Pop stood vigil outside, and several television crews were filming.

The show was great, but it was three hours long. Then there were speeches and a minute's silence at the end so when it finished it was very late. We only had five minutes to talk in the taxi on the way home.

I stupidly set the conversation to small talk by asking him what he was up to tomorrow at work. Ugh! I also chickened out about inviting him in. When the taxi pulled up at my place, I thanked him, we said goodnight and he was gone.

It feels like I am back to square one.

Sunday 28th June 12.30
TO: marikarolincova@hotmail.co.uk

I just had a phone call from Daniel. He saw me on CNN News, outside the theatre going to watch *Thriller: Live!* and holding hands with a tall, handsome black guy.

'Who is he?' Daniel demanded.

I said it was none of his business.

'I don't like it!' he said petulantly. 'Turning on my TV and seeing you cavorting with some *hunk!* It put me off my egg white omelette!'

I said I wasn't cavorting. I was walking into the theatre.

'Anyway, *you've* got a girlfriend,' I added.

'Not anymore,' he said.

Apparently, Kendal's religious beliefs came between them; she is a Scientologist. He refused to be hooked up to an E-meter and be de-programmed, so she dumped him. I laughed.

'What's funny?'

'Oh, the egg white omelette, the Scientologist girlfriend. You're living the American dream.'

'I miss... things,' he said. 'I miss you.'

'No, you don't,' I said. 'You've hit a bump in the road, and seen me moving on. You're jealous.'

He asked all about Adam – what he does and if I had slept with him. I told him where to stick his egg white omelette. It was quite a nice feeling, after I put the phone down.

Rosencrantz is still on the sofa, still intercepting the post and not talking. I managed to get him to eat some noodles.

Tuesday 30th June 10.18
TO: chris@christophercheshire.com

I had a horrible shock this morning. I was finishing my toast when there was a knock at the door. I opened it and there stood Christian! He was dressed in his emerald green suit. A tiny trilby with a mallard feather was perched on his head. His handsome face was set into an odd look of fear and pity.

'You've got a nerve showing your face on my doorstep,' I said, only a set of Carmen rollers and a housecoat away from being a character in *Coronation Street*.

'I haven't come here to fight,' he said, raising a patronising hand. 'I came to give you these.'

He handed over three credit cards. I said cash would be better.

'Do you know how much money we spent to get Rosencrantz home? Not to mention you broke his heart.'

'I'm sorry, truly sorry, about all that happened,' he said, the mallard feather blowing in the breeze, 'but I'm merely giving back what belongs to Rosencrantz.'

He turned, picked his way down the path and out through the gate.

I turned the cards over in my hand and there was Rosencrantz's name, on all of them.

'Why does Rosencrantz have so many credit cards?' I yelled as Christian climbed into a waiting taxi.

'I am sorry, Coco,' he said.

He closed the door and it drove away.

I'm sitting staring at these cards and contemplating ransacking Rosencrantz's bedroom, something I promised myself I would never do.

JULY

Wednesday 1st July 11.43
TO: marikarolincova@hotmail.co.uk

Last night I waited up for Rosencrantz. When he came in from work, he was pale and drawn with huge bags under his eyes. He saw me sat at the kitchen table with the credit cards.

'Tell me what's going on,' I said.

He flopped into a chair and started talking.

Back in April, a couple of young trendy producers from the Carnegie Theatre in Edinburgh came and watched *Anne Frank: Reloaded* and offered Rosencrantz a slot for the play at the Edinburgh Festival in August.

They said the show was 'edgy' and 'now' and with the press interest it attracted, it could be a big hit.

Christian negotiated a deal with himself and Rosencrantz as co-producers. He also said he would design the show. Many successful careers have been launched at the Edinburgh Festival. The only problem was that they had to find five thousand pounds to book their slot at the Carnegie Theatre.

Christian said he couldn't ask his parents for any money as he had already maxed out his credit cards after using up his trust fund.

Rosencrantz didn't want to ask me, because of the money worries I had with the divorce at the time. So, he agreed to apply for a credit card.

In the euphoria of accepting this 'offer', they didn't think about all the other costs involved, and Rosencrantz ended up putting another *ten thousand pounds* on credit cards for accommodation, advertising and numerous other fees.

Then America happened, and Christian vanished. Rosencrantz said he tried to keep everything going, but most of the other actors involved with the show were 'Team Christian' and jumped ship when Christian did. Rosencrantz has been working flat out just to cover the minimum payments. He has been waiting for the post most mornings so he could intercept the credit card statements before I became suspicious.

'It's such a mess Mum,' he said, and laid his head on my shoulder and sobbed. I was relieved I finally knew.

When he had stopped crying, I asked him to give me all the paperwork to look at. He came back with a bulging folder. I told him not to worry and get some sleep.

This morning Rosencrantz looked like he had slept well for the first time in weeks.

He asked what I was going to do. I told him I wasn't sure yet, but when he gets home from classes, he should quit his bar job. He hugged me and told me I was the best. When he'd gone, I made a big pot of coffee, took a deep breath and opened the folder.

The first receipt was for £7,500, to rent three four-bedroom flats in a building called Palace Apartments. At that price, I had to see them so I clicked on Google Street View. Palace Apartments are far from palatial, in fact they are far from anywhere. They are bedsits in a tiny terraced house in Leith, several miles from the centre of Edinburgh. I recognised it as the road Ewan McGregor runs down at the beginning of *Trainspotting*.

I phoned the number on the invoice and an old Scottish lady called Mrs Dougal answered. I asked how each bedsit could sleep four people?

'Och, they'll all bunk doon together,' she chuckled. 'Actors aren't shy.'

I apologised and explained I would have to cancel. She told me that Rosencrantz had paid in the knowledge the £7,500 wasn't refundable.

'How can you justify charging so much?' I said.

'Leith is very cosmopolitan now,' she said. 'The Royal Yacht *Britannia* is permanently moored here. It's very reasonable.'

She said I should log on to edfringe.com. I did and she was right, she is reasonable. A coffee shop on the Royal Mile is renting out its stock cupboard to the Cambridge Footlights for *ten grand*.

Thursday 2nd July 19.58
TO: marikarolincova@hotmail.co.uk

Rosencrantz went to see Ethel last night in her new flat. He told her everything, and she gave him a thick ear!

When he came home and told me, I phoned her up, furious.

'Well, someone's got to give 'im a thick ear,' she said.

'What exactly is a 'thick ear'?'

'Well, it was more a clip round the ear, a wallop...' she said.

'You hit him!'

'Is there a mark on 'im?' she said.

'No, not that I can see.'

'I didn't do it 'ard... You think 'e'd dare run up all that debt if you'd threatened 'im once in a while with a thick ear, a clout or a wallop? I always say, 'walloped kids are 'appy kids'.'

Can she be right? Rosencrantz did seem happier when he got home. Once the physical violence was over, Ethel had made him his favourite; salmon sandwiches with the crusts cut off and Angel Delight.

After another day on the phone, I can't get any of the money back. I have two days to pay off these credit cards before even more interest is added. The APR is 22%.

Also, three missed calls today from Adam.

Saturday 4th July 13.15
TO: marikarolincova@hotmail.co.uk

I didn't sleep, so I came down to the allotment early, put the kettle on, and sat on my bench chain smoking. It was hot and sunny, which made me feel a little better. Around nine Adam came tramping up in the heat, the dust swirling around him. Tight white t-shirt and football shorts. Woof! I realised I hadn't called him back.

He came and stood by the bench and asked if I was ignoring him. I said I was sorry and that things had been manic. He sat down, and I told him what has been going on. To my horror, I began to cry.

'I'm not turning on the tears!' I said, mortified.

He put his arm round me. I put my head on his shoulder

and we watched some crows pecking around in the dust. He smelt all fresh and showered.

'I'm reading your book,' he said.

He undid his rucksack and pulled out a copy of *Chasing Diana Spencer*.

'Why didn't you tell me?'

'I tried to. Three times,' he grinned.

'Sorry, again,' I said wiping my eyes. 'Where did you get it from? It's out of print.'

'The library,' he said.

'What do you think about it?'

'Could do with a lick of paint but it does have free parking.'

'Not the library, my book.'

He leaned towards me, his nose touching mine. 'I'll tell you, if you kiss me.'

'No! Tell me first,' I said.

'You're interrupting our first kiss?' he smiled.

'I'm an insecure creative, tell me!'

He leant in and kissed me. He tasted delicious.

'Sorry, I've been smoking,' I said weakly.

'Shh, don't spoil it,' he said and kissed me again.

It's funny how you just know how to kiss... I mean, if someone asked me to break down the process of kissing on a diagram, I would have a hard job, but our mouths instinctively worked in unison, just enough tongue and tenderness. He even gave my lip a little bite, which was a thrill. He pulled away, giving me his dazzling grin.

'Ten out of ten, and your book is brilliant.'

He hugged me tight. We sat in silence for a moment.

'So. You're stuck with this theatre?' he said.

I told him we had nothing to put in it.

'Well, what about turning *Chasing Diana Spencer* into a play? I saw *The Woman in Black.* It was incredible, and they did it with virtually nothing; a bare stage, and a few props. It was all about the story. If you're going to lose fifteen grand,' he said, 'you might as well take a risk and have a ball doing it.'

We stayed chatting for a couple of hours. He is so much fun to be around. He asked me over to his place for dinner on Sunday night. What do you think? About the play idea? *And* him kissing me, of course.

Sunday 5th July 12.34
TO: chris@christophercheshire.com

Marika told me to phone Angie and make sure I know where I stand. If I want to go ahead with this play, I need her to formally release me from our contract.

Angle's response was a pleasant surprise.

'Oh babe, that is thinking outside your box,' she said. 'A Coco book I can't sell, but a Coco play at the Edinburgh Festival could be lucrative. Hey! How about a Coco musical?'

'A musical?'

'God, yes!' she said. 'Musicals make tons more money than plays. You know *Jerry Springer: The Opera*? I was stood round the piano in the Battersea Arts Centre bar when Richard Thomas was composing it. If I'd known how huge it would be, I'd have invested, but back then I just got pissed and screamed at him to play 'Lady in Red'.'

I didn't know what to say.

'Coco,' she said excitedly. 'I'll go in on the costs fifty

percent, that's seven and a half grand, in return for a fifty percent stake.'

'But, I've never written a musical,' I said, taken aback.

'Course you can,' she said. 'I was looking again at your Greg-O-Byte proposal. It's brilliant, and you did that in an evening.'

We are having coffee tomorrow to talk about it. I came off the phone excited, then realised – I can't write music.

Monday 6th July 00.01
TO: marikarolincova@hotmail.co.uk

Thank God for Chris. He has seen virtually every musical at least three times. I went over to his in a blind panic.

'This is huge,' he said.

'I know,' I said, pacing up and down. 'And I can't do it!'

'What do you mean, you can't do it?'

'I can't write music.'

'You know you only have to write the book and lyrics,' said Chris.

'Haven't I already written the book?'

Chris explained that the script of a musical is called 'the book'.

'You see. I don't even know that,' I wailed.

'I'm talking to a guy on gaydar at the moment who is in his last year at the Royal Academy.'

'Don't change the subject,' I said, helping myself to a glass of his expensive decanter whisky.

'No,' said Chris. 'I mean we could get him to write the music. He's a student, he needs credits for his CV.'

He logged onto Myspace, and played a song from this guy's musical, called *Jackie Stallone's Psychic Arses*. It was very good, and before I knew it, Chris was instant messaging him to come to the coffee meeting tomorrow with Angie. He poured me another whisky and cleared his throat awkwardly.

'Coco,' he said, 'would you let me be the director? I will do it for nothing. You can use my house to rehearse...You loved the British Airways Air Steward Charity Panto I directed, and they're a bitchy lot to co-ordinate, what with all their layovers.' He looked at me pleadingly. 'I need a career... I'm going mad with nothing.'

'Okay,' I said.

'Really?'

'Yes, I would love to have you involved.'

He hugged me, and then he reminded me I had a date with Adam at seven, and it was already six fifteen. I raced across Regent's Park, wellies flapping, and into the Baker Street Tesco Metro. I grabbed a basket and was working my way through to the wine section when I ran into Adam. He was reading the back of a ready-prepared moussaka and had frozen lasagne in his basket.

'Damn,' he grinned. 'Busted. What would you prefer, Greek or Italian?'

I said Italian. He then went on to ask what dessert I wanted, and before long we were food shopping together.

When we reached the wine aisle, there was a middle-aged woman running a sampling promotion. She gave Adam a sample of Bordeaux then asked if his 'lady friend' would like some.

'Here you go, lady friend,' he winked.

She looked at us both, and her look didn't seem to judge that I was out of my league. When we got outside, we realised we had spent nearly an hour shopping, and our date had begun.

We both stood there.

'Look,' he said. 'Do you just want to come back with me? Not that what you are wearing doesn't look great, but I presumed you weren't going to come to mine in wellies.'

I looked down and laughed.

'I've got a great outfit laid out on my bed,' I said.

'The Wellington boots are actually doing it for me. You look like a girl who...'

'Likes getting dirty,' I said. 'I mean, muddy.' I blushed.

'Come back to mine,' he said. 'We're having fun.'

There was a real sparkle in the air. I said okay.

He owns a little ground floor flat off Baker Street, a modern cosy Victorian conversion with scrubbed pine furniture and wood floors. There was no sign of another woman's work, a recently departed ex, etc.

He poured us some wine and I nosed round his living room whilst he put things away in the kitchen.

He has acres of DVDs and books, a big cinema-style TV and some dark squashy sofas. The only visible alarm bell was a PlayStation with controllers and a stack of games.

I realised I had drunk all my wine when he was beside me topping up my glass. He squatted down to put some music on. As he put his arm out to grab a CD from the shelf, his shoulder muscles strained against his white t-shirt. I instinctively reached out, slid my hand under the material, and onto his warm back. He turned to look at me with a lopsided grin. He stood and began kissing me deep and slow.

I pulled off his t-shirt, he pulled off mine and expertly unhooked my bra. I slid my thumb under the waistband of his football shorts and pulled them down. Before I knew it, we were naked, our warm bodies pressing together. We sunk into the sofa and had sex, twice. I cannot remember the last time I did it twice. We drank wine and talked and Adam was starting to look like he could go a third round when I realised it was nearly midnight and I had the meeting to prepare for. We hadn't eaten any of the food we chose and I said I had to go.

As I was pulling on my clothes, he looked disappointed, and I felt a bit cheap. Should I have stayed?

I slopped home in my dirty wellies replaying our dirty evening in my head.

Tuesday 7th July 12.01
TO: alangford@thebmxagency.biz

Chris has asked me to forward the minutes of this morning's meeting to you. I am not sure he knows how to take proper minutes.

MINUTES OF MEETING, TUESDAY 7th JULY

09:00 Christopher Cheshire, Coco Pinchard, Jason Schofield and Angie Langford met at the Café Nero in Old Compton Street. But there were no tables available. It's full of poofs in their workout gear, either going to or from the gym. We decide to move to the BMX Literary Agency office.

09:12 Angie Langford's office (BMX Literary Agency). Proper introductions, I have never met Angie before. (Nice shoes.) None of us have met Jason Schofield our composer. He is twenty-one, handsome and plays a sample of *Jackie Stallone's Psychic Arses*. He is hired. Yay!

09:35 Angie Langford unveils the poster image she has mocked up for the show. We have to submit this to the Edinburgh Fringe office to make the festival programme deadline, which is 5pm today. Angie says she will call the Carnegie Theatre after 5pm and tell them that the show is no longer going to be *Anne Frank: Reloaded* but *Chasing Diana Spencer: The Musical.*

09:50 Coco Pinchard who has been a bit mute up until now rushes from the meeting.

09:53 Meeting moves to ladies' toilets. Coco Pinchard won't come out of the lavatory cubicle, saying she does not 'get' musical theatre, and says she was the only one in the audience who didn't cry at the end of *Blood Brothers.*

09:59 Coco Pinchard is coaxed out of toilet cubicle. Jason Schofield reminds Coco Pinchard that she needs only to write an hour-long musical, as this is the length of theatre shows at the Edinburgh Festival.

10:02 Coco Pinchard rushes back into cubicle wailing that she can't get her whole book across in an hour. Angie Langford lights cigarettes.

10:03 Coco Pinchard calms down but Jason Schofield has a mild asthma attack.

10:15 Meeting reconvenes in office. Jason Schofield by open window with his inhaler. Coco Pinchard will write a rough draft of *Chasing Diana Spencer: The Musical* over the next few days. Jason Schofield will read the book. I, Christopher Cheshire, will put an advert in *The Stage* newspaper for actors and Angie Langford will draw up contracts and set up a limited company so her accountant can fiddle the tax easier.

Tuesday 7th July 14.13
TO: adam.rickard@gov.co.uk

Hi, I just realised I don't have a personal email address for you, just the one at your work in the health and safety department. Could I have your personal one?

I had a wonderful time last night. I should have stayed, but I am new to all this and I really like you, and the last time I slept with anyone other than my ex-husband, in the same bed, was twenty years ago. When I mean sleep, I mean actually sleep, not that I have done anything else with anyone. Just so you know.

It looks like this musical is going ahead. I have to start writing it today as my agent Angie and friend Chris have zoomed into action and made a lot happen. I am trying not to freak out.

I would like to see you again.

Coco x

Wednesday 8th July 21.34
TO: marikarolincova@hotmail.co.uk

The script is coming along very nicely. I spent the day up at the allotment, absorbed in writing. Adam knocked on my shed door just after five; he had come from work with pizza and wine. I had promised myself to take it slow but we ended up having a rerun of the other night, in my shed, under the table of old flower pots. At one point Agatha and Len walked past, and they must have heard one of the flowerpots fall and break. They stopped.

I heard her say, 'What's that noise, Leonard?'

Footsteps came closer, crunching on the dry grass outside the little window.

'Look, she's left a whole pizza out!' said Len hungrily.

I heard him try the door handle.

'Len!' hissed Agatha. 'Come away!'

All throughout this, Adam had put his hand over my mouth, and carried on... It felt rather thrilling.

Afterwards he asked if I wanted to come back to his and chill out with a DVD but I had to keep writing. Now I'm really worried he thinks I am a slut.

Thursday 9th July 17.39
TO: rosencrantzpinchard@gmail.com

You're going to see Nan tonight, aren't you? Could you do me a favour and ask her if she is free tomorrow to help us to open and sort applications for *Chasing Diana Spencer: The Musical*? The living room is full of envelopes.

Thursday 9th July 18.44
TO: rosencrantzpinchard@gmail.com

You can tell your Nan thank you, but minimum wage is £5.80 per hour, not £10 as she is claiming. On this occasion, though, I can go up to £7 per hour to reflect, as she puts it, her 'life experience'.

These are the roles we are casting for:

Queen Elizabeth II, Queen of England, the Commonwealth, the High Seas etc. etc.

Prince Phillip / Prince Charles (played by same actor with interchangeable prosthetic ears)

Camilla Parker Bowles

Lady Diana Spencer

Hans Von Strudel (Queen Elizabeth's hunky footman)

Male Actor 1 To play various parts: servants, French, old and young

Female Actor 1 To play various parts: servants, French, old and young

Friday 10th July 19.24
TO: rosencrantzpinchard@gmail.com

We have just received a couple of CVs from your old drama school principal, Artemis Wise, and his wife. They want to audition. He heard that the show is on in a 3pm slot, so he can appear in it without violating his court appointed terms. He is electronically tagged with a 7pm curfew until he is sentenced for embezzlement in the autumn. His CV is quite good, but apart from him being on bail, he is not right for Prince Charles, or his wife for Camilla Parker-Bowles. She is much more suited to Princess Anne, but I have had to cut Anne and her talking bulldog. I've also had to jettison some of the other minor royals. The Duke and Duchess of Kent have gone, along with Fergie, Andrew, Edward, and Sophie. As in real life, they don't do enough to justify paying for them.

Tuesday 14th July 10.00
TO: marikarolincova@hotmail.co.uk

Just spent the most hectic week writing in the shed. Adam has been visiting at the end of most days with food and wine, and then...

I keep telling myself I am a liberated working woman, who has to fit her sexual needs around her busy career, and if that means up against a gro-bag in a potting shed, so be it. Adam has invited me to a work 'do' tomorrow evening, so that means something, doesn't it? I am not just his allotment slag.

I finished the first draft of the play this morning, and when I got home, Rosencrantz was in the kitchen scraping mould off the last piece of bread with his Mach 3 razor.

'This is the only food in the house,' he said. Then he asked if he could audition for the play.

I have been dreading this moment. His ego is as fragile as an eggshell. What if he auditions and we have to say no to him?

He looked up at me with his gorgeous brown eyes. He was wearing his flat cap and jumper with holes in. Clutching his bread crust, he looked like a sort of Oliver Twist (albeit one who has an iPhone and access to a fridge which makes ice).

'Yes, of course,' I heard myself say before I gave him a twenty and bundled him out of the door to get some decent food.

Wednesday 15th July 22.44
TO: marikarolincova@hotmail.co.uk

Adam phoned at lunchtime to confirm he would pick me up at seven for the 'Summer Ball'. He had said, 'work do' the other day, not formal ball! I didn't have time to have our first argument, so I said it was great and I would see him at seven.

I had meetings with Angie and Jason all afternoon about the auditions tomorrow, and I didn't get away until four thirty. I raced over to Oxford Street where I had ordered Rosencrantz to meet me for an emergency shopping session.

I have spent most of the last two years in jeans so I asked Rosencrantz what's acceptable formal summer evening wear for women now. He showed me a picture from *Heat Magazine* of Nicole Richie, elegant in a white maxi dress and gladiator sandals. I was wary of white, especially maxi white, but he insisted I would look great. We hit Top Shop and he found as close a match as he could.

However, in a white maxi dress and brown gladiator sandals, I looked like Charlton Heston in *Ben-Hur*. All I needed was a shield and spear. I think my tantrum was more to do with tiredness and lack of food but I stormed out of Top Shop, refusing the other things he had picked out.

We tramped around Oxford Street for a little longer but it was packed and sweltering. Mindful of the time, we called it a day and came home.

I ended up in my faithful old outfit. The one I used to wear for summonses to see the Headmaster or parents' evenings. A close-fitting black skirt, a flower print top that showed some cleavage and knee length black boots.

I had toyed with the green skirt but I'd already worn it three times with Adam. I still hadn't had anything to eat, but

I decided not to and keep my stomach looking flat until we sat down for dinner.

The doorbell went just before seven, as I was drying my hair. Rosencrantz came upstairs,

'There's like a dude at the door, asking for you?' he said.

'Did you let him in?'

'No. I said I would check with you.'

'Well, did you ask his name?'

'Yeah. It's Mr Rickard.'

'That's Adam, you idiot!' I said. 'Go and let him in!'

'But he's like fit!' said Rosencrantz.

'No need to sound so shocked.'

'You're dating him?' said Rosencrantz.

'Yes. Look, I haven't got time to do this, and he is standing out on the doorstep.'

We rushed downstairs and I let him in. He was dressed in a black suit, no tie and a white shirt with a couple of buttons undone to show some chest; handsome as anything. I introduced him to Rosencrantz and Adam was very relaxed and sweet.

As we left for the taxi, Rosencrantz whispered in my ear, 'Fucking hell Mum, like way to go.'

'That's enough from you,' I hissed back. 'Watch your mouth. And do the washing up.'

We were dropped near the London Eye and we walked along the Thames Embankment *holding hands*.

'I want you,' Adam growled in my ear.

My stomach unfortunately growled back louder.

The Summer Ball was held in a boat on the river, artfully draped with flowers and paper lanterns. Twinkly music drifted towards us. The tide was out, so the boat was grounded on the shingle riverbed.

With it being a health and safety department Summer Ball, you might have thought this was ideal, no water to fall into. But no. The gangplank was now at a very steep forty-five-degree angle so the ladies were being asked to take off their heels, in case they slipped. I showed the man on the door that my boots only had a slight heel but I was still ordered to take them off.

Adam looked mortified. I unzipped my boots but they wouldn't budge. My feet had swollen in the heat. After much tugging, a queue had started to form behind us. Eventually I had no choice but to hold onto the rail with my legs in the air whilst Adam pulled. It wasn't my finest hour.

The flowers and lanterns continued inside, but there were no tables.

'Where do we eat?' I asked Adam.

'Oh,' he said, grabbing some champagne from a passing waiter, 'it's just drinks, I thought we could eat later.'

'Great,' I said, as my stomach growled its protest.

We weren't permitted out on deck, of course, due to health and safety regulations, so we were all shut in the boat. It was sweltering. Adam took me to meet his work colleagues, introducing me as 'Coco'. Not 'my girlfriend' or 'my date' or even 'my friend'. He made me sound like some avant-garde uni-named performance artist. I was on my fourth glass of champagne when we made it round the boat to Adam's boss, Serena. Up until now, his colleagues had been a bunch of humourless men and territorial women, but Serena, a mature blonde, had a twinkle in her eye.

'You must think we're the ultimate health and safety cliché!' she said, looking at everyone sweating in the heat. 'If I had it my way we'd be out on deck with our feet in the water.'

She asked how long Adam and I had known each other.

'Oh, not long,' I blurted. 'He was wary about letting me into his pants. He said they might contain nuts!'

Serena's eyebrows shot up into her hairline as she smiled blankly and excused herself. Adam's face clouded over and he released my hand.

'What?' he hissed. 'You're talking about my balls to my boss?'

'It was a joke,' I said. 'A health and safety themed joke... obviously off the mark but I should get something for making the effort. They're a tough crowd!'

'You're pissed, aren't you?' he frowned.

I had never seen him look angry before.

At that moment the tide began to rush in and the boat started to rock. Inside was getting hotter and the mixture of no food, no sleep, and too much champagne weren't helping. I suddenly realised I was about to throw up.

'I've got to get some fresh air,' I gulped to Adam, whose indignant mouth was flapping like a beached carp.

He followed me out. To my horror, as I reached the exit, I began to heave. Everyone in the shoe queue stepped back in alarm as I gave a very good rendition of a cat trying to bring up a hairball. I gave an almighty retch and threw up all over the gangplank. I turned to Adam, who looked disgusted.

I felt so ashamed and ran past the shoe queue. I didn't stop running until I reached Waterloo Station and found a taxi. When I got in, I had a long cold shower. I thought being with Adam was too good to last.

Thursday 16th July 20.35
TO: marikarolincova@hotmail.co.uk

Thank you for being nice, but I am a screw-up. I shouldn't have run away. There was no time to think about last night. I was up at six for auditions. Jason, our composer, had to be in college, so Chris hired his old music master from school to play the piano. Clive must be a similar age to Ethel. He was limping and unshaven in a long, ragged winter coat.

'Will you be okay to play?' I said, as he eased himself gingerly onto the piano stool.

'Yes, dear lady,' he said. 'Doctor Theatre will work its magic.'

We took our seats behind a long table and the first actor came in. He was awful, but Clive seemed to come alive. As he thumped out a number from *Les Misérables,* I noticed a white tag on his wrist, and a blue gown protruding out from under his long coat.

'Has he come from hospital?' I whispered to Chris.

'Yes,' he whispered back. 'But don't say anything. He is very proud, and has fallen on hard times. I was glad I could help.'

The morning whipped past as actors came and went. Some were great. Lots were awful.

In a break, I told them about Adam. They said not to worry, and that they had all, at one time or another, thrown up *over* a lover without being dumped. Clive went one better and said that in 1964 he had thrown up on Princess Margaret's muff at Ronnie Scott's. He said she was a great sport and refused his offer of dry-cleaning money...

After lunch, it was Rosencrantz's audition. I don't know who was more nervous, him or me. I was going to wait outside, but the only things I had seen him do were school nativity plays, and a disco dancing Anne Frank, so I stayed.

'What a handsome lad,' said Angie, when he came in.

He blushed, calmed himself and did the most beautiful speech from *Henry V* where King Henry is on the battlefield addressing his troops. He was so magnetic. We all gulped back tears when he'd finished.

His song – 'Hey Big Spender' – was a little less impressive, but it showed off his voice, and they decided to cast him! I have just broken the news to Rosencrantz and he is so happy, which makes all of this recent slog seem worthwhile.

Friday 17th July 19.44
TO: rosencrantzpinchard@gmail.com

I won't be home again until late. I am working on lyrics with Jason for Queen Elizabeth's opening number. We need to find seven words to rhyme with Regina, but we are so tired, we can only think of one. The pressure is on as we start Monday.

Please eat well. I have bought some food. Angie has also given us a load of Tamiflu; she got some on the quiet from her doctor, should we get swine flu. It is all in the news about it being a pandemic but I just think its media scare-mongering. Remember the SARS scare? I spent a fortune on white face masks for you, your father and me and it came to nothing.

Mum x

Saturday 18th July 18.44
TO: marikarolincova@hotmail.co.uk

How are you love? Looking forward to a long summer holiday? I heard a school in Chiswick has had to close early, due to a swine flu outbreak.

I finally found time to phone Adam and say sorry, leaving a message on his voicemail. He has just replied via text;

> OK THX COME OVER TOMORROW NITE
> WE CAN TALK.

It's over. I know it, but would it be that bad? I haven't had time to think the past few days. I just want to sleep… Let's meet up soon.

Saturday 18th July 19.02
TO: adam.rickard@gov.co.uk

Great. Will see you tomorrow. I am just going home for a bit of anal.

Saturday 18th July 19.04
TO: adam.rickard@gov.co.uk

That was the auto correct! Not me! My email meant to read 'I am just going home for a bit of a nap!'

I am tired, I am not, and I never have…

Anyway. Looking forward to seeing you tomorrow.

Coco

Sunday 19th July 22.34
TO: marikarolincova@hotmail.co.uk

I made an effort to tidy myself up and I bought wine and some very expensive cheese. I went round to Adam's with an apology prepared, but there was no answer. I rang the bell several times but he stood me up!

I went to the allotment, but he wasn't there either. I saw his plants were drying out. I didn't water them.

I sat on my bench, ate all the cheese, and drank the whole bottle of wine until it got dark. Len loped past behind, tapping his stick. I sank down on the bench.

He stopped at the back of my shed and I overheard a heated conversation he was having with another old guy. They were arguing over who would look after a large cutting Len had nicked from a grapevine at Hampton Court Palace.

'I've 'ad it down me trousers all day,' whispered Len.

The other old guy agreed to keep it in his biscuit tin until the fuss died down.

I stayed and smoked in the shadows until they moved away. When I got home, I watched the news. At the end of *London Tonight,* they ran a piece on the oldest grapevine in England, at Hampton Court Palace. Someone had managed to give a steward the slip in the Grape House and steal a cutting. The steward said that the culprit must have had to be quick and quiet to outsmart them.

Quick and quiet? Len! The string holding his trousers up whistles when he walks.

Nothing from Adam, he must have deliberately stood me up.

Monday 20th July 18.12
TO: marikarolincova@hotmail.co.uk

It was first day of rehearsals today and I am amazed at what we have achieved in two weeks. Chris had emptied his living room, apart from Daniel's old piano, and it is now our rehearsal room. There is a big square of masking tape marked out for the size of the stage.

A stern young New Zealander called Byron, who introduced herself as the stage manager, greeted me at the door. Her mousy waist-length hair was pulled back into a ponytail and she had on a ZZ Top t-shirt. She handed over a name tag, with my name spelt as 'Cocoa'.

Jason was warming up on the piano, Chris and Angie were huddled in the corner over the script, and the actors were milling about making tea. Part of me wanted to run. It was all so scary.

'Here she is,' said Chris, swooping over with a hug.

Byron brought Angie a cup of coffee.

'No, no, no love,' she said. 'I drink it white.'

'Do I look like a char lady?' Bryon snapped, grabbing it back and slopping coffee over Angie's Jimmy Choos. A lesser man/woman would have apologised, but she stalked off to the kitchen.

'She's a bit fierce,' I said.

'But she's fucking good,' said Angie, dabbing her shoes with a hanky. 'Done all the West End shows.'

Then Rosencrantz arrived. We had walked over together, but he wanted to wait outside for a couple of minutes so he could arrive without his mother. He said it would be better for his street cred. The actors all greeted him like a long-lost friend. Byron stomped back with Angle's coffee then clapped her hands.

'Can you lis-ten,' she said. 'Our writer would just like to say a few words.'

I looked blank.

'Where is Coco Pinchard, the writer?' She saw me, and beckoned me over. 'Chaup chaup. You're first on the call sheet for today... You did *look* at the call sheet I emailed?'

'Um. No,' I said going red.

'Why naught?'

'I don't know,' I said and sheepishly went and stood by the piano.

'Hi everyone,' I said. The actors all looked at me expectantly as if I had so many answers. 'I'm Coco the writer, not Cocoa the hot drink,' I said pointing to my name tag.

The actors laughed hysterically as if it were the funniest thing they had ever heard.

'I know we have a great team and hopefully a hit on our hands.' I went to say something else but Byron stood up and started everyone clapping.

'Graaayt, now for a few housekeeping issues. Rehearsals start at *tin* every day, so you need to be here by quarter to tin to warm up chit and hev tea. Anyone here late will be fined five pounds for every fuff-teen minutes.'

'That's not fair,' I said to Chris, a bit loudly.

Byron's nostrils flared.

'Is there a prawblem?'

'No,' I said sheepishly.

'Then, please don't interrupt during housekeeping.'

We spent the rest of the morning playing icebreaker games. I hadn't played hide and seek for years, and after initial protests, we all were rather carried away. Angie, being the most competitive, got stuck inside Chris's sofa bed, and after lots of fruitless pulling Byron had to cut her free with a band saw.

After lunch, it was the decisive moment when we sat down, read the script, and sang through the songs. *Thank God*, it read well. Everyone laughed and cried in all the right places, and before I knew it, Byron was barking at us to put the chairs and tables back. She even yelled at Chris for leaving a teacup on his own windowsill in his own living room.

Rosencrantz and I walked home full of joy, gossiping about the cast. I didn't realise it would be so much fun.

Tuesday 21st July 19.28
TO: chris@christophercheshire.com

Have you heard from Marika? I keep trying her Blackberry, but all I get is pips.

Nothing either from Adam but then, that's his loss.

You did a great job directing today. I know, thanks to Byron, you didn't get to say much but you had gravitas and filled us all with confidence. You should lose the beret though. xxx

Tuesday 21st July 21.27
TO: chris@christophercheshire.com

Marika has swine flu, well has *had* swine flu. Her school in Dulwich closed early for the summer holidays because of it, and she has been delirious. Not with happiness, but with a high fever. Her Blackberry died and she couldn't find the charger so she had no numbers for anyone. She contacted the swine flu call centre and a teenager diagnosed her over the phone, and asked her if she had a swine flu buddy. She said that, no, she didn't. They told her to ask a neighbour to collect her some Tamiflu, which he did, poking it up through the banister on a stick.

She is better now but I am riddled with guilt. I have a load of Tamiflu here, and we should have taken more notice. I should have been her swine flu buddy. I went over to Dulwich and made her a big pot of soup, the only thing I can really cook, and have lent her *The Sopranos* box set.

Wednesday 22nd July 15.56
TO: marikarolincova@hotmail.co.uk

It seems swine flu panic has kicked off amongst the middle classes, now that Wimbledon has finished. Meryl just caught me on Skype.

'I just had to phone you,' she trilled. 'Look! We're having a swine flu party tonight!' On cue, Tony lumbered past with an inflatable pig and several balloons. 'That's Tony,' she said, in case I'd forgotten. 'He's putting things up.'

'Aren't they warning people not to have these parties?' I said.

'We all want to get it as quick as possible,' she said. 'Before the strain mutates.'

'Before it's resistant to antibiotics?'

'No, before too many of the *wrong sort* get it,' she said. 'By the time it's passed through the Enoch Powell Estate over the way, who knows what the virus will be like.'

I tried to warn her about the symptoms but Tony, carrying a big tray of glasses, distracted her.

'I told you! We're all drinking from the same glass,' she said. 'Now put those back in the sideboard!'

I took the opportunity to shout 'goodbye' and disconnect.

Wednesday 22nd July 09.01
TO: marikarolincova@hotmail.co.uk

Morning hun, did I give that guy Marek from Slovakia my email address? I just received this:

ATTACHMENT
TO cocopinchard27@gmail.com
FROM marekfzobor@azet.sk

Hello Coco,

You like the naughty, bad lady? You remember? I am Marek, the boy that you had one night in Slovakia with on your birthday.

I had a great evening with your love and examination of your body, which still has tip top condition after 42 year.

I am dreaming many nights of you lying naked on the agricultural land, recalling my tongue over your body.

My band Zobor is making a concert tonight at the Hammersmith Apollo. Want to participate? We could make a grab to bite something to eat then and then go back to my hotel for some warm intercourse.

I live in Travel Lodge Hammersmith. It have very good

transport links. Use the telephone if you wish to speak with me.

Marek Z.

I will have to reply to him later, but I have to go to rehearsals. You feeling better?

Coco x

Wednesday 22nd July 09.43
TO: chris@christophercheshire.com,
      rosencrantzpinchard@gmail.com

Jason has asked to see a different version of the last scene in Act One. It is up in my allotment shed amongst paperwork. I am dashing up there now. I will be at rehearsals ASAP.

Wednesday 22nd July 23.54
TO: marikarolincova@hotmail.co.uk

When I arrived at the rehearsal, Chris was waiting for me in the hall.

'I'm sorry, there was nothing I could do,' he said.

I went into the living room and sat behind his old piano was Daniel, playing one of the numbers for the actors.

Byron launched herself out of her chair and came over hissing, 'You're late, agin!'

'Why is my ex-husband here?' I hissed back.

Byron said that she'd had to advertise for an emergency pianist via Gumtree. Jason has gone to hospital about his hand. He injured it the other day during another competitive warm-up game of hide and seek. She then fined me five pounds.

I asked Chris why we couldn't have hired his friend Clive, but he has apparently had a relapse, and is in hospital being detoxed.

'I'm sorry, Cokes,' he said. 'We're up against it with time, and at the moment I just need someone who can play... Byron found him, I had to say ok.'

At that moment, Byron called a tea break, and I went over to Daniel.

'Hello,' he said smugly.

His ponytail was longer and he was even more tanned.

'Why aren't you in America?'

'I'm in London for meetings about a *Whistle Up the Wind* West End transfer.'

'So why are you darkening my door?'

'I Googled your musical, saw the advert and thought, what a fun way to spend a free day and play my old piano. Plus, you're paying me a hundred quid to be here.'

Byron came over with a scowl for me, and cup of tea for him.

'We are? I mean, yes we are,' I said. 'So stop wasting time and familiarise yourself with the second act.'

And I stomped off to look at a box of tiaras, which had just been delivered.

As the day wore on, I got used to him being there. I had forgotten how good he is, and if I'm honest, he gave the score something. I couldn't put my finger on it but it seemed to have a little more heart and soul.

We finished at six and I invited him home for some Chinese. We both seemed to be in competition to see who could be nicer. No one mentioned the elephant in the room i.e., his torrid affair, desertion, and our bitter divorce.

Halfway through his crispy seaweed, Rosencrantz slammed down his chopsticks.

'You guys are freaking me out,' he said. 'I'm finishing mine upstairs.'

He went off and I poured Daniel some more wine. He leant over and stroked my cheek,

'My Coco,' he said.

I looked into his eyes. He went to kiss me, but the sound of his phone cut through the moment. I picked it up off the coffee table to pass it over. As I did, I saw the display, which read 'SOPHIE SNOW WHITE'.

I started to laugh.

'What's so funny?' he said.

I held up his phone.

'You always manage to make me forget what a complete bastard you are.'

His mouth opened and closed.

'I swear on my mother's life, I ended it,' he said.

I chucked the phone at him. Then mine started to ring.

'Okay, Miss Goody Two Shoes,' he said. 'Who's phoning you? Maybe this is *your* bit on the side?'

Daniel made a grab for it and answered. It was Marek. I had forgotten to get back to his email.

Daniel held it out to me,

'Some guy says he wants to lick your vinegar...'

I took it, mortified. I said thank you for the invitation (to the gig) but that I couldn't make it. When I hung up Daniel was smirking.

'Not so innocent,' he said. 'Two men on the go, one a child by the sound of him.'

This escalated into a huge fight. Many accusations were thrown, plus a pot plant from me. It stopped when

Rosencrantz came down the stairs in his pyjamas.

'Shut up!' he screamed. 'Parents... you are divorced. Deal with it. My sleep shouldn't be disturbed because deep down you actually want to be together in your screwed-up little world...'

We looked at each other in shock. We apologised and Rosencrantz stood over us whilst we cleared up the exploded yucca plant. I then went up to bed and Daniel slept on the sofa.

Is Rosencrantz right? He's not. I am sure of it.

Friday 24th July 18.07
TO: marikarolincova@hotmail.co.uk

It was another eventful day. I seem to have so many. When I got up for rehearsals, Daniel had left a note wishing me luck with the show and that he'd gone to see Meryl and Tony before heading back for the next leg of *Whistle*.

I then bumped into Agatha at the allotment after rehearsal. She told me Adam had been rushed to hospital on Sunday. His daughter Holly found him, collapsed at home. He had contracted swine flu and, mixed with his asthma, it was serious. He seems too strapping and sexy to suffer from asthma. He was probably lying on the floor whilst I was outside cursing him!

Friday 24th July 10.47
TO: marikarolincova@hotmail.co.uk

I went to visit Adam in hospital. He was sitting up and looking good even through illness. He does have the most wonderful pectorals. I wanted to rub Vicks into them. I think the nurses had the same idea. I have never seen nurses so attentive.

Question: If all patients were good looking would the NHS be more or less efficient?

I was surprised how upset I was, and relieved to see him. It was apparently touch and go. I apologised for the Summer Ball, which now seems like an age ago. He smiled weakly and said he was pleased to see me. I only stayed a little while, as he was tired. He squeezed my hand tight and asked me to visit again. I promised I would come tomorrow.

Saturday 25th July 18.01
TO: adamrickard@bedsideentertainments.co.uk

Hi you,

Thought I would send a message via Bedside Entertainments. However, be careful, they charge an arm and a leg.

We had our first run through of the show tonight. It was a shambles, a bit like a load of contestants on *The Generation Game* trying to perform a play they have only just seen, only it wasn't funny. I blame Byron; she had banned them from holding scripts. The piano playing was rather off too. Jason has damaged a ligament in his hand but he is soldiering on with ice packs in between numbers.

We are doing a preview show next Friday above a pub in Camden. Do you think you will be well enough to see it? My friend Marika is coming and she would love to meet you; she has only recently recovered from swine flu.

Coco x

P.S. You want me to bring you any Vicks? ;-)

Sunday 26th July 21.30
TO: marikarolincova@hotmail.co.uk

It seems that when I visit Adam, the nurses love to come and interrupt. Tonight, he had his blood pressure taken three times. The nurse lingered on his bicep for longer than I thought was necessary.

I didn't know if I should say anything but it's still not established if I am his girlfriend. Do I have a claim on him? He let me put Vicks on his chest. It got quite intense as I slowly rubbed it in, he grabbed my hand and looked at me longingly. Then the bloody ward sister came in and ordered me out, even though it was five to, and visiting is until eight.

'We go by my watch,' she said, her eyes flashing.

She watched over me as I gathered up my things. I felt scared to even give him a peck on the cheek.

Monday 27th July 11.15
TO: marikarolincova@hotmail.co.uk

Adam was discharged at seven this morning. I went over to his flat to see him before rehearsal. I just missed his daughter Holly, who had brought him home. I made us a coffee and he asked if I would come over tomorrow night and meet her properly.

I hesitated, which didn't go down well. I told him that I have a million things going on, and that maybe it's a bit fast. This went down even worse. He said as my *girlfriend* I should meet his daughter.

'I didn't know I was your girlfriend!' I said.

'I invited you to the Summer Ball!' he said, looking stung.

'Where you referred to me as 'Coco'!'

The atmosphere became rather frosty. I plumped up his cushions, and said I had to go to rehearsal.

Why is this all happening at once? Two months ago, I had no relationship and acres of time but now, everything is screaming for my attention. Byron fined me, again, for being late. I am down £30 and it's my bloody show.

I have to go back to Adam later. I said I would pick up a prescription for him.

Monday 27th July 19.55
TO: marikarolincova@hotmail.co.uk

At lunchtime, I rushed to the chemist, then over to Adam's with his antibiotics and got back to rehearsals a minute late. Byron fined me, again. Then I realised I had left my iPhone on Adam's coffee table.

I went back after rehearsals to be met with a furious look. You know what he did? He spent the afternoon reading through the sent emails on my iPhone. He wanted to know why I hadn't told him about sleeping with Marek in Slovakia, or about Daniel staying the other night. He read everything I had written. About him, about my divorce. Everything.

We had a nuclear row. He told me I wasn't the woman he thought I was, and that I was 'just like the rest'.

I grabbed my phone and stormed out, shaking. Should I have told him about Marek? I know Adam had asked me on a date *before* Slovakia. Is that grounds for cheating these days?

I clicked back through my messages and saw that I had indeed gone into detail about my night with Marek and that I had told Adam, and I quote 'I haven't slept with anyone since my husband', when in fact I had.

I cannot believe he went through my phone messages. He seemed so confident.

Tuesday 28th July 15.15
TO: marikarolincova@hotmail.co.uk

Nothing from Adam. I conducted an informal poll during today's rehearsal. So far, everyone except Byron said they had looked, or would look, through the messages on a friend/loved one's phone.

Tuesday 28th July 23.01
TO: marikarolincova@hotmail.co.uk

Rosencrantz has left his phone on the kitchen table and gone up to bed. I am not going to look.

Tuesday 28th July 23.12
TO: marikarolincova@hotmail.co.uk

Still not looking.

Tuesday 28th July 23.51
TO: marikarolincova@hotmail.co.uk

Okay! I couldn't stop myself. I looked. It was empty apart from a text message, which said,
'HI MUM. TOLD YOU YOU WOULD LOOK!

LOVE R X'

He heard my shriek and came downstairs.

'You should give this guy Adam another chance,' he said when he took his phone back. 'Maybe he's only guilty of really liking you. More importantly, he's like well fit.'

Wednesday 29th July 23.40
TO: marikarolincova@hotmail.co.uk

Went up to water my allotment, but once again was side-tracked doing rewrites for the preview tomorrow. Agatha was roaming around, and collared me.

'It seems once again you're getting the cheapest office space in central London,' she said, lighting a roll-up and indicating my dead tomato plants. 'To think poor Mr Bevan laid down his life on this allotment.'

I said he'd had a heart attack hoeing.

'Well, be that as it may, you are in breach of contract,' she said. 'You are using this space for commercial purposes. I'll need you to vacate by the end of the month.'

I smiled and looked her in the eye. I asked her if Len had managed to plant his Hampton Court grapevine, or if it was still down his trousers. The colour drained from her face.

'Oh, so you're in on it too?' I crowed. 'That's rather serious, isn't it? Thieving from royal property.'

Agatha huffed and puffed, saying maybe she was being harsh and that all I need to do is 'buck up' with my watering. 'And if you need any manure,' she said, 'I'm sure I can spare a sack.'

Ha ha!

Angie can't come to the preview tomorrow; her child prodigy author has had a tantrum and is refusing to deliver his next manuscript. She has to drive up to Oxford and bribe him with an Xbox 360.

I am willing to give Adam another go, but he has to ring me. Doesn't he? Two wrongs don't make a right, do they? I lied, but he invaded my privacy. Surely, we are quits...

However, he should ring me. Shouldn't he?

Friday 31st July 23.59
TO: angielangford@thebmxagency.biz

We got through the preview of the show. In the audience was myself, Chris, our friend Marika, and a baying pack of out-of-work actor friends of the cast, who whooped and cheered at every sentence. I wish my ex-mother-in-law had been able to see it; she is always blunt and honest.

Clive, who played piano at the auditions, came along. He looked even more dishevelled than before. He said the show 'has legs'. I agreed with him, but the legs are rather wobbly.

Jason's hand is much better. He has to go back to hospital for more steroid injections tomorrow, which should see him through August.

Chris has taken Rosencrantz and the rest of the cast to Cathedral. Nothing good ever happens for me there, so I came back to continue working.

I have sorted out the train tickets to get the cast up to Edinburgh on Monday. I have the Queen's state robes on a thirty-degree wash, now I am off to bed.

AUGUST

I am a bag of nerves about travelling up to Scotland. I should have gone and got drunk with the others. Rosencrantz has been showing me photos on his iPhone from Cathedral. They all blagged their way up to the VIP 'pulpit' and were posing with a look-a-like of the Pope. Rosencrantz has also been saying who 'got off' with who. It is as follows:

Clive and Byron (there is a forty-year age gap)

Chris and Jason (Chris was seen popping a painkiller into Jason's mouth, *seductively*, for his bad hand)

Beryl and Hugo (weird, says Rosencrantz, as Beryl plays The Queen and Hugo plays both Prince Phillip and Prince Charles)

Rosencrantz said he could have got off with Andy Lobster, the blond good-looking actor who plays Hans von Strudel the Queen's butler. Everyone is convinced he is 'bi-curious'.

The only person not to 'get-off' with anyone was Spiffy Mc Cready, who plays Camilla Parker-Bowles. She, apparently, is asexual.

What kind of business is my son going into? I should have made him take that job Ethel got him when he was seventeen, photographing criminals at the police station.

Sunday 2nd August 10.15
TO: angielangford@thebmxagency.biz

Jason has phoned me, very, very upset. He had to go back to hospital this morning. The ligament in his hand is more damaged than they thought and he has been advised not to play the piano for three months! He is pulling out of coming to Edinburgh. He is devastated, so am I.

WHAT DO WE DO? We don't even have a CD with the music on!

Sunday 2nd August 10.40
TO: angielangford@thebmxagency.biz

Chris has suggested hiring Clive... He is barely out of rehab but I don't think we have any other choice. Clive doesn't have a mobile phone/email address or fixed abode, but according to Rosencrantz, he went back to Byron's last night. I am going to drive up to Byron's house in Walthamstow and talk to him. I only hope he is coherent. Byron is always going on about how she brews beer in her airing cupboard.

Sunday 2nd August 15.01
TO: angielangford@thebmxagency.biz

Chris and Rosencrantz came with me to Byron's house in Walthamstow, 'to protect me'. They can't weigh more than eighteen stone between them, but the thought was nice.

Byron has a room in a huge student house. When she answered the door, she was still in her dressing gown, and untouched by the hand of Clive. It seems Rosencrantz had got his gossip wrong.

Clive only came back to Byron's after confessing *he didn't have anywhere else to go*. Beryl had crashed on Byron's other sofa. She was sitting in a long Frankie Says Relax t-shirt, which looked odd with her Queen Elizabeth II wash and set. Byron was still in the same ZZ Top t-shirt; I have never seen her wear anything else.

I asked Clive if he would consider coming to Edinburgh, and being the pianist for all twenty-six of our shows.

'Something told me last night to lay off the sauce,' said Clive, with tears in his eyes. 'I'd be honoured,' and he kissed my hand.

I am still a little worried, he looks in a bad way, but at this late stage, we don't know any other brilliant pianists who can come and work for us for a month, on non-equity rates and at twelve hours' notice.

I went upstairs to use the bathroom, and on my way out, Beryl was waiting for me on the landing.

'Coco,' she said with a low voice. 'Can you tell me something, honestly? Do you think I can act?'

'Um... yes, you're very good,' I said.

'You hesitated,' she said.

'Well, you threw me? I hired you on the basis that you *could* act.'

'It's Hugo,' she whispered, with tears in her eyes. 'He had a small part in the comedy film, *The Naked Gun.*'

I looked blank.

'Jeanette Charles,' she said, 'was also in *The Naked Gun*, she played Queen Elizabeth II, you know when Leslie Neilson has to save the Queen... She's the most famous Queen-a-like.'

'Oh yes,' I said, remembering.

'Hugo says if this musical transfers to London, you will replace me with Jeanette Charles.'

I assured Beryl that she is fabulous and perfect and will be my Queen whenever, wherever. I realised how horrible actors can be. Hugo is very jealous of Beryl. On a selfish note, however, it was a good endorsement of her faith in the project.

We bade farewell and took Clive with us. After we dropped off Chris, Clive asked if we could talk, alone in the car. Rosencrantz excused himself, and went indoors.

'Coco,' he said holding my hand. 'You might just have saved my life and know I will do you proud. I will champion your show day and night. I will lie down in the mud so your shoes remain spotless. I am your devoted servant.'

He hugged me. He was skin and bone.

'You only need to play the piano, but thank you,' I said.

When we got in, I ran him a deep bath and gave him a pair of Daniel's old pyjamas. I put his clothes through on a hot cycle. The only things in his pockets were a scruffy little address book and his tin of tobacco.

Sunday 2nd August 19.30
TO: marikarolincova@hotmail.co.uk

We all slept in late, then Rosencrantz made a huge brunch of eggs, bacon, beans, and toast. Late afternoon I took Clive up to see the allotment and we watered everything. It shouldn't need doing for a couple of days. I left you some gin and tonic in the shed.

The ground was rather bumpy, and Clive is very frail.

He had to put his arm through mine for support.

'Oh Coco, this is wonderful,' he said. 'I always wanted a little piece of England to call my own.'

He then knelt beside me and recited from Shakespeare, "This blessed plot, this earth, this realm, this England.' Richard the Second.'

He took my hand and kissed it.

Someone cleared his throat. We turned and it was Adam. He was tapping his empty watering can on the ground. Clive let go of my hand and held his out to Adam.

'Good evening, I'm Clive Richardson. How are you acquainted with this marvellous woman?'

'Adam Rickard,' he said, shaking Clive's hand and eyeing him suspiciously. 'So, you're off tomorrow, Coco?'

I said we were leaving at 6am. There was an awkward pause. Clive made for the shed, but wobbled so I grabbed his arm again. Adam looked at me petulantly.

'Well, good luck. I have to go,' he said, and turned and walked away.

'Affair of the heart?' asked Clive, as we watched Adam stamping along the rows and out onto the road.

I merely nodded. I have no time to try to fathom the workings of his mind. I still have so much to do: pack, plan our route, plus the stuffed corgi hand puppets have finally arrived, and each one needs a squeaker sewn inside.

Monday 3rd August 12.00
TO: chris@christophercheshire.com

I wish we were on the train with the rest of you. London to Edinburgh in four and a half hours would be bliss.

Rosencrantz and I are tootling along quite well but I think we will be much later than the promised 3pm. I took a wrong turn at the last motorway junction and ended up coming back towards London. We only realised when we stopped for coffee and saw the same waitress. I should have twigged when we passed The Angel of The North, twice...

Monday 3rd August 23.57
TO: marikarolincova@hotmail.co.uk

We finally arrived at ten this evening. I feel sick. I think it's nerves, and all the shortbread we have scoffed since passing Hadrian's Wall.

Edinburgh was warm and buzzing with activity, even late at night. Banners for the Festival were being strung between lampposts. We passed the Royal Mile, which is the main high street in Edinburgh's old town. It is cobbled and filled with gothic stone buildings, several churches, and quaint little shops selling whisky and thick jumpers. This will be the Festival nerve centre for the next month. Everyone will be out in all weathers; buskers, fire eaters and actors promoting their shows, giving out flyers and performing on stages dotted along the cobbles which stretch up to Edinburgh Castle sitting floodlit on the hill.

When we found The Carnegie Theatre, we joined a queue of cars for the loading bay. I couldn't wait to see where the show would be performed. I had this twinkly vision of a little theatre with polished wood and plush red seats. This was dashed quite quickly. The Carnegie Theatre is, in fact, a series of disused vaults in an old abandoned abattoir. We weren't allowed in because the fire brigade had to pump out water before they can unstack the chairs.

We unloaded our props on a small square marked out in the loading bay. A sign was taped above it, which read:

CHAFING DIANA SPENDER: THE MUSICAL

Three squares down, there was a huge fake plastic balcony, covered in fake plastic grape vines. Boxes of wine and cups were stacked up to the ceiling. I walked over and saw the sign, which read:

REGINA BATTENBERG'S WINDOW BOX WINEMAKING LIVE!

Rosencrantz noticed me standing with my mouth open and came over.

'I wanted to tell you, but we thought it was best you didn't know, whilst you were writing.'

'What?'

'We found out last week. Regina Battenberg is doing a chat show here.' He put his arm around me.

'In the same theatre?'

'Yup.'

'In our theatre?'

'She's got the 7pm slot… Were we right not to tell you?'

I suppose it made sense, but now I have a horrible, horrible feeling about being here, being compared and ridiculed. The pressure is even greater.

A girl in a hard hat came over and told us to get moving as the cars were backing up. I didn't have time to think and we unloaded the rest of the props and costumes.

Palace Apartments were no better. Everyone was waiting on the pavement in the dark with their suitcases. As we got there, Mrs Dougal, the landlady, arrived to let us in. She was wearing a kilt and a headscarf and showed us where we have to feed in fifty pence pieces for the electricity meter.

Quite why the actors applauded this, I don't know. They seem to applaud most banalities told by anyone with a little authority. When Mrs Dougal had gone, we chose our rooms. I am sharing with Chris, and Rosencrantz is with Clive. Palace Apartments was once a proud, elegant Victorian terraced house, but plasterboard partitions appear to have been thrown up with no regard for ambience. The bay window in the front room is chopped in half by a thin wall running along the middle, and where it doesn't quite meet the glass, bog roll has been stuffed in the gap.

However, the actors all seemed thrilled, having apparently stayed in far worse. Spiffy was telling everyone how she was concussed when the ceiling collapsed on her once during a tour of *Arsenic and Old Lace* with Lesley Joseph.

'I still did the matinee,' she said proudly.

Byron, to her credit, has been amazing. I went to see her in the little office she had set up in what looks like the old scullery.

'You heard about Regina Battenberg?' she said.

'Yes,' I said.

My eyes began to well up and to my surprise, Byron hugged me. The ZZ Top t-shirt was kicking out a whiff, but I was grateful and hugged her back.

'I may be a complit butch,' she said, looking me in the eye, 'but I think thus is a fantistic show and I'm only a butch because I want it to be a big hit.'

'Thanks Byron,' I said.

She then showed me how she had hacked into the Wi-Fi signal in the pawnshop next door so we can look at our online ticket sales. We have sold nineteen tickets for the whole run. It doesn't even equate to one ticket for each show, but it is a start.

I know Regina Battenberg is going to wipe the floor with us.

Tuesday 4th August 23.44
TO: marikarolincova@hotmail.co.uk

We did our dress rehearsal today. Our theatre, The Carnegie Main, is one of six venues in the old abattoir. It has three hundred seats. As we were arriving, the show on before us, *One Man Titanic*, was finishing its dress rehearsal. We had to help the actor out of his costume when one of his funnels got jammed in the doorframe.

I asked Byron if he had been using a special aroma machine because it stunk of seawater, but apparently, it's from real seawater leaking in. The Leith is tidal and The Carnegie Main sits below the water table.

We used up all the time we had for our technical rehearsal so we didn't quite get to the end of the play, which was alarming. Chris had a crisis when he saw that the stage is triangular as opposed to the square shape we have been working with, so now the positioning of the actors is wrong.

When we finished, Hugo had to be rushed to hospital. Byron had mistakenly bought model aeroplane glue instead of latex glue for his stick-on Prince Charles ears.

'Ah, this is Edinburgh for you,' said Clive. 'It'll get better!'

We have sold two tickets for the first show tomorrow.

Tuesday 4th August 12.00
TO: angielangford@thebmxagency.biz

I have just been to The Carnegie Theatre box office and none of the journalists who received our press release are coming. We have only sold *two* tickets out of three hundred for today.

The actors have been giving out flyers on the Royal Mile since eight. I made them do it in costume, to help with publicity. I thought Rosencrantz would attract the gay audience if he wore the speedos he has in the Cannes beach sequence. It's very cold though. He went blue at ten thirty and he's being cared for by a couple of Polish girls in a sandwich bar. They have wrapped him in catering foil.

Hugo is making everyone depressed. He keeps repeating how his life as an actor is a joke. He had to sit in casualty until two this morning in huge prosthetic ears. Byron is mortified.

Tuesday 4th August 17.12
TO: angielangford@thebmxagency.biz

The two paying customers in the audience were a nice couple from Lowestoft. I sat a couple of rows behind them with Chris. They were very polite afterwards, and said they would 'spread the word'. I am tempted to follow them and cut the brake cables on their car. It was a disaster. We had forgotten lines, people falling over, and Spiffy had a wardrobe malfunction with a jammed chinstrap, so Camilla Parker-Bowles was still wearing her riding hat when she was in the bath with Prince Charles.

The cast is meeting for an urgent rehearsal in the living room of Palace Apartments. There was barely room for the actors, so Clive offered to take me out for afternoon tea.

We went to The Elephant House tearoom, where JK Rowling allegedly scribbled the first Harry Potter novel on napkins, sheltering from the cruel Edinburgh wind. She must have cleaned them out. The little napkin I got with my scone could hardly fit a limerick.

During his second scone, Clive very politely brought up the subject of money. I was mortified that, in all the chaos, he hadn't been paid. As I fished in my bag for his envelope of cash, he asked me if I knew of a reasonable tailor. His ragged clothes are not much against the Scottish weather. I said he could get a lovely suit for under fifty quid from George at ASDA.

'Let's tally ho then!' he said, excitedly.

ASDA is a little way outside Edinburgh and as we drove, the sky seemed to get greyer, which made me more despondent. Clive's mood also dropped when he realised that George at ASDA was not an in-house tailor.

I heard him mutter, 'Stiff upper lip, Richardson,' to himself as he selected a decent off-the-peg suit, and a lovely warm coat.

As we reached the checkout, my phone went off with a message from Byron. We have only sold one ticket for our show tomorrow. I turned to the chewing gum rack and tried not to cry.

'Come on, dear girl,' said Clive, handing me a napkin. 'Now is the time for guts and guile.'

On our way back I drove slowly past The Carnegie Theatre. Outside was a huge queue for Regina Battenberg's show.

'I've never given much cop to British wine,' said Clive loyally. 'Only good for sterilising wounds.'

When we returned, Chris said the rehearsal had been a success. They were all tucking in to take away and singing show tunes at the tops of their voices. I came upstairs to lie on my camp bed. I don't know if I can take a month of this. It's a bit like I am on a school trip... I am thinking about Adam again.

Wednesday 5th August 16.30
TO: angielangford@thebmxagency.biz

No audience at all today. We did sell the *one* ticket, but the person turned up late and the theatre refuses to admit latecomers. It's a shame because it was much better, everything worked well, and the actors were far less nervous.

Hugo and Beryl were very unhappy in the bar afterwards. They told Byron, who told Chris, who told me, that we should have observed the theatre tradition that if the actors outnumber the audience then they don't 'go on'. I am worried there will be a cast revolt. Right now, getting seven people to buy tickets seems like a tall order.

After a stiff drink, I went to the box office and spoke to a camp young chap in huge Jarvis Cocker-style glasses.

'Why didn't you paper the house, darling?' he drawled.

I looked at him, confused.

'Paper the house,' he repeated.

He saw my confusion.

'Darling. Paper means free tickets, house means theatre. The Carnegie gives you a hundred tickets per show per first three previews, helps with the word of mouth.'

I asked if everyone was papering.

'Oh yes, everyone's houses are thoroughly papered.'

'What about the Regina Battenberg chat show?'

'*Heavily* papered,' he said knowingly.

Byron offered to resign when I told her. She started beating her breast and saying she had 'lost face' and 'brought shame on her profession'.

I poured her a drink and said she wasn't going anywhere. Without her this will all fall apart. She's the only one who can get the actors up to give out leaflets in the morning.

Friday 7th August 06.00

TO: marikarolincova@hotmail.co.uk

Regina Battenberg was on ITV's *This Morning* yesterday morning, doing promo for her chat show. What with the exposure to millions of viewers and the fact she gives her audience free booze, I can never compete.

No one is buying our tickets, and the few that have done seem to only have bought one to get out of the rain. Yesterday we had a smattering of old people with their wet coats slowly giving off steam.

I miss seeing you, my house, and pootling around the allotment. I need space! Sharing a box room with Chris is fine but he has been having nightmares about the show and keeps shouting out in his sleep. He woke me up at five so I came for a walk up to Calton Hill. I am sitting smoking on a beautiful monument. It is based on the Parthenon in Athens. A row of huge pillars sits on a marble base. It has no real purpose, and it is quite extraordinary to see it shrouded in mist, on a hill in Scotland.

Below me, Edinburgh is twinkling in the dawn. Today is

a big day – we have a reviewer in from *Scotsgay* magazine. Byron is getting everyone up at seven to be on the Royal Mile by eight. I know the actors, especially the older ones, aren't going to like it.

'We don't operate before ten,' they keep saying. I have now had to bribe them with proper cigarettes. They all smoke roll-ups.

Have you seen Adam at the allotment? If so, how was he looking? Did he ask about me? When are you coming to visit?

Friday 7th August 18.40
TO: angielangford@thebmxagency.biz

Ten in the audience today, which halted a cast revolt. *Scotsgay* sent a teenage Royalist. He was horrified with just about everything in the show. He found Charles and Camilla's singing sex scene crude, and he hated how Lady Diana Spencer is played as a rather dim Sloane Ranger. He said we were committing treason. Well, he didn't say it to me; he spent twenty minutes talking to Rosencrantz who told me. *Scotsgay* goes to press tomorrow.

Regina Battenberg's chat show sold out today. Her special guests were Keith and Orville.

Saturday 8th August 15.30
TO: angielangford@thebmxagency.biz

Just an update on figures:
Reviews: None, we are not in the new edition of *Scotsgay* and no one at their office is taking my calls.

Audience members: Eight.

Hours it has rained today so far: Twelve.

Chris woke me up at three-thirty this morning shouting, 'I've cursed the play!'

Morale is very low. We all got soaked this morning, and the heating is off in the flat. No one has any fifty pence pieces. As of now, we haven't sold ANY tickets for tomorrow.

The only good thing is that I have managed to avoid Regina Battenberg, which is easy; she wouldn't be seen dead in Leith. She is staying in the penthouse at The Scotsman Hotel.

Sunday 9th August 17.00
TO: marikarolincova@hotmail.co.uk

Today plumbed new depths for the show. When four people turned up to watch, Beryl and Hugo refused to go on stage. No amount of cigarettes could get them to change their minds. Spiffy accused Beryl and Hugo of being unprofessional, and soon a week's worth of pent-up emotions was released.

I had to go on stage and announce, over the arguing backstage, that the performance was cancelled. The audience, consisting of two elderly couples, left, but then reappeared two minutes later to demand a refund. The Carnegie told them they hadn't authorised the cancellation, so we were liable.

I have never felt so depressed as when I was rummaging around in my handbag to give them their money back. The backstage argument then spilled out onto the stage as Queen Elizabeth slapped Camilla Parker-Bowles across the face.

Prince Charles stepped in and tried to separate them. Clive, who was watching in horror, began to improvise some dramatic music. For a moment, one of the pensioners looked unsure about his refund, but his wife snatched the money out of my hand and pulled him away.

It was then that I walked out. I took a back road away from the hordes of tourists on the Royal Mile and made my way through the winding streets, smoking furiously. Then my phone went. It was Angie saying she had landed at Edinburgh Airport. The Carnegie Theatre management has called an emergency meeting to discuss 'ongoing audience attendance issues'. There was yelling and shouting in the background. I asked what was going on.

'There's photographers all over the airport,' said Angie. 'Kate Moss is flying in.'

'Is she coming to the Festival?'

'Look,' said Angie pausing. 'You'll probably hear anyway, she's here to do Regina Battenberg's chat show. It's attracted huge media attention. Kate Moss rarely speaks, let alone does interviews.'

We are waiting to go into The Carnegie Theatre Manager's office. Angie is muttering to herself and Chris is in tears, saying that everything he touches is doomed to fail.

Sunday 9th August 18.04
TO: marikarolincova@hotmail.co.uk

The Carnegie Theatre Managers are Inga and Orla Shaw, identical twin sisters in their early twenties, and they hate us. They had wanted *Anne Frank: Reloaded* and through Angie's underhand dealings, we foisted *Chasing*

Diana Spencer: The Musical onto them. Now it was payback. They were dressed very Hoxton cool in matching blue Victorian lace dresses with a high frill collar and space age reading glasses. I could see they were trying to be cool, but they looked a bit like the twins from *The Shining* off to see something at the IMAX.

Angie was feisty, but we had no trump card to play. On Tuesday, they want to move us to another of their venues called The Carnegie Fun Bags. Which are two tiny inflatable cubes in a car park at the top of the Royal Mile. It has twelve seats.

We are doing a swap with a show called *Twitterati,* something to do with tweeting on Twitter, and video screens. It has become huge and people are clamouring to see it.

Angie asked them what would happen if we refused. They said we would be liable for the first 40% of gross ticket losses.

We agreed and left. I cried, Chris cried, Angie had a tear in her eye, but it could have been smoke. I think I am going to get the show settled in the new venue and come home. I now have to go and tell the cast.

On our way out, we saw Kate Moss arriving for her interview with Regina Battenberg. There were so many flash bulbs that I feared for epileptics.

Sunday 9th August 20.24
TO: rosencrantzpinchard@gmail.com

Chris has done what he always does when things go tits up and booked himself a suite in a hotel. I have come too, to get away, and keep an eye on him. Angie has flown back to

London. She didn't say much; we are both going to lose a lot of money and I think she is finally about to cut me loose.

How is the cast? I've put a bag of fifty pence pieces on top of the meter, plus cash for a take-away on the table in the hall of Palace Apartments. The one I feel worse for is Beryl. I had no clue she had a casting director coming on Tuesday who is interested in her for a part in a film. The show will look awful on a four-foot-square inflatable stage.

If you want to get out, there is a bed here.

Mum x

Sunday 9th August 23.33
TO: marikarolincova@hotmail.co.uk

I called Daniel from the phone in my hotel room. I don't know why. I suppose I just wanted to talk. He was always good to talk to. I told him all about the show, and I told him I missed him... which I don't. I miss the idea of him.

He admitted that *Whistle Up the Wind* is in trouble. Middle America hates it.

Audiences come thinking it's the sequel to *Whistle Down the Wind* and get confused/angry or bored. They just did a week in Springfield, Massachusetts and the huge venue was only a quarter full. They are all waiting for the phone call to say it's closing.

'I might need a place to live,' he said.

I panicked and put the phone down. I could see where this was going, and in my vulnerable state of mind, I might end up asking him to come back. It rang a few times, but I ignored it and turned off the light.

Monday 10th August 14.45
TO: marikarolincova@hotmail.co.uk

I was woken by the phone next to my bed, shrieking in the darkness. Fearing it was Daniel, I let it ring out. Then my iPhone began to trill. It was Rosencrantz.

'Mum, it's me. Wake up,' he said excitedly. 'Tell the concierge I'm your son, and that he should let me up to your room.'

'What?' I said, looking at my watch. 'It's two in the morning!'

'I've just seen the front page of tomorrow's, well today's, *Sun*,' gabbled Rosencrantz. 'You're not going to believe this. On the front page, there's a picture of Kate Moss, and she's holding our poster, the poster for *Chasing Diana Spencer: The Musical!*'

The concierge came on the line and asked if I knew who this excited young man was. I said I did, and to let him come up. By the time Rosencrantz arrived, I had made some tea. He handed me the newspaper.

The picture was a close-up of Kate Moss sitting outside a pub on the Royal Mile with Regina Battenberg. Kate was laughing at something Regina was saying and in her hand was our poster.

The *Sun* headline read:

KATE HELPS REGINA GET OUT OF HER BOX

My iPhone rang again, it was Angie.

'Have you seen this?' she said. 'I just spoke to the pap who sold the picture. He says that Kate wasn't really looking at the poster, she used it to fix the wobbly table outside the pub.'

'Oh,' I said disappointed. 'So, she didn't want to see the show?'

'Course not. She folded it up and shoved it under the table leg. But in the picture, she *looks like* she's planning to see it!'

Angie hung up.

'Talk about luck,' said Rosencrantz. 'Remember that book *Skinny Bitch*? It sold a packet after Victoria Beckham was pictured holding it.'

'What are we getting excited about?' I said. 'The fact we're the reason Regina Battenberg's lager doesn't get spilt?'

'This is how the noughties work,' shrugged Rosencrantz. 'It's not about getting things on merit or hard work, it's all about opportunity and branding.'

I said I was going back to sleep, that this was all ridiculous, and I wasn't about to get worked up about our poster being used to fix a wonky table leg.

An excited Chris woke me at ten o'clock the next morning.

'Why didn't you wake me up? Byron just phoned,' he said. 'We've sold a hundred tickets for today's show. The box office has only been open an hour!'

My mouth fell open. By the time I got dressed and down to the Royal Mile, today's show only had thirty seats left.

The difference in the cast is incredible. All the fighting has been forgotten; they are brimming with excitement at the prospect of a full house. Just before 2pm, the show sold out!

We are about to go in, Chris and I are going to have to sit with Byron at her technical table as there are no spare seats!

Friday 14th August 16.02
TO: marikarolincova@hotmail.co.uk

It's been an amazing few days. After Kate Moss was pictured holding our poster, on the front page of *The Sun*,

Chasing Diana Spencer: The Musical became THE must-see show at the Festival. By 1pm on Tuesday, we had sold out every ticket for the rest of the run and there were requests for press tickets and interviews from every newspaper and magazine covering the Festival.

Inga and Orla Shaw seemed to be the only ones who were not pleased. They said that due to an 'unprecedented surge' in ticket sales, they were unable to move us to The Carnegie Fun Bags.

'It's due to the complexities of refunding,' said Inga, sour as ever.

'We still think the show a little too *mainstream* for us,' said Orla.

I reminded them they have an old biddy in a giant fake window box doing a chat show, but they stalked off, their matching Beatrix Potter dresses swishing in the breeze.

Byron has stapled quotes from some of our reviews on our posters. These are my favourites:

The Scotsman 'The audience went wild! Toe tapping songs and a brilliant story, I laughed, I cried, I tried... to buy another ticket, but it's sold out!' ★★★★★

The Sun 'Book before it sells out! It's a hit! It's *the Sun* what done it!' ★★★★★

Scotsgay 'We saw it first, *before* it became a diva of a show. We loved her then and we love her now. Tickets are like this seasons Fendi, a must-have!' ★★★★★

Did you see *The Independent* today? They did an article about the show and it's led to me being booked to go on BBC1's *Saturday Kitchen* tomorrow. I am a last-minute replacement for Anne Widdecombe, who has the flu. I am driving back down to London for a few days. Do you fancy a catch up?

Saturday 15th August 16.00
TO: chris@christophercheshire.com

I'm glad you didn't see *Saturday Kitchen*. However, they say no publicity is bad publicity...

The gorgeous Chef Jean Christophe Novelli hosted it. I had to perch on a stool in the studio kitchen, whilst he cooked steak and kidney pie, and we talked about the Edinburgh Festival.

I had stupidly left my iPhone on, and it rang during the live show. I tried to ignore it but he told me to answer. He then grabbed my phone and put it to his little radio mic.

Ethel's voice boomed into the studio.

''Ere Coco, that Anne Widdecombe is on the telly, I never knew 'ow much she looked like you.'

There was a pause and Jean Christophe told her she was live on BBC1.

I wanted the floor to open up and swallow me, but Ethel continued chatting away.

'Ooh! I'm on telly!' she said. 'Oh yer gorgeous, you are, if I were forty year younger...'

She went on to ask if Jean Christophe was single, and when he said 'no', she still tried to set me up with him.

'Go on Jean Christophe, give Coco a kiss, you'll make 'er day!'

He gathered me up in his arms and kissed me full on the lips, to the squeals of Ethel echoing through the studio.

'Slip 'er the tongue, Jean Christophe!' she shouted. 'Not all 'er eggs are past their sell-by date!'

I could have killed her.

After the show, the producers were thrilled at such a 'hilarious' segment. Jean Christophe was very sweet, kissing my hand before his car took him off to meet his girlfriend at Claridges.

He made me think of Adam. I wonder if he was watching and, if so, I hope he was a bit jealous.

Sunday 16th August 12.30
TO: chris@christophercheshire.com

I have been to see Ethel in her new flat. It's in a nice little block, just off Catford High Street. There is a warden on the front door and a communal lounge, but apart from that, it's self-contained. The IKEA furniture looks quite good. She still can't get over the fact that it all belongs to her.

'I've never 'ad nothing I've owned before,' she said, stroking the sofa.

I remember Daniel telling me that, growing up, even their toaster was rented from the Co-op.

Jean Christophe Novelli gave me a signed cookbook for Ethel. She is still excited about having been on television. Everyone in the sheltered housing is talking about it. I met her new 'best friend,' an Australian woman called Irene who reads palms. When Ethel cleared away our coffee cups, Irene offered to do a reading.

'You're going to meet a tall, dark handsome stranger,' she said, examining a crease in my palm.

'She's done that already,' shouted Ethel from the kitchen. ''E's a beautiful dark man, but she buggered it up.'

'Ah yes,' said Irene, looking closer. 'Yes, love could be something which eludes you, but,' she said, leaning into a crease by my little finger, 'I do see a companion... a cat. You're going to get a lovely cat.'

I asked her to tell me about my career.

'I just see cats,' said Irene. 'Maybe you'll open a cattery?'

'Tha's a good idea Irene...' shouted Ethel from the kitchen. 'This writing business will never make 'er rich.'

I want to be back in Edinburgh, I miss it all. The buzz on the Royal Mile. The roar of the crowd before our show begins.

Marika is moving into my spare room. Her landlord has vanished; he hasn't paid the mortgage on her flat for six months and it's been repossessed. She thought she had until October, when her tenancy agreement ran out. I am about to go over with the car to collect her and all of her stuff.

Monday 17th August 17.44
TO: chris@christophercheshire.com

Marika persuaded me to go to the allotment today. We finished moving her stuff late last night and after waking up late morning, she said we must go and enjoy the sunshine.

I really didn't want to see Adam, but Marika was putting

on a brave face about losing her home so the least I could do was risk seeing him.

I raided Marika's suitcases for summery things to wear. I haven't been on a proper shopping spree in ages, and I picked out a cool tracksuit. When we got to the allotment, I began watering, Marika opened a deck chair, stripped down to a string bikini, and began to oil herself. You should have seen the old guys, ha! Not a lot of digging was done.

After a late lunch, Marika was sunbathing and I came out of my shed to see a young woman, thirties, blonde with a thong riding high above her low-cut jeans, bent over picking sweetcorn from Adam's allotment.

'Um, excuse me?' I said.

She looked round and took off her shades.

'What?' she said.

I was about to tell her off, when Adam came out of his shed (shirtless, in denim shorts, woof) saying, 'What's wrong?'

Then he saw me.

'Coco, I thought you were in Scotland?'

'I'm back for a few days... Who's your friend?' I said.

'I'm Tonya,' she said, with a hint of attitude. 'Who are you? One of his mother's friends?'

Tonya looked like she knew exactly who I was. I thought Marika was asleep, but she came alive, leaping out of her deckchair saying, 'You want a slap, you cheeky bitch?'

Tonya folded her arms. 'What did you call me?'

'You know she's too young to be his mother's friend,' said Marika.

'I wouldn't know, I've never met his mother,' Tonya said, backtracking.

'Just know. I'm watching you,' said Marika, putting her shades back on and sitting down.

Adam looked at me with something in his eyes; I don't know if it was longing or regret, or just that he was embarrassed. Tonya was now rather scared of Marika, and told him to hurry up.

I went back to my watering. They gathered their sweetcorn up in a plastic bag, locked up, and walked down the path, disappearing in the dust. Tonya put her hand in the back pocket of his denim shorts and turned to look at me. I went into my shed for a cry. Marika followed and gave me a hug.

'He's moved on, already,' I blubbed. 'He's letting her eat his corn on the cob.'

'She's probably some old slapper off match.com,' said Marika.

It didn't make me feel any better.

Tuesday 18th August 18.00
TO: rosencrantzpinchard@gmail.com

I had a meeting today with Angie. A representative from The Edinburgh Festival Awards phoned her; they are coming to see our show! Securing a nomination would be a very big deal. *Jerry Springer: The Opera* won numerous awards at the Edinburgh Festival in 2002, and then transferred to the West End. Don't tell the cast though. Hugo only had his aunt in last week and he was over-acting.

Nan phoned tonight, she is coming up to see the last show with Meryl and Tony. During the Festival, as you know, the hotel prices triple so Meryl is looking into hiring a static caravan, outside Glasgow.

Thursday 20th August 21.00
TO: marikarolincova@hotmail.co.uk

It is good to be back in Edinburgh. I have tried to forget about Adam and enjoy what is happening now. I have seen many weird and wonderful shows. *One Man Titanic* was rather good yesterday. I let Mike, who performs all of *One Man Titanic*, buy me a drink in the bar afterwards. He is my age, a little nervy, but handsome enough. He apologised that his iceberg wasn't very big. He ran out of fifty pence's for his electricity meter and half his ice cube trays defrosted. I was about to offer to drive him to ASDA and buy him some ice, but Rosencrantz dragged me away.

'You can do *much* better,' he said.

Can he detect my fear of singledom?

Beryl and myself were invited on *Lunch with The Hamiltons* this afternoon. It's another theatre chat show hosted by Neil and Christine Hamilton. They were both very nice. Christine looks much less scary than when she was heckling Martin Bell on that playing field. I think having a fringe has helped.

I finally bumped into Regina Battenberg today, on the spiral staircase down to the bar. She was wearing a huge fur shawl and carrying her dog, Pippin.

'Congratulations, darling!' Regina shrilled.

I looked round, then realised she was talking to me.

'Thanks,' I said.

'I've been meaning to pop over and see you!' she lied. 'You must be so grateful to me, what with darling Kate Moss giving you all that fluke publicity.' She leaned in and tapped her nose. 'Don't tell anyone, but I gave her the poster!' She then hugged me. Pippin growled.

'What a great idea, Pippin!' said Regina. 'Pippin just said

you should come and be a guest on my show today!'

I looked at her, and then Pippin, and realised she was serious. She grinned enthusiastically.

'How about it?'

'Yes?' I said.

'Super! I've been needing a replacement for Anne Widdecombe, the poor old girl has terrible flu!'

My heart sank, and it sank low. I got Chris to come with me. We were shown to reserved seats in the front row. I had been told that Regina would signal for me when to go on.

The lights dimmed and an announcement blared, 'Please put your hands together for the one and only Regina... BATTENBERG!'

A hysterical ripple of whooping ricocheted round the auditorium as the curtain swished back to show Regina sat with Pippin on the fake balcony, which was slowly sliding out of the wings towards centre stage.

Regina was not the best host. The main guest was a veteran of the Second World War who had the terrifying experience of once meeting Adolf Hitler. What could have been an incredibly interesting interview was ruined by her banal questions, of which there were only three:

Did Hitler have a dog?

Do you think Hitler's little moustache was a 'stick on' one?

Did you crap yourself?

The rest of the time she talked about herself. Then I heard her ask me to join her on stage. Up close, the harsh lights glistened on her thick face powder, clinging to the tiny hairs on her lined face. Her black eyes were like bottomless pits, and her slash of red lipstick seemed to have a life of its own. She informed the auditorium that I was here for the final segment of the show called 'How to make window box wine!' before directing me to stomp on some grapes in a plastic washing-up bowl.

As her assistant was drying my feet, she pulled a dripping corn plaster out of the bowl.

'I think you left something behind, cheesy feet,' she said, holding it up and gurning to the audience, who all collapsed into gales of laughter.

'Can we have a big hand for Coco Pinchard! The only contestant to make cheese *and* wine!'

Afterwards we went straight to the bar. I was furious at being set up, even more so at Chris for laughing the loudest.

'I thought you were in on it too!' he said.

If that bitch shows up for *my* show, she can piss off!

Friday 21st August 16.44
TO: angielangford@thebmxagency.biz

Regina Battenberg returned the favour and came to see my show. She got in, even though it was sold out. The theatre put out an extra chair for her, on the front row. She was also allowed to bring in Pippin!

Hugo wasn't happy. He is allergic to animal hair and he sneezed so hard that one of his false ears came off.

I was annoyed, as we had a representative from The Edinburgh Fringe Awards in. Afterwards I went to the box office and asked why she was allowed to bring him in; she's not blind, and Pippin is not a Guide Dog.

'Miss Battenberg is exempt, due to the Britt Eckland clause in our health and safety policy,' said the boy in the Jarvis Cocker glasses.

'What?' I said.

'The Britt Eckland clause,' he repeated.

Apparently, Britt Eckland did a show at the Edinburgh Festival a couple of years back, and refused to go anywhere without her little dog. The local council caved in, and designed a 'Britt Eckland clause' so that celebrity dogs can be exempt from health and safety legislation.

'It's paved the way for dog-carrying celebrities like Paris Hilton and our own Regina Battenberg to visit the Edinburgh Festival,' said the Jarvis Cocker boy excitedly.

I don't know what is more ridiculous – the clause, or the fact that Regina Battenberg is classed as a celebrity. She did approach me in the bar afterwards, to offer her congratulations. She was wearing a character turban with a (real) stuffed budgie on it, and said it was 'fantabulous', which isn't even a word. She calls herself a writer?

The man from The Edinburgh Fringe Awards seemed to love it too. When we came home, I bought Hugo some anti-histamine.

Sunday 23rd August 16.45
TO: angielangford@thebmxagency.biz

Man from Edinburgh Awards was in again. He laughed very hard. Ears stayed on (Hugo's that is).

Monday 24th August 16.01
TO: angielangford@thebmxagency.biz

Awards people in again. This time there were three of them and they made a lot of notes. Beryl twigged who they were during her finale song, 'I'm a Regina, I Don't Sing in A Minor'.

Wednesday 26th August 16.17
TO: angielangford@thebmxagency.biz

More awards people in. I watched them even more closely; they looked bored and didn't laugh. They have now seen it four times. However, I see it most days, still laugh, and I wrote it. Is that sad?

Thursday 27th August 12.10
TO: marikarolincova@hotmail.co.uk

The nominations have just been announced in *The Scotsman*.

Chasing Diana Spencer: The Musical has been nominated for three Edinburgh Festival Awards!

Best Musical; Coco Pinchard & Jason Schofield, Best Newcomer; Beryl as Queen Elizabeth II, and Best Direction; Christopher Cheshire.

I am utterly, utterly thrilled, most of all for Chris.

'I could be a real professional theatre director,' he said, his eyes lighting up.

The ceremony is on Saturday night in the ballroom at the Assembly Rooms.

Do you want to stay with us when you come and see the show? Chris's parents have just said they are coming. He was shocked. His mother rarely strays north of Harrods... She has already asked how the exchange rate is for Scottish pound notes.

I am sad now it is all coming to an end. It's been like one long party here these past weeks. Edinburgh never sleeps and we have seen more theatre than you can imagine. Plays run day and night. Have you seen Adam, or the terrible Tonya?

Sunday 30th August 07.14
TO: marikarolincova@hotmail.co.uk

I have walked up to Calton Hill, and I am looking out over Edinburgh in the morning mist. I haven't really slept much because...
WE WON!!!!
WE WON ALL THREE AWARDS!!!
I wished I had been a bit more sober during the ceremony. Byron had been in charge of buying drinks for us to have, before the taxis arrived to take us to the ceremony. I had given her a hundred quid for champagne, but because she is a stickler for budgets, she refused my money and spent only what was left in the kitty from our original £15,000 budget which was £3.09.

In Leith, £3.09 buys six litres of White Lightning Cider, which rendered us all, apart from Clive, rather plastered. Everyone looked so elegant; even Byron finally shed the ZZ Top t-shirt and was persuaded into something more formal, namely A Hard Rock Café Dubai t-shirt with leather waistcoat.

The Edinburgh Festival Awards were fun, terrifying, and rather competitive. Each show nominated had their own table, dotted around the ballroom.

The Edinburgh Fringe Award itself is a piece of slate

about the size of a large book, framed in wood, with the name of the winner in silver writing. I am afraid I did a bit of a Gwyneth Paltrow at the podium when I accepted on behalf of Jason and me.

I looked around the room, at the actors, Chris, Byron, Angie, Regina Battenberg (who was typing on her Blackberry), all the hangers on and industry people, and my eyes came to rest on Rosencrantz. He was looking handsome as could be in his tuxedo, his face full of hope and pride.

I thought, after all that has happened, he is the most important thing in my life, the one I am most proud of. He dreamed of putting on his own play, with Christian, yet when it was all taken away from him, he conducted himself wonderfully. He has never moaned, even when we were wet and cold and I made him wear speedos on the Royal Mile. I said my award was for him.

When I sat back down next to him, he had tears in his eyes,

'You're like wicked mum,' he said.

He meant 'wicked' in the cool sense, I think.

Chris was also emotional and directed his speech to his parents.

'Mother and Father, I now have a career. A profession, so you can't marry me off. I have work to do!'

He was gutted when I told him afterwards that it hadn't been televised.

Beryl was rather bewildered when she went up to accept her award.

'Best newcomer? I've been doing this for thirty years... I was a Benny Hill girl.'

Regina Battenberg was nominated in the solo show category, but lost out to *One Man Titanic*. I wished the ceremony *had* been televised, if only to see the look on her face when she lost! I was pleased for Mike, though, his ice issues have continued to plague him.

On Regina's table were various producers, publicists, Pippin, and Dorian, my old agent! When Regina went off to hobnob, I sat beside him.

'Coco!' he said grabbing Pippin, who was trying to eat the centrepiece on the table. 'Well done. You know if you'd have come to me with the play idea, I'd have gone with it...'

I gave him a thin smile. 'Really? I thought I was a loose cannon?'

'No, I was misquoted. I said 'loose woman',' he wormed. 'You know, like the girls off that lunchtime show. They're great!'

'I've heard Regina is going to leave you,' I said. 'Right now, she's discussing a media deal with BBC Worldwide.'

Luckily, at that very moment, Regina was sat at a table engrossed in conversation with Alan Yentob, the former BBC television controller. Dorian went pale and began to sweat. On cue, Pippin peed down the front of his shirt!

After the ceremony, Angie had to fly back to London so I went outside to have a cigarette with her before she left. I'd run out of Marlboro Lights, so asked if I could nick one.

'See,' she said. 'I told you I didn't want you nicking my fags at award ceremonies... But I'll let you off this once, you did great, babe.'

'*You* did great, babe.'

'I've done even better,' she said, hugging me. 'We've got a meeting next week with the Trafalgar Studios. They want to talk about transferring us to the West End!'

I was going to go home after the cigarette but hearing that spurred us all on to a pub crawl and then, at 2am, to CC

Blooms, a gay bar in Leith.

I don't know how they are going to perform the last show today.

Monday 31st August 13.41
TO: angielangford@thebmxagency.biz

I'm hiding in Byron's little office, on her computer in Palace Apartments. The soundtrack to *Chasing Diana Spencer: The Musical* is booming throughout the house. Byron made a recording of the last show. It sounds awesome. The actors are all singing along with themselves, packing, and cleaning so hopefully we will get our security deposit back from Mrs Dougal.

I have so much to tell you! Everyone came to see the last show. Marika, Meryl, Tony, Ethel, and Chris's parents.

Clive swears by Doctor Theatre, and it worked for the actors. You would have never known half of them were throwing up just beforehand. The performance was perfect. There was no time to get sentimental afterwards and Byron collared me to help with the 'git out' (get out). All the costumes and props had to be loaded into my car boot, and we had to leave the premises.

As I was parking the car outside Palace Apartments, my phone bleeped with a text message. It was an unknown number, which said,

SUM1 SPECIAL IS HERE TO SEE YOU.

I wanted to text back but my bloody phone died and my charger was packed in the bottom of my suitcase under all the props in the car. I parked the car and then walked back into the city centre where I had promised to meet everyone in The Carnegie Theatre bar. My mind was racing. What if it is Adam? I tried to remember if I had deleted Adam's number in a fit of rage, but I hadn't. Also, wouldn't he say that he was here and not talk about himself in the third person?

When I arrived at the bar, I found Chris in the foyer showing his parents his Edinburgh Fringe Award.

'Darling, it's a piece of slate off a roof?' said his mother Edwina as her anorexic frame buckled under the weight. 'Shouldn't awards, well ones that matter, be golden?'

'Now Edwina,' said his dad. 'This is a real achievement for Christopher.'

There was an awkward moment where they should have hugged, but he broke it by saying they had dinner reservations, and they left.

'Don't worry,' I said. 'At least they came.'

And I took him into the bar.

It was crowded, and as I looked around expectantly, there in the corner was Meryl, Tony, Ethel and... Daniel!

I didn't know what to do. Meryl waved, and called me over saying, 'Oh Coco! We loved the show, aren't you clever!'

'You know, I saw the Queen Mother once,' boomed Tony, red in the face. 'Well, I'm sure it was her, but she was in disguise. You know, once she took those hats off, she could be anybody.'

'Oh gawd,' said Ethel. ''E's on about the Queen Mother again, why would she go to a car boot sale in Milton Keynes?'

I looked at Daniel.

'Hi Cokes,' he said, bashfully.

'Ooh! Look 'oo it is Coco,' said Ethel. 'It's Danny. Did ya get me text message?'

'That was you?'

'Yeah, look. I got me one of them Chinese telephones,' she said holding up a brand-new iPhone. 'I'm gonna get Rosencrantz to put me on Twitter.'

'What are you doing here?' I said to Daniel.

''E's got a surprise!' said Ethel. 'Danny wants to say something,' and she dragged off Meryl and Tony.

Daniel smiled. He was wearing a black suit and his long hair was greased and tied back with an elastic band.

'Can I get you a G&T?' he said. 'How about some dry roasted peanuts?'

'You still haven't told me why you are here? What's the surprise?'

'Your phone call, the other week, you wanted me back...' his face dropped, 'didn't you?'

'No!' I said, incredulous. 'No. I was low, and I'm sorry if I gave you that impression.'

'So now the show is a success, you don't want me?'

'You're telling me that YOU are the surprise? You really think that you being here is some kind of special treat for me!' I was becoming shrill. Daniel looked at his shoes.

'*Whistle Up the Wind* has been cancelled.'

'Leave me alone and go home,' I said.

'Let's try again,' he said, taking my hand. 'Really try, forget all the silly stuff.'

'Silly stuff?' I shouted.

I grabbed his pint of lager and poured it over his head. Then, grabbing a bowl of dry roasted peanuts off the bar, I emptied it on top of his greasy wet hair.

'*That* is silly stuff. Cheating and divorcing me is a whole other load of words!'

Daniel stood there dripping, with clumps of dry roasted

peanut dust congealing on his face.

Ethel appeared holding out her new iPhone. ''Ere let me take a photo of you two!'

She saw Daniel and her face dropped.

'Ethel,' I said, 'I will never get back together with your scumbag son.'

I stalked off and found Marika. We went for a conference in the ladies loo.

'What's going on?' she said.

'Oh, an unwelcome surprise guest.'

'You mean Adam?'

'No, Daniel has appeared.'

'No. Adam was at the show,' said Marika. 'You didn't get my text?'

'What? No. My phone is dead. Adam is here?'

'Yeah, I'm sure it was him, he sat a few rows behind us. He waved to me.'

I was trying to take this in when the toilet door opened, and in came Ethel.

'Danny's in the bog with Meryl's travel wash,' she said. 'I knew it was a long shot you taking him back, I just didn't want 'im in me spare room. Me 'n' Irene are using it for Tarot readings, we're making a mint. Tha's how I bought the Chinese telephone.'

Then Rosencrantz came in.

'Oh Rosencrantz, you were brilliant,' said Ethel ruffling his hair. 'You're like a young Rock Hudson.'

I asked him if he had seen Adam. He said no. Then Ethel took Rosencrantz to the bar for a drink. I looked at Marika.

'Are you sure it was Adam?'

'I think so, yes.'

'This is stupid,' I said. 'I've just won an award and heard

we could be transferring to London. I'm obsessing about two stupid men.'

Then Ethel rushed back into the bathroom.

'Are you two done?' she shouted. 'Only my Danny's knocking seven bells of shit out of some bloke!'

We ran out. Daniel was rolling around on the carpet with another guy. Ethel was screaming,

'Wallop 'im son! Remember the boxing lessons yer father gave you!'

I realised I knew the middle-aged guy. He was a reviewer from *The London Evening Standard,* called Al Malone. Daniel produced his own musical in 1988 called *Do-Ray-Moi.* It was a whimsical and rather crap tale of an obscure French piano teacher. It ended up being a load of French girls with hairy armpits dancing around Daniel as he bashed out discordant tunes on the piano, whilst I had busted my arse painting a huge mural of the Eiffel Tower.

Al Malone had reviewed *Do-Ray-Moi* calling it 'Woeful artistic hand relief'. Daniel always said if he ever saw Al Malone again, he would punch him.

The fight came back onto its feet and Al seemed to get the upper hand, landing a blow to Daniel's face. He staggered back into a fruit machine, his nose pouring with blood. Al hit him again, and again.

'Leave 'im alone, yer bastard!' shouted Ethel, scrabbling in her handbag. 'I'm gonna film this on me new Chinese telephone, an' give it to the pigs!'

She didn't get the chance because then, like a dream, in rushed Adam pulling Al away from Daniel. Al realised Adam was at least a head taller and backed off. Meryl and Ethel ran to Daniel.

'Hi Coco,' said Adam.

We looked at each other.

'Your show was wonderful.'

'I've really missed you,' I blurted. 'And I'm sorry about not explaining, things, I wasn't cheating, unfortunate timing, if that makes sense.'

'Sorry I turned into... an obsessive girl,' he said.

He pulled me into his chest for a hug.

'Hang on,' I said pulling away. 'What about Tonya?'

'What about that old guy you're dating?'

'What?'

'Him,' said Adam pointing across the room at Clive, who was playing darts with Byron.

'You thought me and Clive were dating?'

'Yeah, you were holding his arm, and he was wooing you when I saw you at the allotment.'

'The ground was too bumpy for him,' I laughed. 'He's lovely, but no.'

'Oh,' he said looking embarrassed. 'I only went on a few dates with Tonya. Then I realised, you're my girl. That's why I'm here.' He grinned.

Tony lumbered past, red in the face, saying, 'Good job there, mate, breaking it up. You just pipped me to the post, I was about to intervene myself.'

We looked over at Daniel. Meryl was gobbing on a hanky and cleaning the blood off his nose. Ethel was pulling chunks of pineapple and cheese off a cocktail stick to make a splint. Adam put his arms round me,

'Can we try again?'

I nodded. He leant in and we kissed. It was a real knee-buckling kiss.

Meryl came back and told us she had put Daniel in a taxi back to his Bed and Breakfast. Chris, Rosencrantz and

Marika joined us.

'Where's your father, Chris?' asked Meryl. 'I did so want to meet Sir and Lady Cheshire.'

'She brought one of your napkins to sign,' said Tony.

Meryl flushed red but still let Chris take it with him, to be signed later. Ethel looked around at everyone and bit her lip.

'I'm sorry, I can't keep it in any longer. Meryl's up the duff!'

Meryl gave Ethel a look, then smiled at Tony,

'We were going to wait for my twelve weeks but yes, I am pregnant.'

'Meryl,' I said, 'congratulations.'

We all hugged and Meryl began to well up,

'I'm going to be someone's mummy,' she sniffed. 'We're so happy.' Tony hugged her close.

''Ere,' said Ethel. 'Tell 'em what Irene said.'

Meryl shot Ethel a look, 'No, they don't want to hear that, thank you.'

'No!' said Ethel. 'It's spooky. It's about when they, you know, did the business.'

Meryl went red but Ethel carried on.

'Meryl and Tone 'ad a bonk, you know, made the baby, after their Rotary Club Dinner on the twenty-sixth of June. The same night Michael Jackson died.'

Ethel looked around for effect.

'Irene is very psychic, and she says that their baby IS the reincarnation of the King of Pop, Michael Jackson.'

No one knew what to say. Adam and Rosencrantz raised their eyebrows, and I saw Chris and Marika turn away and smile. Ethel raised her glass.

'To the reincarnation of the King of Pop!'

I felt so sorry for Meryl, who once again had to experience Ethel stealing her thunder.

We stayed talking in the bar until late. I let Marika have my bed at Palace Apartments. Adam had booked us a room at The Scotsman Hotel.

We finally made it back to the hotel at four-thirty in the morning. He led me up to a beautiful room with a view over the city, slowly waking up in the first light. On the pillow of a four-poster bed sat a small green box, which made me think, Tiffany! I opened it, and nestling on the little satin cushion was a beautiful silver necklace.

'Is this real Tiffany?' I said.

'No rubbish,' he said, holding up the box.

'I've wanted one of these since...'

'Christmas?'

'Yes. How did you know?'

'Well, I did read all of your emails,' he said, with a grin.

He gently took it out of the box and secured it around my neck.

'But I didn't get you anything.'

'I know how you can make it up to me,' he said, as we sunk back into the soft cover of the four-poster bed.

SEPTEMBER

Tuesday 1st September 10.01
TO: angielangford@thebmxagency.biz

Hi love, just a quickie, I will be back in London next weekend. Daniel begged, again, to let him stay, but I said no. He can move in with Ethel until he finds his own place. However, he has exacted his petty revenge. The iPhone, which he gave me for Christmas, is still in his name, and he is now demanding it back to use for himself. His got crushed in the fight and he says he cannot afford to buy a new one. I have to organise a replacement phone and a new number, so I will be offline for a week or so.

If you need to pick up those copies of *Chasing Diana Spencer* for the producers at the Trafalgar Studios, Rosencrantz will be around all week, as will Marika and Clive. He is going to be staying for a while so he can get himself together. He deserves it far more than Daniel does.

I had better go. Adam is waiting in the car and I have to put this phone through the door of Daniel's Bed and Breakfast.

We are going to drive down to London over the next week, stopping off along the way. Adam has booked some lovely hotels. I have never seen the Lake District or

Yorkshire, and we might even go and have a look at Dublin!
See you soon to conquer the West End!
Lots of love, Coco

A NOTE FROM ROBERT

Hello, and a huge thank you to you for choosing to read *The Not So Secret Emails of Coco Pinchard*. If you did enjoy it, I would be very grateful if you could tell your friends and family. Word-of-mouth is one of the most powerful tools, and it helps me reach out to new readers. Your endorsement makes a big difference! You could also write a product review. It needn't be long, just a few words, but this also helps new readers find one of my books for the first time.

If you'd like to get in contact with me, and tell me what you thought about the book, or just to say hi, you can find me through my website www.robertbryndza.com.

If you enjoyed *The Not So Secret Emails of Coco Pinchard*, you should check out Coco Pinchard's next adventure in, *Coco Pinchard's Big Fat Tipsy Wedding*! Until then...

Robert Bryndza

ALSO BY ROBERT BRYNDZA

COCO PINCHARD SERIES

The Not So Secret Emails of Coco Pinchard
Coco Pinchard's Big Fat Tipsy Wedding
Coco Pinchard, The Consequences of Love and Sex
A Very Coco Christmas
Coco Pinchard's Must-Have Toy Story

STAND ALONE ROMANTIC COMEDY

Miss Wrong and Mr Right

KATE MARSHALL CRIME THRILLER SERIES

Nine Elms
Shadow Sands
Darkness Falls

ERIKA FOSTER CRIME THRILLER SERIES

The Girl in the Ice
The Night Stalker
Dark Water
Last Breath
Cold Blood
Deadly Secrets

ABOUT THE AUTHOR

Robert Bryndza is an international bestselling author, best known for his page-turning crime and thriller novels, which have sold over four million copies in the English language.

His crime debut, *The Girl in the Ice* was released in February 2016, introducing Detective Chief Inspector Erika Foster. Within five months it sold one million copies, reaching number one in the Amazon UK, USA and Australian charts. To date, *The Girl in the Ice* has sold over 1.5 million copies in the English language and has been sold into translation in 29 countries. It was nominated for the Goodreads Choice Award for Mystery & Thriller (2016), the Grand prix des lectrices de Elle in France (2018), and it won two reader voted awards, The Thrillzone Awards best debut thriller in The Netherlands (2018) and The Dead Good Papercut Award for best page turner at the Harrogate Crime Festival (2016).

Robert has released a further five novels in the Erika Foster series, *The Night Stalker, Dark Water, Last Breath, Cold Blood* and *Deadly Secrets,* all of which have been global bestsellers, and in 2017 *Last Breath* was a Goodreads Choice Award nominee for Mystery and Thriller.

Most recently, Robert created a new crime thriller series based around the central character Kate Marshall, a police officer turned private detective. The first book, *Nine Elms*, was an Amazon USA #1 bestseller and an Amazon UK top five bestseller, and the series has been sold into translation in 15 countries. The second book, *Shadow Sands* was an Amazon charts and Wall Street Journal bestseller, and the third book, *Darkness Falls* will be published shortly.

Robert was born in Lowestoft, on the east coast of England. He studied at Aberystwyth University, and the Guildford School of Acting, and was an actor for several years, but didn't find success until he took a play he'd written to the Edinburgh Festival. This led to the decision to change career and start writing. He self-published a bestselling series of romantic comedy novels, before switching to writing crime. Robert lives with his husband in Slovakia, and is lucky enough to write full-time.

Made in the USA
Middletown, DE
03 February 2022